THE GRAVEDIGGER'S DREAM

Book I – Rivers Wild Series

DON BEST

Brimstone
Fiction

THE GRAVEDIGGER'S DREAM BY D. BEST

Published by Brimstone Fiction
1440 W. Taylor St. Ste #449
Chicago, IL 60607

ISBN: 978-1-946758-52-1
Copyright © 2021 by D. Best
Cover design by Elaina Lee- www.forthemusedesign.com
Interior Design by MeaghanBurnett.com
Additional art, map and glossary by Elizabeth Best
Available in print from your local bookstore, online, or from the publisher at:
www.brimstonefiction.com
For more information on this book and the author visit: www.donbestauthor.com

Brought to you by the creative team at Brimstone Fiction: Rowena Kuo and Meaghan Burnett

Library of Congress Cataloging-in-Publication Data
Best, D.
The Gravedigger's Dream / D. Best 1st ed.
Printed in the United States of America

CONTENTS

To the people of the Amazon,
who have been gracious and
hospitable to us beyond words.
Muito obrigado!

ACKNOWLEDGMENTS

To ...

... Elizabeth, my lovely wife, encourager, and first reader ...

... Rowena Kuo and Meaghan Burnett, the visionaries at Brimstone Fiction ...

... Keith Osmun, my talented editor ...

... J. Tucker White, our most excellent proofreader ...

... Regina Eberle, Lucivan and Claire Ferreira, and Siobhán (at Bite-Size Irish) for helping me fine-tune the cultural and linguistic elements in this book ...

... Graham Greene, Kurt Vonnegut, and Gabriel García Márquez, who have been my beacons of excellence and creativity ...

... My Heavenly Father, from whom all blessings come.

NOTE TO READERS:

A guide to Portuguese words and phrases may be found (by the curious) at the end of the book. See the Table of Contents for page numbers.

CHAPTER ONE

A MAN HEARS SO MANY WILD STORIES. WHO KNOWS WHAT'S TRUE?

Maybe truth is like the Amazon, always on the move. Roughed by the wind in the morning and calmed by the moon at night, it changes mood and color with every twist of light.

I spoke these thoughts to the Irishman one night, and he just smiled. "The truth will always be true," he said. "No matter how the wind should turn."

Such a peculiar man! He spoke Portuguese worse than a child, so I could hardly understand him. And sometimes even when I did understand him, I didn't understand him.

Some people say Michael O'Hannon was an idiot or a fake or a demon in disguise. But I say *this*: Mick was hungry for the truth and never afraid to speak.

Duba, our do-nothing leader, liked to blame the foreigner for all the troubles we had in Jacaré.

Que besteira! We were up to our necks in trouble long before Mick showed up.

1

For years, I'd blame our troubles on the women. And would say to my own woman, "Ana, if it weren't for all this gossip and complaining, half our problems would disappear."

And she'd sit there in silence, suffering my attacks. Because I taught her to respect me.

One night, I spoke it to her while the Irishman was sitting at our table. I said to her, "Woman, if you and your friends would quit complaining and stop all this gossip, most of our troubles would vanish."

I looked over at Mick for some manly confirmation. But he was biting his tongue, determined not to speak.

"Isn't that so?" I prodded him.

Mick tilted his head a little to the right, mulling the thing over, and said softly, "Complaining is like a rash that spreads from one person to the next. Before you know it, the whole family's got it, then the neighbors, then the whole village. Itching all the time."

"That's it!" I blurted. "Itching all the time!"

"And gossip is worse," he went on. "It smears your neighbor with a kind of mud that can never be washed."

"Exactly!" I bellowed. "I wish the other hens were around to hear this."

"But let's be honest," the Irishman said. "It's the *men* who do most of the drinking, isn't it? And most of the fighting? And abandon their families, don't they, to chase other women?"

Puxa vida, that stung me pretty good—like a fish hook in the ear!

I didn't speak to the man for a long time after that, because he humiliated me in front of my woman. But in a slow and grudging way I realized that he was after the truth, the way an *onça* pursues its prey.

Since we had no library in Jacaré, my Great Aunt Leona was our village memory and talking encyclopedia. She was the oldest woman in the Amazon, I'm sure, and probably in all Brazil. Who else could remember the rubber ships that steamed up and down the river to Manaus? By age and experience she commanded our respect.

When I was young and not so young, Leona would walk me back through the groves of rubber trees and tell me stories of the long ago. Together, we'd inspect the old V-shaped scars climbing up the bark, marking the years of wealth, and imagine the taps still there, drip, drip, dripping latex into little tin buckets.

If the encyclopedia fell open to a different page, she would walk me down to the river, to that special place of hers. I still remember the last of those walks, when we stood on the shore together.

"Did I ever tell you about the wreck of the *Pelican?*" she asked.

"Twenty-three times," I said. Indeed, I'd heard stories about the *Pelican* for as long as I could remember hearing.

She ignored my remark and pointed her walking stick westward along the shore. "The ship was lost in a storm, where the Rio Cajutuba flows in from the south. About a day and a half on foot. You know the place."

"I know it, Auntie."

Her face lit up when she came to the part about the cargo. "Full of gold and rubber and watermelons," she said. "And also Englishmen."

"No one ever found the ship, Auntie. A lot of people tried."

Leona stabbed her walking stick into the sand. "I swear to God it's there! The gold and the rubber went down with it. The next day, a bunch of dead Englishmen and watermelons came floating down the river. Some of them heaved up right here on the sand."

"Right here where we're standing?"

"That's right. My father carried the bodies into the jungle, took their jewelry and their gold fillings and their fine English shoes, and buried them there. We ate the melons, I remember. No sense in letting them rot."

"We should go home now, Auntie. You're not looking very steady."

"I'm all right," she said. But took hold of my arm as we turned. "For the love of God, who throws all this trash on the ground?" she erupted. "We live like a bunch of pigs."

Twice she stopped me on the path, insisting we pick up an old can and some glass from a broken whiskey bottle. "*Porcos,*" she muttered.

When we got back to her house, I sat her on the bench under the

3

mango tree and brought her a cup of water. The shadows were long now and the air surprisingly cool.

"I have news for you," I said. "*Big* news."

Her old brown eyes grew wide, sparkling with curiosity. "Tell me boy!"

"I can't just yet. We have to wait a few minutes."

She shooed me away with her hand. "*Puxa!* Why bring it up if you're not ready to say it?"

"So you can enjoy the anticipation," I said.

Leona folded her little bitty arms over her little bitty chest and sat there tapping her foot. I was taken again by the enormous size of her feet, which seemed to be the only part of her that hadn't shrunk away with age.

"I want you to know that I'm not much enjoying the anticipation," she said. "And the mosquitoes are coming out."

"All right then." I sat down beside her and pointed her off to the east, where a three-quarter moon peeked over the trees. "See that?"

She looked at me like I was a fool. "It's the *moon*," she said. "I've seen it there before."

"Yes! It's the moon. But look at this, Auntie!" I pulled the strip of newspaper out of my pocket and smoothed it out over her lap.

She peered at it a moment and grew even more agitated. "You *know* I can't read, Zemário. So just tell me what it says!"

"They sent a man to the moon, Auntie! About three weeks ago."

"What?"

"The Americans sent a ship to the moon."

"A ship to the moon?"

"Yes! See right here. See the picture? That's men walking on the moon."

Leona peered at the photo for a while, then up at the moon—just clearing the trees now—then back at the photo again. "It doesn't look at all like the moon," she said. "And they don't look much like *men* either."

"That's because they are dressed in space suits, Auntie. Specially made."

She looked at me with soft, pathetic eyes and patted me on the

4

knee, the way a mother might indulge her idiot son. "You mustn't believe everything you read in the papers, Zé."

"No, but it's true, Auntie! They sent a ship to the moon. They *did*."

She nodded and gave me a smile that was full of grace and whimsy. "Tell you what," she said. "I'll believe in *your* ship if you believe in *mine*."

Years before, in the early days of the dictator, I was drafted into the army and trained into a military police unit in Manaus. Much of the evil that's infected me—and also the guilt—started in the army, where I learned how to drink and brawl and spend myself with prostitutes.

On the 20th of March, just three weeks after I'd been promoted to sergeant, Luiz Gasolina strutted into the lobby of the Banco Federal with a pump shotgun in his hands, laughing hysterically, high on God-knows-what.

I might have stayed a sergeant, with a sergeant's pay and a sergeant's perks and a sergeant's pension, had it not been for Gasolina. When I think back on all the people I hate, he always floats to the top, like a turd bobbing in the river.

Five of his gang came with him, with two more outside—men who would just as soon kill you as spit. From one end of Amazônia to the other, Gasolina gloried in his reputation, christened in the tabloids as "Luiz the Laugh."

Standing on the balcony above the lobby, I had no way of knowing that two of my men were already dead, their throats slit in broad daylight, lying on the sidewalk in front of the bank. I had told them to stay on their feet, to quit daydreaming, to stop sneaking around the side of the building to grab a smoke. But who can tell a nineteen-year-old anything? I myself—the old man in the squad—had just turned twenty-three.

Thinking back to that moment when "The Laugh" came striding into the bank, I realize how confident he must have been. He and his men were hardened outlaws, in their thirties and forties, armed with shotguns and pistols. We were nothing but a bunch of kids—some of us barefoot—equipped with assault rifles that we barely knew how to use.

How can I not believe in hell when I saw it erupt through the surface of the earth that day? And saw the Devil standing in the midst of it, *laughing*.

Gasolina shot the man in front of him just to get our attention, then waved his men forward toward the tills.

Scared witless, I angled my weapon on the lobby below and fired. Two or three people went down. Who knows who? Private Mendez, off to my side, was firing too.

Gasolina's eyes ran up to meet us—like a jungle rat. With an easy, practiced swing he raised his shotgun and killed Mendez, then pumped up a cartridge for me.

I edged along the balcony, firing at him. But his was the better shot. It caught me across the shoulder and cheek and sent me stumbling backward through a door, into the ladies' room. Trickles of blood drooled down my arm and into my trembling hand. I kicked the door shut, threw the bolt, and crouched beside the toilet.

There were more shots. The cries of the wounded. Then silence.

I don't know how long I slumped beside the stool, dripping blood on the floor. Ten minutes maybe. Maybe longer. Finally, more from desperation than courage, I unbolted the door and crawled out onto the balcony, dragging my weapon behind me. Down below, the hole in the lobby, where hell had broken out, had sealed itself up. Only the carnage remained, and the Devil's hot, sulfuric stink.

The numbers were grim. Three of my men were dead, plus seven civilians, including the vice-director of the bank. Most of the casualties, the investigation showed, were hit by machine gun fire—*our* fire—coming from the balcony and the back of the lobby, where two of my men had been posted. Who knows how many rounds they fired into the lobby—maybe with their eyes closed—before they broke and ran?

According to the papers, the bandits had left just one dead and one wounded behind. They reported that Gasolina had escaped without a scratch, with 37,220 cruzeiros in his bag. According to some of the witnesses, the bandit leader came dancing out of the bank and hopped into the back of a blue Bandeirante, which whisked him and his men out of town. Some said he left trails of money floating in his wake, thrown from the truck as a blessing to the poor.

Week after week the newspapers pushed the story, ever more critical and mocking. "It's not so much the outlaws that people need to fear," they wrote, "But the ignorant clowns in the military police!"

I'll never forget the jeering headline that ran above one of their editorials:

Three Dead, Two Fled, One Hiding in the Toilet

Some time later, when the gang was caught, I learned that the firefight in the bank had not been quite as one-sided as the newspapers portrayed it. Gasolina had not "danced" out of the lobby, and certainly wasn't "laughing." One of my bullets had in fact shattered his left knee. His men had to carry him out of the lobby and lay him in the back of the truck, where he almost bled to death. After March 20th, Gasolina never ran again, or walked without a cane. And if he danced at all, it would have been clumsy as a goose.

The news would make me happy.

But not for long.

Late in the afternoon of the 20th, the battalion nurse picked eleven shotgun pellets out of my left shoulder and arm, and five from my cheek, including one that came within a half-centimeter of my eye.

"Will the girls still love me?" I said.

"Better than ever," she lied.

CHAPTER TWO

Two months after the shootout with Luiz Gasolina, I was summoned to battalion headquarters to see my commanding officer, Colonel Mateus Izquerda.

It was clear to me, entering his office, that this was the day of reckoning that would end my career as a soldier.

I had already been tried and convicted, tried and convicted, tried and convicted by the newspaper writers and editorialists, who fed upon my bloodied reputation like a school of piranhas. From one story to the next, the "bank robbery" had evolved into a "wild shootout," the "wild shootout" into a "bloody massacre," and the "bloody massacre" into a "national disgrace." Somewhere along the way, Gasolina and his gang were mostly forgotten, while I'd become a *bufflaw*—that is, half buffoon and half outlaw.

Nor did I get much sympathy or encouragement from my fellow soldiers, who treated me like a dose of the clap.

Even so, my heart did not convict me.

I found Colonel Izquerda standing at the corner of his desk that morning, as though posing quietly for a portrait. He was a long, slim razor of a man, who could cut you quick. I noticed, while still at a distance, that he smelled of lemons and gunpowder, and that his sliver of a mustache was freshly trimmed.

"At ease, Sergeant," was all he said. Then, with clear green eyes, he began to measure me, muscle and soul, the way a fisherman examines his nets.

Finally, he wrinkled his nose, as if some putrid odor had wafted into the room. "I am in the unhappy position of having to demote you," he said. "According to my orders, it's to be done without a hearing, without a court-martial, and without any further review of your case. Do you understand?"

"Yes, sir." Bad as it was, it wasn't as bad as I'd feared.

"You are demoted not because you've done anything wrong, Sergeant, but because our noble president has involved himself person-ally in the case and feels that we should toss a chocolate to the press, so they might shut their mouths."

I could think of nothing to say, except that I wanted to leave. And that, of course, I dared not say.

He walked around the back side of his desk and took a seat, then pointed me to a rigid, leather-backed chair to my right. "Please, Sergeant, sit down."

But it was the door I wanted, not the chair. "Would it be all right if I stood, sir?"

"Of course." He glanced down at some papers that were spread out before him, which must have pertained to me. "You're from the Isle of Fair Winds?" he said, already knowing the answer. "On the Amazon, isn't it?"

"Yes sir."

"A beautiful place, I imagine."

The word "beautiful" struck me as odd. I usually thought of my island as "poor" and "forgotten."

The Colonel leaned forward, resting his arms across the desk. It was the first and only time I can ever remember an officer smiling at me. "I want you to know, Sergeant, that I am not demoting you," he said. "In fact, I have plans to *promote* you."

I had no idea what he was talking about.

Nor did he choose to explain, but led me down a different path.

"What do you think of our supreme president and protector of the republic?" he asked. There was a dose of sarcasm in the way he rolled the titles off his lips.

"I don't know, sir. Where I come from we're just scraping by. There's not much time for ... ah ... *politics*."

He gave me a knowing look. "The people are taught, by subtle and not-so-subtle means, to keep their mouths shut and their opinions to themselves. Isn't that so?"

His silence prodded me to answer. "I guess so, sir."

"On the island there, in the village of Jacaré, what do your friends think of our most *excellent* president? Tell me the truth."

"I don't know, sir."

"Let me put it this way, Sergeant. Would they place him among the eagles? Noble, valiant, soaring?" His hands took off from the desk with unexpected grace, describing the wings of an eagle in flight. "Or would they place him among the *urubus*, scrabbling along the ground with his cronies, picking at the carcasses of dead animals?"

"I don't know, sir. I couldn't speak for them."

"Very politic, Sergeant. But if you were *pressed*?"

"If I were pressed ..." The words failed me and plunged us into silence.

"Well?" he said finally.

"With the urubus, sir. Most of them."

"Count them as patriots then!" he exclaimed. "Like me. Like *you*, Sergeant!"

"Yes, sir." Oh God, for a simple ticket out of the room. It was all I wanted.

He stood up and rounded the desk, facing me up square and a little closer than I liked. "The winds are changing, Sergeant. They will blow the old order away ... just ... like ... *this*." He blew out a little puff of air, as though to extinguish a candle.

I couldn't possibly be hearing what I thought I was hearing—*from the mouth of my commanding officer!*

The Colonel brightened and steered me onto yet another path. "You *must* come to the party Saturday night, Sergeant. My daughter's birthday. Seven-thirty sharp. And no excuses. You know where my home is, don't you? Across from the depot, with the bougainvilleas along the front?"

Out of dumbness and numbness I agreed. "Yes sir. I'll be there."

"Then you shall have the great privilege of meeting my daughter, Esmeralda," he said. "And she the great privilege of meeting you."

The Colonel's house was ablaze with lights and overfilled with guests, who spilled out onto a large, tree-lined veranda. I was stunned by the richness of his tables and the endless flow of drinks, including some imported wines and bourbons that must have cost a fortune.

An odd mix of family, military and bureaucrats meandered from room to room, sometimes mingling and sometimes not, served at every turn with fresh drinks and trays full of lavish food. How poorly dressed and out of place I felt, yet never stopped to wonder—so naïve was I— why the Colonel should invite a lowly sergeant to his party. And other noncoms too.

Promptly at nine, the waiters withdrew and the guests were ushered into an enormous sitting room, festooned with dozens of peach-colored balloons.

Then, as from a dream, Esmeralda appeared—the birthday girl— imparting a vision of excellence that has haunted me ever since.

Though only ten, she was already a perfect flower, blooming with health, intelligence and charm. She smiled with straight white teeth and showed off her dimples on fine rosy cheeks. She moved around the room in her violet petticoats, like a fairy princess, introducing herself with politeness and poise. I tried, for half a moment, to place her on the island with our barefoot boys and dull-eyed girls, and found the stretch too painful.

Suddenly the princess was standing right before me. With a smile, a curtsy and a single word she delighted me—*"Encantada!"*—then moved quickly on, little knowing or caring how much damage she'd done.

Later, under the doting eyes of her father, Esmeralda recited a long, enchanting poem—easy as you please—then moved to the piano and played us a waltz.

As the last note sounded and the applause died away, the Colonel proudly announced that his daughter was studying algebra and English.

I didn't know what algebra was.

Still don't, really.

But I do know *this*: Esmeralda was so wonderfully different from the ragged, pot-bellied kids in Jacaré that she seemed a different species altogether.

So came my first real glimpse of excellence. And with it a world of discontent and trouble.

A few days after the party, with images of Esmeralda still spinning through my mind, I was summoned again to the Colonel's office. But this time I was met by his plump adjutant, Sergeant Ribeiro, who led me into an adjoining room that was walled on the north and east by a pair of magnificent windows. Never had I seen such workmanship in glass, with delicate splines of wood weaving here and there—like spider's lace—set with panes so clear that I might have poked a curious finger through them. Between the windows, cutting the corner, were a pair of doors trimmed out in lime-colored glass and polished bronze. These opened into the Colonel's private garden.

To my right stood a row of massive bookshelves packed with history and philosophy and fiction—anything a man could dream. That so many books could be assembled in one place and owned by a single man seemed a miracle to me.

The adjutant, who treated me with great deference, showed me to a table and chair that looked out over the garden. "The Colonel regrets that he couldn't meet you in person this morning, Sergeant Licata. You are free, until noon, to relax here and read whatever you like." He gestured toward a short stack of books on the edge of the table. "The Colonel took the liberty of selecting a few of his favorites, but you can read whatever you want."

Like a frog plopped down in a jewelry store, I took my awkward seat and wondered what combination of lucky stars had placed me there.

Sergeant Ribeiro disappeared briefly and returned with a bottle of ice-cold beer, served on an elegant tray with a slender glass. How could I, a poor, rough-cut man from a poor, rough-cut family, be mistaken for a scholar? I dared not tell him that I could scarcely read, and write but poorly, for fear that the dream would melt. As he opened the beer and poured it for me, I casually took one of the books from the Colonel's pile, opened it before me, and pretended to understand it.

Over the next fourteen months, freed from my normal duties, I spent every Monday, Wednesday and Saturday morning in the Colonel's library.

As if by magic, a tutor appeared beside me the second week, insisting that I put aside the thick literary classics and invest my time in a first-grade reader.

It was Ribeiro, of course, who'd uncovered my crude charade and reported it to Colonel Izquerda. Nothing in the least bit changed, except for the regular appearance of my tutor, José Nery, a learned old man who had apparently been everywhere and done everything.

All modesty aside, I was the greatest student that Nery ever had. He told me so. Within a month I had vaulted to a sixth-grade reader and was gobbling up words and phrases the way a chicken pecks ants. Two months more and I was reading better than most college students and would for the simple pleasure of it spend an hour or two with the dictionary opened across my lap, enchanted with words.

Nery himself would sometimes select a book or pamphlet for me to read—*The Price of Liberty*; *Common Sense*; *The Patriot's Call*. Other times, I was left to choose whatever I wanted.

At six months he pushed me into writing, which came so quickly and naturally to me that the old man would sometimes cackle with delight.

One morning, toward the end of my enlistment, Nery walked me into the Colonel's garden, I with my glass of cold beer and he with his gourd full of maté tea.

"You have a wonderful gift for letters, Mister Zé," he said. "To watch you grow like this has given me enormous pleasure, and also a pound of sorrow."

"Why the sorrow, Doctor Nery?"

He stopped and sipped from his gourd, then spoke very softly. "Not many of us come to realize our gifts," he said. "Here in Brazil, we are like seeds without water, leaves without light. Could it be, I wonder, that a young Érico Veríssimo lies hidden among us, here in the city or there in your village? Maybe another Einstein or Mozart, waiting for his chance?"

The thought struck me hard and drew up memories of my island home, of kids with no school, no books, and no future. "What can we do?"

Nery stood there for a long moment, gazing at me. His face, weathered by time and boundless experience, suddenly brightened. "We must speak out against the madness, Zé. Against corruption and nepotism. Against the heavy fist of the dictator. If not us, then *who*?"

"Yes, sir," I replied. But it was not a military response I'd given him. It was the yearning of my heart, persuaded now to act.

I knew by rumor and intuition that some of the other noncoms were visiting the Colonel's library. Yet none of us ever crossed the other's path. Though I might have guessed at their identities, their true names and numbers remained a mystery. We must have known—*all* of us— that we were being groomed for a mission that was radically different from our current oath and duty.

It wasn't until the very end of my enlistment, with only a month to go, that the Colonel walked me deeper into his confidence.

I had come to headquarters at 0800, expecting to find Sergeant Ribeiro, my books, and a cold beer.

But it was the Colonel himself who met me, standing at the corner of his desk, in much the same position that I'd first encountered him.

I saluted him, with genuine respect, and stood there at attention for a while before he finally said "at ease" and fixed his gaze upon me.

"You are a most excellent student, Sergeant. Dr. Nery speaks very highly of you. *Glowingly*, I would say."

"Thank you, sir, but—" I pointed to the pair of chevrons on my sleeve. "I am only a corporal now."

"You may be a corporal so far as Brasília is concerned, Licata. But *here* ..." He put his index finger to his temple. "And *here* ..." He placed his other hand on his chest. "... you remain one of the finest sergeants in my battalion."

"Thank you, sir."

"Next month, when you muster out, I want you to continue under my command, with full pay, living among your friends and family."

I swallowed hard and could scarcely find my voice. "How could that be, sir?"

"As a *patriot*," he said. He brought his fingers together in perfect union and raised them to his chin, as though to pray. "Brazil is like an orphaned child, Sergeant. Poorly fed, poorly schooled, and worst of all, poorly loved by those who govern her." His hands flew apart and became a pair of tight-fisted hammers. "We can change it, Zé! If we stand together and fight, we can *change Brazil forever!*"

"Yes, sir!"

The Colonel lowered his voice, almost to a whisper. "You'll need to work quietly, recruiting others, helping us to build an army of patriots. I wish I could tell you more. Hundreds and hundreds have already rallied to the cause. But we must, above all, be silent and discreet until the time is ours. You must *never* mention my name, Zé. From now till the end of the world, or till we bury the dictator—God speed the day! —I am nothing but clouds to you. Do you *understand?* Nothing but *gathering clouds.*"

"Yes, sir."

"Are you willing?"

I was so full of adrenaline and patriotic zeal that I would have died upon his order. "Yes sir, I am!"

Thanks to the Colonel and his immaculate daughter, to José Nery and a library full of fertile thinkers, I had come to see my country in a different light, through the eyes of her suffering, through the eyes of her bondage, and especially through the eyes of her promise. Birthed now within me was the dream of a new Brazil, freed once and forever from the blood-suckers and tyrants, a place where justice and opportunity could thrive.

As a parting gesture, Colonel Izquerda walked over and put his hand on my shoulder, the way my father never had. Though years and years have passed, I remember yet that touch—full of courage and camaraderie—which should be the due of every son.

CHAPTER THREE

I RETURNED FROM THE ARMY TO A WORLD THAT HAD NEVER HEARD of Luiz Gasolina, never learned of my disgrace and demotion, never read a word of Castro Alves, and never dreamed that Brazil might someday become a great prince among the nations.

At first look the Isle of Fair Winds was just as I remembered it, blessed with every imaginable tree and fruit. With acerolas and bananas, with mangos and taperebá, with caju and pineapples, with guavas and açaí, with passion fruit and papayas. Something beautiful was always ripening overhead or flowering underfoot.

But in Jacaré, where most of us lived, a lot of faces were missing and the pulse of life had weakened. On my second day back, I found my brother Zorion busily packing his bags, headed off to the gold fields on the Rio Tapajós.

"I won't be coming back," he said. "The house is yours, and the land. Do what you want."

Other friends and family had run off to Manaus or Santarém to seek their fortunes. But what were their chances, I wondered, with no education or skills? Here on the island, at least we have some land to call our own. Fruit from the trees. Fish from the river.

In the city, you can starve to death and no one ever notice.

Everyone knew everyone on my island home because most of us were related in one way or another. It's a wonder, with so much intermarriage and promiscuity, that the kids didn't all have six fingers and armadillo tails.

I myself have three uncles and five aunts, more than forty cousins, more than thirty nephews and nieces—who can count them all?—not to mention my brothers, whom I'd rather not mention.

My father, a poor, unschooled man, thought he might somehow elevate our family's position by giving his sons long, elaborate names. For reasons that were never explained, he seized on the letter Z as being especially dignified, maybe even aristocratic. Thus, he named my six brothers Zequinha, Zavan, Zacarias, Zeusef, Zorion, and Zinildo. I, the seventh born, drew the name Zemário. Zemário Luan Vasconcelos dos Santos Licata. Thankfully, over time it was whittled down to Zé.

My father had no idea how to discipline his boys—how could he teach us something that he'd never known? So, in the wee hours of some drunken morning, long, long ago, he seized upon a plan that was simple, impartial, and thoroughly mad. Each of us boys, being seven in all, would take responsibility for a given day of the week. Seven sons for seven days. Why, it was a stroke of genius!

So we drew straws among us, and Thursdays fell to me. No matter what kind of accident, injury or crime should occur within our family, if it happened on a Thursday the blame was mine. My oldest brother, Zequinha, always took responsibility for Fridays, Zinildo for Saturdays, Zacarias for Sundays, and so on down the line.

Though no one could argue with the system's impartiality, it removed any incentive for us to reflect upon the stupid and evil things we did and try to change our ways. Rather, it encouraged us to lie, manipulate and betray one another at every turn. When I took a beating for one of my brother's *besteiras*, the first thought in my head was not, *"How can I change to keep this from happening again?"* but rather, *"How can I get even?"* Thus I kept a careful record of crimes and countercrimes and countercountercrimes, ever plotting revenge against my brothers.

The results were predictable. My father came to hate his sons, and we to hate each other. When the old man passed, only I and Zorion bothered to attend the funeral, and spoke not a word to one another. The family had to hire mourners at fifty centavos apiece so that someone might actually come to the mass and weep for his passing.

Not only did everyone know everyone in Jacaré, but everyone knew *everything*. If something happened in the morning and you hadn't heard about it by sunset, you were either deaf or out on the river fishing.

The reason we all knew everything about everybody was because our shacks were clumped in close together and made of thatch. With no glass in the windows, our fights and prayers and orgasms were broadcast freely into our neighbors' ears, whether they wanted to hear them or not.

In addition to all this unplanned communication, the island was equipped with a gossip vine that wound its way into every little corner of our lives and shot its prolific tendrils into the lives of other villages too. Who needed telephones when there were so many busybodies and gossips at work? Secrets were as rare as the hair on a bald man's pate.

How much easier our lives might have been without all the venomous chatter and strife that came pouring through the vine. Little Aparecida, my second cousin Geraldo's youngest daughter, was deaf as a stone. Yet she appeared to be the happiest soul on the whole island. Hearing the foolishness that came out of our mouths and battered our ears, I sometimes envied the silent place where Little Aparecida dwelled.

I gloried in my role as returning hero, let ride the story that the wounds on my cheek and arm were suffered in hand-to-hand combat with communist guerillas, and flashed the news around that I had real cash money in my pockets. On an island where most everything is bartered—roosters for rope, *farinha* for fish hooks, beans for batteries

—cash was rarer than a dancing dog. Only a few of us actually handled money in our day-to-day lives: There was Chico, my second cousin, who owned the beer shack and the only electric generator within a hundred kilometers; Tatianni the whore, who accepted no credit; Padre Xabrega, who got a monthly stipend from the diocese and a portion of the weekly offering; Witch Alzira, who sold potions and spells; old man Domingos, who raised cattle; and a few pensioners who received payments from the government.

And *me!* Home with my army pay and more on the way.

With my pocketful of money and fabricated glory, I courted the prettiest girl in the village, Ana Paula Bezerra. More truly said, I courted her father, who was somehow persuaded, despite my family's sordid reputation, that I had a future. If it was mostly passion that led us to the altar, rather than love, it seemed plenty at the time.

For three days straight we lay together, so closely intertwined that I could scarcely tell where my body ended and hers began. On the fourth morning, at first light, Ana put her lips to my ear, kissed me on the lobe, and whispered, "We will have eight children, I think. Four boys and four girls."

"Why eight, my love?"

"Because I was born on the eighth of May," she said. "And you on the eighth of February. And we were married, at the perfect moment, on the eighth of November."

"Ah-ha!" I laughed. "Our lucky number!"

A few weeks later, when we lost our first baby, I took up my bottle and my shovel and buried the embryo out back. I couldn't tell if it was a boy or a girl. Only that its luck had run out.

Through those early days of marriage, I never stopped thinking about the revolution and the Colonel's covert order to gather a troop of rebels. There was no shortage of candidates on the island, but to catch a man alone and sober and willing to listen was not so easy. My best chances came at night, when I'd go fishing with my friends. Abacaba and Chocolate, both fishermen and second cousins on my father's side, were recruited in the ease of their own canoes.

Though they lived in stoic silence, their hearts were full of anger. I had only to prick them with a word or two and out it came, like pus from a boil. Had there been any hope in the midst of our ignorance, any relief in the midst of our poverty, any aid in the midst of our disease, we might have taken a different way. But age and hard experience had made us cynics. Progress, if it existed at all, was a mist that sailed the further shore, forever fading into the distance.

Chocolate, as it turned out, was easy to recruit. When the moment of decision came, he looked back over his shoulder at me, a fish in hand, still wiggling on the hook, and said simply, "Count me in."

Somehow, I'd expected a lot more reluctance from him—*a lot more thought*.

He grinned over my surprise, just briefly, and tossed the fish into the bottom of the canoe. "My son's only ambition, now that he's old enough to think, is to get off the island," he said. His expression soured at the thought, as though he were peering into a grave.

I turned the canoe around and paddled us back through the stretch of water we'd been fishing, hoping for another strike.

Chocolate shrugged and baited the hook. "What do I have to lose?" he said. "At least we'd be *trying*, wouldn't we? Trying for something better?"

I nodded at him. "Yes."

His smile was ripe with sarcasm. "Better than dying in your sleep, isn't it?"

CHAPTER FOUR

THE WIND STIFFENED OFF THE RIVER AND BEAT ACROSS OUR campfire like a wild bird. Flurries of hot orange sparks swirled up from the flames—up and up and up some more—till they were waltzing with the stars. When I squinted just so, they all became campfires, lighted from one end of Brazil to the other, each with its band of patriots.

Our little camp was hidden on the eastern tip of the island, far from the nearest home, where only the jungle rats and scorpions lived. Cutting saplings and thatch from the jungle, we had built a little *barraca* and dug a fire pit in front.

Our meetings were set by the cycles of the moon, always in the small hours of the morning, always with plenty of drink.

My hands could never speak poetry the way the Colonel's did. And my voice lacked his tenor and honey. Yet I could paint an honest dream for my men, from the palette of my own heart. "I see a day when Jacaré will have its own school," I told them. "Its own health post, and electricity for every house. Can you see it? Can you *imagine* the day?"

The Voice took a drink of *cachaça* and passed the bottle on. "One more shot of this and I'll be able to see *anything*," he laughed. "Or maybe nothing." He reached around and picked up his old guitar, tuned it up, and commenced to play. His voice rang out, rough and beautiful, as though the wind itself were singing:

> "They spun a web for me
> And I be caught in the middle, caught in the
>   middle
> They spun a web for you
> And you be caught in the middle, caught in the
>   middle
>
> "Freedom come to visit,
> But she never come to stay, never come to stay
> Speak up, O sweet Brazil
> But careful what you say, careful what you say
>
> "They spun a web for us
> And we be caught in the middle, caught in the
>   middle
> Take up the fight, beloved
> Or be forever disappeared. Forever disappeared!"

The bottle circled around the fire for the fourth or fifth time. When it came to Abacaba, he finished off the last of it and belched so loud that it rattled the banana leaves.

If we were drinking a little too much (or even a lot too much) we were convinced now that it was different than ordinary drinking. Ours was *heroic* drinking, in the time-honored tradition of warriors bracing themselves for battle. And if our tales were a little too long and filled with bluster, they were still a cut or two better than life's ordinary *papo*.

Thus we persuaded ourselves that everything among us should be heroic. Our cause was heroic. Our songs were heroic. Even our belching was heroic.

"Does there have to be a lot of killing?" said Leaky. We called him that on account of his bladder problems, which sent him into the bushes all the time and left him smelling vaguely of urine. And sometimes not so vaguely.

"Of course, you idiot! It's a revolution!" Chocolate snapped. His face was young and softly toned, like cocoa powder, except for a pinkish birthmark that splattered his ear. Despite his name, the man was sour as a pickle.

Leaky ignored the remark and leaned off to one side, looking at me through the top of the flames. "But how many, Zé? How many would have to die?"

"I don't know," I said. "As few as possible." But I couldn't muzzle the darker thought that followed. "As many as it takes, Leaky." I had a sudden memory of bodies strewn across the floor of the Banco Federal, of burnt powder in the air, of blood pooling darkly on light gray marble.

The Voice, whose real name was Vinícius, had been quiet as a flower. Now he let his thoughts sing out. "How do you think our dictator got to be dictator in the first place?" he asked. "Was it honesty and hard work that put him in the palace? Integrity and fair play?"

"*Porra!*" Chocolate cut in. "Butchering his enemies! *That's* how he come to power. Or buying them off."

Leaky chewed on the thought and spat into the fire. "But if we have to kill a lot of people to get rid of him, how does that make us any better than he is?"

Chocolate gave him the fast and ready answer: "Because we're fighting for freedom! *Para libertar o povo!*"

Leaky hoisted himself up and shambled off into the night to relieve himself. Unfortunately, he wandered upwind and not very far, which left the rest of us privy to his business. Once he was back and seated by the fire, he found himself under immediate attack.

"Look," said Chocolate. "Could you please find yourself a favorite tree and stick with it? Somewhere *downwind*, okay? No one wants to be smelling that, blowing through the camp." He fanned the air around his nose. "*Credo*, it smells like kerosene and sour eggs. You dying or what?"

Sadly, though none of us knew it at the time, Leaky *was* dying, and confirmed the fact about four months later.

That night, invited to the first-ever meeting of my rebel squad, he made the right decision for himself. "I don't want to kill nobody," he said. And never came back.

The Colonel's first letter came on a line boat in the middle of August. The envelope was small and plain, with no return address. Across the front it said:

Zemário Licata
Isle of Fair Winds
Jacaré, Amazonas

Inside was a one-page letter wrapped around a bunch of cash:

Beloved patriot,
    Here is your pay. Equipment to follow soon. Put together a squad of good, trustworthy men. Be discreet. Burn this letter.
    Gathering Clouds

A month later, his second letter came. This one was delivered to my door by the nervous captain of the *Apocalipse II,* a dirty little freighter that kept no particular schedule.

He came clapping in the rain that morning, about an hour past dawn, and drew my dogs to him like a slab of fresh liver.

I managed to get out of my hammock and call them off before they could do any harm, then walked him through the yard into my open kitchen.

Though the captain was drenched down to his crotch, he seemed happy for the rain, knowing it would keep a lot of curious eyes and ears indoors.

"You are Zemário Licata?" he asked.

"Yes."

He looked past me to make sure we were alone, then whispered, "I have the equipment you ordered. And all the parts." The rain was still dripping off the bill of his cap, off the tip of his nose, off the hairy lobes of his ears.

"Can I make you some maté?" I said. "Some coffee maybe? Something to warm you?"

He shook his head and spoke sternly. "Three crates we got. Because of their, ah ... *weight* ... we should offload them on the beach someplace. Say midnight tonight? You choose the spot. Whether you show up or not, we'll leave them on the beach."

I confirmed the time and set the place, not far from our camp.

"Also this," the captain added. He pulled an envelope from under his shirt, smelling of diesel oil and sweat, and gave it to me.

"*Até mais,*" he said, and without another word slogged off through the rain.

Though the letter bore no return address, I knew the one who'd sent it. Inside, I found two sheets of paper, with money tucked into the fold. The top sheet, probably typed by the Colonel himself, was brief:

Beloved patriot,
Action is close. Be ready at any hour, day or night. Conserve your ammunition. Burn this letter.
Gathering Clouds

Attached to the back was a clipping from the newspaper in Manaus. I noticed by the date that the story was about two weeks old. The headline, set in large, red letters, stunned me:

'Luiz the Laugh' Killed, Gang Busted!

Underneath the headline was a grisly photograph. Five bodies, in various postures of death, were laid side-by-side on the ground. None of them looked happy.

The police hadn't bothered to wipe the blood off the bodies or cover up the bullet holes. In this way they proved their worth to the public and buttered their bread with the local press.

Across the top of the clipping, the Colonel had scribbled a harsh little note:

The bastard's dead!

I pumped my fist and cried aloud, "*Yes!*"

Over and over I read the story, relishing every word, relieved that my name was never mentioned.

Still, the news didn't satisfy me the way I'd hoped.

I read the caption under the photo, identifying the bodies. Gasolina was second from the left. I leaned in closer, savoring the image, thinking back to that hellish moment in the bank when he'd fired his shotgun into my face.

Though the man was riddled with bullets—five at least, that I could count—it wasn't enough to suit me. If anything, he looked strangely unperturbed.

So this is how it ends. This is what justice looks like.

I sat down at the kitchen table and decided to read the whole thing again. A sense of joy was what I wanted, if only for a moment. But that moment never came. When I'd read the last of it again, I felt dark and hollow, as though someone had gutted me out with a boning knife.

I wish I'd been there. To see it up close ...

I put the money away and tossed the Colonel's letter in the fire, then folded the newspaper clipping into a neat little square and tucked it carefully into my wallet.

Under cover of night, with a red moon rising, we hauled the crates up off the beach. Because of their weight and the rough terrain, it took us till dawn to get them into camp.

I'd never seen a group of men work so long and hard with such silence and severity. Step by step, their dreams were becoming real.

Just after daybreak, safe in our camp, we opened the first crate. Inside, packed neat and clean, were a dozen .38 caliber assault rifles. The second box, about the size of a casket, was filled with ammunition. The third, to everyone's delight, contained a .50 caliber machine gun with a collapsible tripod.

Like a bunch of exuberant kids we rushed to assemble the thing, and managed, despite all the clamor and confusion, to have it armed and ready in about twenty minutes.

The machine gun was the wildest thing to ever appear on the island, except for the meteor that tore through the roof of Chico's beer shack a few years back. The little fireball had bounced two or three times across the dirt floor and ended up smoldering at the foot of Chico's hammock, where the man was fast asleep. Sniffing something strange afoot, he'd rousted himself up on one elbow and shouted to his wife, "Hey Edna, you're burning the *fish*!"

Even now, the high point of many a drunk will be that sacred moment when the boys finally persuade Chico to go get his sacred meteor, hidden in some sacred corner of his bedroom, protected in a sacred leather pouch. I've seen the meteor a dozen times or more—a chunk of dark gray iron, pocked with holes, about the size of a baby's fist—but have never been allowed to actually touch it. In fact, no one has ever been allowed to touch it, lest it lose its "sacred essence of outer space," as Chico put it.

But the machine gun inspired a very different kind of reverence. Who could help but admire its smooth blue metal, glistening in the sun, and the easy way it swiveled back and forth on its tripod? Most of all, we loved the sense of power it gave us, to finally force a change.

No one was more deeply impressed than Abacaba. When first he saw the machine gun, his eyes popped wide and refused for some minutes to blink. Wiping the slobber off his chin, he solemnly declared, "It's the greatest thing I've ever seen."

"Don't touch it!" I warned him. And almost said, as Chico would, *Lest it lose its sacred essence ...*

In fact, so foreign was the machine gun to life on the island, it *did* seem to come from outer space.

I made the stupid mistake that morning of letting Abacaba convince me, with his zeal and adolescent charm, that he should have a chance to fire the machine gun. By the time I realized my error and managed to wrestle him off the trigger, he'd scared me white, shredding a row of banana trees off to his left, then sweeping right, blowing away the corner post on the barraca and sending everyone into hysterical flight.

Thus we lost our first big battle.

"Brother, that was fun!" he shouted. *"Really* fun!"

About two weeks after he'd slaughtered the banana trees, Abacaba appeared at my house one night, drunk as an eel. The man was so thoroughly liquored and reckless in his maneuvers that my dogs, though dutifully yelping, decided to keep their distance.

I rolled out of my hammock, grabbed my flashlight and met him at the gate. Once I perceived his sorry condition, I got very annoyed. "What are you doing here, you idiot?""

He stopped for a minute, trying to remember why he'd come. Then it dawned on him afresh: "Let's go see the gun!"

"Shhh! You'll wake the neighbors."

"The *machine gun*," he slobbered. "Let's go!" He took a rubbery step backward and almost collapsed upon himself.

"*Tá maluco!* It's three in the morning. Go home."

"No, but we could go see it," he persisted. "We could! It's still early."

"No it's *not*," I said. "Go home. Get some sleep. You don't want Clara to know you're cheating on her—with a *machine gun* for God's sake!"

He pressed his lips together, working up an apology. "I know I didn't do it good there, that first time," he said. "But I can do it good, Zé! I can!"

"I know you can. Now go home and get some sleep." I put my arm around him and steered him toward the gate.

"Okay," he said. "But remember, she's *mine*."

"What?"

He thumped himself on the chest. "I'm the machine gunner, okay?"

Since I didn't much believe in the grace of God or the dispensations of luck, I had no way of explaining the extraordinary events that followed just three days later: that the tugboat *Fernando Lima* should choose our little stretch of river to break a seal on its propeller shaft; that the captain should tie off on the shore just where he did, not a hundred meters from my house; that the boat's radio operator should come ashore that morning and wander up into our yard; that he should be anxious to share some maté with me and spill the latest news—of the "failed rebellion," he said—of the fighting that had broken out along the Rio Araguaia. From what he'd heard on the radio—*my heart was racing now!*—the government had already killed or captured most of the rebel leaders, including some senior officers in the military. "Day before last," he said, pointing upriver, "we passed a pair of federal gunboats, loaded with troops, searching the villages along the river ..."

The pounding in my chest grew louder, throbbing up into my ears.

They were coming for us! *Coming for me!*

Drops of sweat ran off my chin and dribbled onto the table. Surely they'd betray me.

But on he went with his story, unaware that he was sitting across the table from a dead man.

Thus it was, thank happenstance, that news of the failed revolt came to our village just a breath and a wink before the gunboats arrived.

I called an urgent meeting at the camp that night. All nine of us were present. No fire, no booze and no smiles. We had but one choice: to disband. As for the guns and ammunition, we could either throw them in the river or bury them in the jungle.

"We could stand and fight," said Abacaba.

"*Não,*" I said. "*É não e pronto!*" I knew, without a whisper of doubt, that in a fight with professional soldiers we'd be slaughtered like a bunch of pigs and take a lot of innocents down with us.

We chose a place in the jungle and began to dig. Bad planning found us working with a single shovel and lots of bare hands, clawing out the dirt.

No one said a word. Perhaps the same morbid thought had silenced us all: *We are hooked through the gill and waiting for the knife.*

When it came time to bury the machine gun, I thought Abacaba was going to break down and cry. He gave up his shovel to another man and wandered off into the jungle to mourn.

I got back to my house about sunrise, too exhausted to stay awake and too frightened to sleep. *Maybe I could take the canoe and flee downriver ... hide myself in the marsh. But that would be to abandon my Ana and desert my friends ... to forever live in the shadow of my own cowardice.*

Once my men were trained and ready, I had imagined a big line boat would pull into Jacaré, bristling with patriot soldiers. When I let the dream unfurl, I could see her decks packed tight with rebels, like an endless belt of ammo. With a thunderous cheer they'd greet us—*Viva a revolução!*—as we marched up the gangway to join them.

Sometimes I'd picture Sergeant Ribeiro there at the top of the plank to meet me. Or even the Colonel himself, delighted with my men: "Well done, Sergeant!" Always though, as we pulled away, I could see a vast flotilla of other boats coming down the river to join us, laden with patriot soldiers, who had poured out of their villages like fire ants.

In the best of all these visions, our numbers were so vast and well-organized that the government would recognize the coming tide—the inevitable triumph of democracy—and yield without a fight.

Thus the story might end without much bloodshed, I imagined, and amnesty be given wherever amnesty was possible.

The gunboats came at dawn and anchored off the point, where no one could enter or leave our little harbor without their seeing. They were sleek and ugly, painted the same dead gray that overcast the sky. The larger of the two had a three-inch gun on its bow, trained hard to starboard, bearing right down the throat of our village.

Two full platoons of soldiers came ashore—tough, professional men from the jungle brigades up in Roraima. They moved from house to house, looking for our village leaders. In less than an hour they had rounded up our bumbling president, Duba, Xabrega the priest, and all five members of the village council. One by one they were brought to the village center, to the great cinnamon tree that overspreads the square. There, without a word of explanation, they were forced to huddle on the ground and keep their mouths shut.

In short order an officer appeared, wearing jungle camouflage, a dark blue beret, and the silver stars of a first lieutenant. He ordered Duba to stand up and step forward, and bluntly gave him orders: "Tell your people that I want them here, assembled by this tree, at eleven o'clock sharp. This includes *every living soul* on the island, do you *understand* me? This includes babies, children, invalids, lunatics and marginals, such as yourself."

Accelerated by fear, the order flew from one tip of the island to the other. At the appointed hour, every last one of us had gathered around the cinnamon tree, waiting for the ax to fall.

To my right, smelling loudly of beer, stood my cousin Chico. On account of his runaway mouth and complete lack of discretion, I had told him nothing of our plans and ordered my men to do the same.

"*Meu Deus*," he piped up. "I didn't know there were so *many* of us!"

To my other side stood Aunt Leona, with one hand latched to my elbow and the other leaning hard upon her walking stick. "There's going to be trouble, isn't there?" she whispered.

"Yes, Auntie."

"Well, I hope they do it fast," she said. "My feet are tired."

At a minute past eleven, two squads of soldiers appeared and formed themselves into a circle around the cinnamon tree. With their rifles presented forward, muzzles up, they pushed back the crowd, creating a secure little island for their commander.

The lieutenant came forward and took a slow turn around the circle, looking us over as though we were a bunch of goats. Then he stopped, removed his beret, and spent half a minute preening his slick black hair. When it was arranged to his satisfaction, he replaced the beret and adjusted the angle just so.

Quiet as we were, it wasn't quiet enough. He suddenly drew his pistol, pointed it up into the tree, and fired. Into the hush that followed he barked out his orders: "Shut your mouths now and pay attention!"

A baby cried on. Apart from that there was cold stone silence.

The officer returned his pistol to its holster, pulled a paper out of his pocket and slowly unfolded it. "From the office of our President and Most Excellent Protector of the Republic," he read loudly. "Let it be known to every loyal citizen of Brazil that there has been a scattered and insignificant rebellion against the Brazilian people and their government, led by a pack of criminals and communists, and a few sordid traitors within the military. These men, especially the traitors within the military, have brought disgrace upon themselves and their families forever. The heroic military forces of Brazil have easily dispersed these outlaws and executed their leaders.

"Let it be further understood that any citizen lending support or encouragement to the insurrection, in any way whatsoever, will be considered a traitor to his nation and a hostile combatant, and treated as such, under the full application of military law."

The lieutenant folded away the paper and gazed out across the crowd. "Is it possible that some of you know Colonel Mateus Izquerda, commander of the third battalion of military police?" He waited for the question to sink in, then bluntly added: "I should say, the *late* Colonel Izquerda." He walked patiently along the edge of the crowd, waiting for an answer.

My heart was pounding again, intent on giving me up. *Was it possible they didn't know who I was? That somehow my name had slipped through their fingers? Maybe the Colonel had kept no files. Or managed to destroy them before the sky fell in.*

The officer stopped and shouted over our heads. "Let it be known among you, and remembered, that the Colonel involved himself in insurrection and disgraced himself to death. Thus he will not be buried with military honors. Nor will he be buried with civilian honors. In fact, he will not be buried at *all*."

With a wave of his hand he signaled to a third squad of soldiers that was grouped beside the church. Two of their number came forward and positioned themselves under the cinnamon tree. The soldier on the left carried a box, about half a meter square, wrapped in burlap. The other held a length of iron chain and a crimping tool.

Under the lieutenant's watchful eye, they chose a stout, low-hanging branch and wrapped the chain around it. With grim efficiency, they lifted the box, ran the chain through an iron ring on top, and crimped the ends together. When they backed away, the box was left there hanging, about shoulder high, so that everyone could gawk and wonder.

The officer walked briskly over to it, pulled out his pocket knife and cut away the burlap. Underneath it was a stout little cage made of banded iron. Inside, lying on the bottom, was something gnarled and gray.

"What in God's name is it?" Leona gasped.

On the other side of the crowd, downwind of the cage, people were murmuring and melting away, holding their noses.

As the cage swung gently around, a hand appeared, severed at the wrist. The fingers were grotesquely bent and grasping, devoid of grace, devoid of poetry, devoid of power.

The lieutenant had moved himself upwind and stood idly by, trimming his fingernails with the knife. When just enough time had passed, he put the blade away and shouted out, "Is it possible that Colonel Izquerda has friends here in Jacaré who will mourn his passing?" He walked expectantly along the edge of the crowd, looking from one person to the next. "No? Not a single friend?"

Silence.

"Surely there's *someone* who will say a kind word for the Colonel?"

Chico leaned over to me and whispered, "I think maybe he was more popular when he was whole."

I tried to shush the fool, but it was too late. The officer was coming over to investigate.

"You there, with the whispers. Are you a friend of the Colonel's?"

My cousin wagged his silly head. "No. I don't know the Colonel." Then, with wide-eyed innocence, he added, "Don't know his *hand* either."

The lieutenant was right in front of us now, craning forward. His face and neck, especially on the right, had been pocked by disease.

When he turned just so, the scars looked like they'd been impregnated with bits of fried sausage.

His gaze fell hard on Chico. "Are you the town poet, little man? The storyteller?"

"No," he answered. "I'm the clown."

The officer's mouth twitched at the corners. "Clowns are good, so long as they keep their acts clean."

He turned suddenly, as if he'd sniffed something foul, and looked me straight on. "How about you? Are you a friend of the Colonel's?"

Somehow I managed to look him in the eyes and lie. "No sir."

Now he'd noticed the scars on my cheek and leaned in closer to examine them. No one had ever gawked at me quite so rudely. "Shotgun?" he said.

"Yes."

"I hope the other man looks worse than you do."

"The other man is dead," I said.

He nodded approvingly. "Do you tell stories, Mr. Shotgun? Are you the town minstrel?"

"No sir," I said. "There's no one like that here."

"Yes there is," Chico spouted. "The Voice. He sings pretty good."

The lieutenant smiled darkly. "The Voice? Which one is that?"

Before my cousin could point him out, the officer abruptly turned and shouted, "Which one of you is The Voice? Speak up. *Now!*"

From out of the crowd, off to our left, stepped Vinícius. "Here."

The lieutenant walked quickly over, seized him by the arm and led him into the shade of the cinnamon tree. "Kneel here," he said, pointing to a spot beneath the cage. "I want you to *sing* for us! Something full of spark and glory."

Vinícius knelt, his face abandoned, desperate for a song.

"Go ahead!" the officer snapped. "Inspire us!"

Poor Vinícius was on the verge of speaking, or maybe singing, when the lieutenant pulled out his pistol and shot him in the head.

It took several hours before the first of the women screamed. Or maybe it was days. Suddenly the man behind me was throwing up, splattering vomit on my feet. Aunt Leona was sobbing uncontrollably.

Her head fell hard against my shoulder, splashing tears across my sleeve. Or maybe they were *mine*.

"You! Shotgun!"

The officer was calling me out. "Get over here!"

I loosened Auntie's arm from mine and pushed Chico into the gap. "Hold her!"

"Get over here!" the lieutenant barked.

I walked numbly forward, passed through the line of soldiers, and stood silently before him. It was going to be quick now.

He pointed his finger at the ground, where Vinícius lay. "You see this man here?"

"Yes."

"This man needs to be buried."

"I see."

"I want you to go get a shovel and I want you to bury this man. Right *here*. Right under the cage."

It seemed impossible even to draw another breath.

"I want it done by sunset," he said. "I want everything *tidied up*." He turned and bellowed into the crowd, "This cage remains here forever! You touch it, you forfeit your hand! You move it, you forfeit your life!"

So ended our glorious revolution.

And so began my career as a gravedigger.

Thus did the enemy place a curse upon us, meant to bind us with fear and poison our chances. Whether by design or not, they had defiled the most beautiful tree on the island—the great cinnamon. In its glory, blooming white, it was visible halfway across the river and filled the whole village with its fragrance.

The urubus came first, clinging ponderously to the side of the cage, picking away at the Colonel's hand. Then the ants, taking everything but the bones. And finally the sun and wind, to bleach them white.

Some say the Colonel's hand began to move, empowered by his anguished spirit, struggling to free itself from the cage. Whether that

36

or the trickery of the wind, the bones *did* move, bit by bit, till the fingertips latched hold of the iron mesh and protruded through the gaps.

With such evil hanging from its limbs and murder buried at its roots, the grand old tree forgot how to flower, then to leaf, and finally died.

After the soldiers had gone, when I was able to think again and act, I dug out every centavo I owned—all my soldier's pay and more—and took it to Padre Xabrega.

"I want you to pray for my friend Esmeralda," I said. "She's very young, Padre. Her father's been killed. Probably her mother too ..."

"Why not come and pray for her yourself?" Xabrega said. "There's a mass tomorrow morning."

"No, that won't work, Padre. Listen, she may be on the run, from people who want to harm her. I don't know for sure."

Xabrega looked befuddled.

"I want you to line up all the Saints you can," I said. "Whichever ones apply."

He shrugged and looked off into his memory. "I don't know. I'll have to think."

I grabbed his hand and pressed the cash down into his palm. "However many prayers this will buy ... that's how many I want. You *understand*?"

In the months that followed, when I found our table empty and the fishing poor, a sneering voice would sometimes come and whisper, "You fool! Why would you waste your money on prayers when you scarce believe in God?"

The answer, I knew, lay somewhere in the gap between "scarce" and "believe."

CHAPTER FIVE

A FEW WEEKS LATER, ON MY TWENTY-FIFTH BIRTHDAY, AN ODD PIECE of freight showed up on the boat from Santarém.

The cargo master himself—one João Silveiro—appeared at our gate that day, about midmorning.

Yes, my name was Zé, I told him. But no, I'd ordered nothing from Santarém, and had no friends or relatives there. Three times I asked him the nature of the cargo, and three times he dodged the question, pressing me to come along and see for myself.

Unaware that an earthquake was about to shake my life forever, I grabbed my fishing cap and followed him down to the river, sure there'd been some mistake.

Once aboard, João walked me back through the cargo deck, past cases of bottled beer and bags of onions. When we came to the bulkhead, near the stern of the boat, he pointed me to a cardboard box that was tucked back under the sink.

"All yours," he declared, with what can only be described as infinite relief.

A baby lay quietly in the box, peering sternly up, as though to say, *"What took you so long?"* He was wrapped in an old dish towel, so potently stinky that it overpowered the putrid odor of the onions. A long drizzle of snot ran out his little nose, bridged the lips on his little mouth, and dangled tenuously off his little chin.

"What's this got to do with *me*?" I blurted.

João pulled the box out from under the sink, untied the tag from the baby's toe, and handed it to me. It said:

> *To Zorion's better brother, Zé Licata*
> *Isle of Fair Winds*

"You're Zé Licata, right?" he said. "Zorion's brother?"

There was no way to worm my way out of it.

"This is the Isle of Fair Winds, isn't it?"

My mind raced back to the last time I'd seen Zorion, packing his gear for the gold fields. In the other room that morning was his latest splash ... some Peruvian girl ... *what was her name? Yelenda!* She'd been packing too, I remembered—blouses and bitterness, lingerie and loathing—grim as a hand grenade. Zorion was headed for Itaituba that afternoon, up the Tapajós. And she ... *where was she going? Santarém!*

I remembered whispering to my brother, pointing through the doorway. "What about *her*?"

He'd waved her off like a housefly. "Flamed out," was all he said. In less than a month, his irresistible "princess" had somehow become a pest. And also, apparently, pregnant.

I looked into the baby's clear green eyes and saw my reckless brother grinning back. Sure as seeds beget seedlings, the boy was my nephew.

"Gutsy little guy," the cargo master said. "Two days on the river and he never squawked once."

I leaned over and considered the little poot up close. Truth is, he was neither cute nor innocent, the way babies are supposed to be. Rather, he seemed immersed in heavy thought, pondering, I guess, why the world had plopped him down in such poor circumstances. Had he been able to speak, the questions would have been tough: *Why this fire in my crotch, and this awful itch? Why this gnawing in my tummy? What's happened to Mama?*

Indeed, I thought. *What happened to Mama?!*

39

João was growing restless. The boat was soon to leave. "Here, you need to sign this manifest," he said.

Maybe I could turn this thing around. Send the baby back to—

"Forget it," he said. "There's no return freight on this guy. Besides which, you'll never find her. She was hell-bent for other parts."

"You read minds, do you?"

He hacked up a wad of snot and spit it into the sink. "The girl gave us fifty cruzeiros for our trouble," he said. "The baby's *yours*."

Too confused to think, I stood up and took the clipboard from him, and a stubby little pen.

"I've carried some pretty strange cargo in my day," the man said. "But never a baby. Alone, like this."

I couldn't make any sense of the papers he'd given me.

"One time, I remember, we took a canister of refrigerated bull sperm to a cattle breeder over in Óbidos. Always wondered, you know, how he got them sperm into the ... ah ... you know, the place where sperm goes ... without getting trampled or gored or—"

"I always wondered that *too*," I said sarcastically. "Look, I don't know what you want here."

"It's the fifth line there," he said, jabbing it with his finger. "Since we got no category for babies, I just scribbled him in as 'livestock.'"

I took a deep breath and signed the thing. What else could I do, leave him under the sink? Throw him in the river?

João took back his clipboard and shrugged. "What you gonna do?"

I bent down and peeled the sticky dish towel off him, then lifted him out of the box. "You can burn all that," I said. "Box and everything."

The cargo master pinched his nose. "*Ishh* ..."

I washed the baby off in the sink, from tip to toe, then held him up, all fresh and dripping clean. He was so delighted by the change that he just peed out into space.

João jumped back, but the splatter caught his shoes. "*Porra!*" he squealed. "Watch where you're aiming that thing!"

When the boy was through expressing himself, I swung him back over my shoulder—the same way the dockers were slinging their bags of onions—and carried him off the boat.

The cargo master leaned out over the railing and yelled after me, "He won't give you no trouble, *senhor*. You'll see. He's a quiet one."

He was quiet all right, and I on the verge of panic. What would Ana say, me bringing home a baby? She and I had been through some wild and bitter turns on the procreation front; a string of miscarriages —was it three now, or four?—that certainly weren't my fault. And maybe one that was.

The first thing out of her mouth, I knew, would be, *"How long we keeping him for?"*

"Till Zorion comes back," I'd tell her. Which probably meant forever. But why say it?

"Didn't he have no diapers or food with him?" she'd ask.

"Just his personality."

"Well what's his name? He must have a name."

And there she'd have me.

Up from the shore a ways, I turned and looked back at the boat, chugging away from the dock. *Rafael* was its name.

And so, from that moment on, was his.

Rafael Licata.

In the cool of the mornings, when Ana went down to the river with the wash, I'd put Rafael in my hammock and swing him back and forth. How he loved to bounce and roll and giggle there, and I to see him so, wiggling around in the belly of the hammock, all close and warm and safe. I'd poke at him through the fabric—"Where'd he go? Where did Rafael go? Is that him *there*?"—and tickle him so mercilessly that he'd run out of laughter and just lay there gasping.

I remember the day he first stood up in the hammock, wobbly as a noodle, clinging to the hem with both hands, peeking out at me with those bright green eyes.

"You're going to be the greatest man that Brazil has ever seen," I told him. "Greater than Pelé!"

He looked me over, under that pensive brow, wondering how such a thing could happen.

"Someday, you will play piano and recite poems," I said. "Learn to speak algebra and English. Have straight white teeth, like Esmeralda's."

I got up off the stool, opened the wardrobe, and pulled my first-grade reader off the shelf. "This here is a book," I said. "Good for learning and edification. The key to most everything on earth."

I opened the cover and read again the inscription that old José Nery had scrawled:

> *To Zé, my best student ever!*
> *If not us, then who? If not now, then when?*
> *With revolutionary affection,*
> *José*

Filled with the warmth of his memory and the bitterness of our failure, I handed the reader to Rafael. "You'll be wanting *lots* of these," I said. "A whole library."

The boy eagerly took it, dropped it into the bottom of the hammock, burrowed down to find it, drooled on it, ripped the back cover in half, dropped it again, discovered it again, chewed on it to see if it was edible, and finally, tiring of the whole thing, chucked it over the side of the hammock.

I stepped back to the wardrobe and pulled out the Colt 45 that I had used in the army. When I mustered out, the Colonel had made arrangements for me to keep it. I was good with it really—good enough to hit a mango at thirty meters.

"I expect you'll need one of these too," I said. "The world being as it is." I took the pistol out of its holster, removed the clip, checked the chamber, and slipped it into the hammock for him to play with.

Though Rafael could barely lift the thing, he loved it from the start. Maybe it was the smell of oil and gunpowder that charmed him. Maybe the shine.

I leaned in close and ruffled his hair, which had come in black and curly, thick as fleece. "Take every chance you dare, boy. You *hear* me?"

He smiled at me, bobbing from side to side, then reached out, as far as his little hand could stretch, and grabbed the tip of my nose.

I picked him up and held him against my naked chest, and smelled the newness of him. I began to love him, just then, in a way that I'd never loved anyone.

It was not long after that, carrying him into the village, that someone first mistook him for my son. "No," I might have said. "He's my brother's boy." But didn't, and never did thereafter.

Whatever the hereditary truth, my heart had made me father.

CHAPTER SIX

WHEN FIRST I MET THE IRISHMAN, WHOSE FULL NAME, I LEARNED later, was Michael Tarron O'Hannon, he was sitting on the back of his boat—the *Jornada de Fé*—with a fishing line in one hand and an open book in the other.

Coming off the river, about an hour past dawn, I nudged my canoe into the shore alongside him. The fishing had gone poorly that night and I'd been drinking heavy. The world felt ragged and empty.

As my canoe slipped past him, he looked up from his book and gave me a little wave. *"Bom dia!"*

"That's no way to fish," I said. "You can't be reading a book with one eye and fishing with the other. You got to *pay attention*."

He smiled enthusiastically, as though he'd been expecting me to come along and insult him.

"You're dense as a post," I said. "You don't understand a word I'm saying, do you?"

He nodded eagerly. *"Um pouco.* Please talk slow."

I got out of my canoe and pulled it up on the sand. "Why are you here, gringo? To snapshot the natives?"

The man understood just enough Portuguese to know I was mocking him, but not enough to defend himself.

I pitched my few small fish up on the shore. "Where do you come from?" I asked.

He shrugged, fumbling for an answer.

I looked at his foreign tennis shoes and his shiny watch. At his sunglasses, cocked back into a mess of curly red hair. "You come from the land of plenty, don't you?"

"Ireland," he said hopefully.

"Why?" I said. "Why would you do such a thing?"

He put aside his fishing line, then the book. And with an exuberant grin, answered, "To fish."

I shook my head at him. "If you knew anything about fishing, you'd know there's nothing in these shallows but piranhas and stingrays."

He laughed and wagged his finger at me. "No, not fish like *that*," he said, pointing to my catch.

I had no idea what the man was talking about. And didn't much care.

Struggling for words, he grinned and pointed to his book. "Scaring the love of God," he declared.

What could I do but laugh at the poor fool? "Well you're off to a good start, Irishman. You got *me* scared."

His smile wilted into confusion. "Wait, that's not it ..." He scratched his head for a long moment, then blurted, "*Spreading* the love of God! That's what I meant."

"Ah, a *missionary*," I said. "Just what we need."

"Yes. A missionary."

A clanging of pots and pans rose inside the cabin.

"So there are more of you, are there?" I said.

His face brightened. "Yes! Me and Josué. He makes lunch."

I knelt on the sand and sacked up my fish. "Well, I wouldn't get too excited if I were you, gringo. Trying to change things here is like plowing the river."

Though the meaning escaped him, he couldn't have missed the tone. There is a certain meanness that whiskey inspires in a man, and its voice is never kind.

"You come here to put an end to our poverty, do you?" I said. "To heal our diseases? You think maybe *that's* our problem?"

He stood up and leaned over the railing, listening hard. Then said something to me that I will never forget: "It is not poverty that kills us, *amigo*. It's hopelessness."

Incredibly, the man had finished my speech for me! I looked back over my shoulder at him, surprised and suspicious. He wasn't quite the fool that I'd supposed him to be.

With nothing left to say, I shouldered my paddle, took up my little sack of fish, and headed off. But turned, for some reason, and called back to him, "I am not always this rude to strangers."

He nodded at me, understanding everything, it seemed, and nothing at all.

I sighed over his sad condition, and mine. "Then again," I said, "maybe I *am*."

CHAPTER SEVEN

By the time Mick O'Hannon came to our village, I had buried dozens of people, including my brothers Zavan and Zinildo, who killed one another over a game of dominoes.

I remember the morning I buried them, feeling very sad that I didn't feel very sad. I wish there was some way to conjure love posthumously. Or even affection. You could sell it by the barrel.

All that was left me that morning, as I marked their graves, were boyhood memories of punch and counterpunch, and the bare-butt whippings we got from my father.

With so many graves to my credit, it was no surprise that Chico came to my house that February afternoon, looking for help. Instead of barging right in, as he usually did, he waited outside the gate, clapping softly, "*E aí, Primo, você está?* It's Chico!"

By the time I got there, my dogs had already dashed out to meet him, wagging their happy tails. Like everyone else on the island, they instinctively liked the man. Maybe it was his eyes that charmed us, always bright and laughing, or his wild black hair, which sprang out in a thousand little curls. But more, we could tell that underneath that chubby exterior lived a man who was perfectly at home with his madness and always ready to make you part of it. If Chico had lived in another time or place, they would probably have put him in an asylum. But on the Isle of Fair Winds, he was our favorite clown, our most daring innovator, and—most important of all—our sole supplier of beer and fireworks.

"Hey Primo, we got trouble down at the river," he said.

Already I didn't like the way that he'd roped *me* into his "we."

I opened the gate and gestured him in, but he held back. Of all the roles that Chico could play, gloomy suited him least.

"What sort of trouble?" I said.

"That foreign guy—you know the guy in the boat?—was up at the shack this morning looking for help."

"The redhead you mean?"

"That's him, Primo. Wandering around like a lost goose."

I thought back a few days, to that sour morning by the shore. The foreigner had tried to be friendly, while I'd been rude as a pig. "So what did he say?"

Chico tapped his finger on his chin, trying to recall. "Truthfully, Zé, I couldn't much understand him. But, understanding what I did, I think maybe someone's real sick down there."

"*And?*"

"Well ..." He shrugged his big, round shoulders. "I gave him a couple aspirin and sold him some toilet paper."

"That's it? You gave him *aspirin?*"

"And toilet paper."

"Well that ought to fix him up."

"And also told him I'd *do* something," Chico added solemnly.

"Well then, go do something."

His eyes flitted off like a pair of birds, perched in the bushes for a while, then suddenly returned. Up came that enchanting Chico smile and his warm, appealing hands. "I was thinking, since you're the undertaker, maybe you could go down to the boat and see what's happening."

"Is someone dead?" I asked.

"No. Not yet."

I gave him a little smirk—the kind he was always giving me. "We'll I don't generally bury folks till they're dead, Chico."

He nodded at me with all the solemnity he could muster. "I know that, Primo. They got to be dead before you can bury them, right? Or even to investigate whether they're ready to almost be buried or not."

I could tell by the wild lights in his eyes and the curl of his lip that he was getting ready to zing me.

"I was thinking though," he said, "since you're a policeman, maybe you could—"

"Stop right *there*, little cousin. I am not the police."

Chico looked shocked by the news, and ready to argue the point.

But I cut him off. "Look, we've been over this before. Repeat after me, *there are no police on the island.*"

He gave me a dark and brooding look, like a little boy who'd been swatted by his teacher.

"Go ahead. Say it."

"There are no police on the island," he mumbled.

"And even if there *was* a policeman, Zé's not him."

His whole body seemed to droop. Even his curls were wilting.

"Go ahead. Say it."

"But you got the gun!" he erupted. "A real *policeman's* gun."

"Having a handgun does not make me a policeman, Chico. You know that."

"Well, why do you keep it?" he persisted.

"To protect myself from all the fools that live on this island," I said.

"So you're not going down to his boat?"

"No, I'm not going down to his boat."

Chico slipped back into that private space of his, where the clown and the lunatic dwelled happily together. "Well," he muttered to himself, "we did all we could, didn't we? We talked to the *undertaker* and we talked to the *police,* and that's about all a man can do."

Having come to an honorable peace, he popped back into the world where the rest of us live. "Okay," he said brightly. "We did all that we could and that's all that we should!" He reached down to pet the dogs, spun himself around on a happy heel and headed off down the path. "Hey Primo," he yelled back. "Come up to the shack later and we'll play us some dominoes!"

After Chico left, I took a couple swigs of cachaça and carried the bottle into the bedroom. The wind blew fresh and noisy through the windows, with rain on its breath. I closed the shutters, sat the bottle on the floor, and eased back into my hammock.

Halfway asleep, on the edge of a dream, something unnatural came upon me. Like a feather it was, and then a brick, pressing against my chest.

I bolted upright in the hammock. "Get away from me!"

But the spirit pressed closer. Without form or sound, it flooded the room and made its message clear. *Go help him!*

I swung my legs out over the hammock and took a long chug from the bottle. "Ana!"

Her voice came in from the yard. "*Oi?*"

"Get in here!"

She came quickly, as she'd been taught, and stood before me with a handful of eggs. "Yes, Zé."

"I want you to get a jug of water, some dried fish and a *palma* of bananas, and take them down to the gringo's boat."

Her eyes fell warily on the bottle. She had never liked my friend Cachaça and my friend Cachaça had never liked her.

"Tell them it's a gift from Zé," I put in.

Ana moved toward the door, but stopped there and looked back. "It wants to rain," she said timidly.

I considered her through a mist of alcohol and splintered dreams. *When exactly had the glow disappeared from her cheeks, and the sparkle left her amber eyes? And why, for the love of God, couldn't she take a simple order?*

"*Porra*, I know it wants to rain, woman! Just do what I say!"

In the merest whisper she replied, "I think it would be unseemly for me to go down to his boat alone."

"What do *you* know about seemly?" I said. But quickly regretted the words and tried to mend them. "Take little Nina with you then, or one of the other girls."

Ana nodded, and was on her way, when I suddenly felt ashamed. "Wait," I called after her. "Get the food together, and Nina, and I'll go down with you."

Death hung over their little boat like a vapor. I could tell by the smell —familiar to my trade—that indeed they would need me soon.

My old friends the urubus had smelled it too. A pair of them sat on the forward rail, flexing their wings, with a dozen more scratching around on the sand. They say that an urubu will eat anything, no matter how vile, *except* for another urubu—because they know what they've been eating. But I'll give them this: they're patient in their work. And when no one's around to dig a poor body a grave, they'll clean up the mess for free.

With the river rising, the *Jornada de Fé* had slipped its lines and swung around toward the beach. An old plank, fractured on one side, ran up from the sand through a gap in the forward railing. We stood close by the bow—Ana with the fish, Nina with the bananas, and I with the jug of water—and clapped. When no one came, we clapped some more. "*Boa tarde!*" I called out. And still no one appeared.

Ana gave me an anxious look that mirrored my thoughts exactly: *Maybe they were already dead* ...

To the east, a curtain of rain was marching across the river toward us. It was five, maybe ten minutes away at best. Behind it loomed a wall of great thunderheads, like a family of giants rising from their sleep.

"There's no one here," Nina said. "Let's get home!"

Rain was splattering the face of the river now and leaving dimples in the sand. A bolt of lightning ripped across the clouds.

With the thunderclap, Nina vaulted backward and nearly dropped the bananas. "I want to get home!"

At that very moment the Irishman poked his head through the forward door, just beside the pilothouse, and climbed up on the deck.

He was way too big for his boat—maybe two meters tall—and built like a tree. His hair, ruffling in the wind, was watermelon red.

"*Olá! Olá!*" he shouted, rushing onto the bow. "Please come up. Please *come!*"

Up the plank I hurried, with Ana just behind me and Nina trailing.

The man seized my hand and pumped it hard. "Thank God you come," he said, in his horrid Portuguese. "*Obrigado!*"

With the rain spitting at our backs, he led us down into the cabin, where the mood quickly changed. So cramped and dark were the quarters, so foul the air, that Ana and Nina hung back at the top of the steps, preferring the rain on their necks to the squalid space below.

A pair of hammocks hung loosely across the cabin, swaying with the boat. Beyond them sat the engine, housed in a heavy wire cage, with a tiny galley and head tucked into the stern. Across the top of the engine, on a bed of rough wood planks, lay a man who was dead already or close enough that he smelled that way.

"Thank God you here," the Irishman said. "I been praying for help."

I sat the jug of water by the bulkhead. "You remember me, then?"

"Yes, the fisherman. But the name of you, my friend, I do not remember."

"It's Zé," I told him. "This here is my wife, Ana. And up there, with the bananas, is Nina, my neighbor's daughter."

"*Meu prazer,*" he said, in a strange and formal way. "I am Mick. Mick O'Hannon."

He pointed to his friend and gestured me to follow. Whatever he said next was lost in a sudden barrage of rain, which beat across the boat like a thousand drummers.

I ducked through the hammocks and followed him aft, till we stood alongside his friend.

Over the clattering rain he shouted, "This is Josué! He got something real bad with his stomach!"

The man was naked to his waist and stank of old sweat and rotten flesh. There were flies everywhere, buzzing around his face and chest, crawling down the holes in his ears. In good health, he must have been a handsome man and strong. Now his cheeks had turned sallow and all the brightness had left his eyes.

I leaned in close and tried to catch his attention. "How you doing, friend? I'm Zé."

It took him a long moment to register the question. "*Mais ou menos,*" he said.

"You Brazilian, eh?"

"*Sim.*"

"*De onde?*"

"*Belo Horizonte.*"

I turned to the redhead. "We need to get some air in here, and flush these damned flies out." But he didn't understand me. "Fresh air!" I shouted. "Open some windows there!" I pointed him along the starboard side, where we wouldn't take much rain. "*Abre as janelas!*"

Josué said something to him in English, and he finally got it.

While Mick opened the wooden shutters, I cracked the rear hatch and propped it with a broom. In came some light and rain and a gush of clean, cool air.

I hurried back to the engine, shooed the flies away and took a closer look. The man had loosened his belt and dropped his pants to ease the pressure around his waist. His belly was swollen and strangely yellowed.

I put my hand on his abdomen and gently pressed. It was tight —*real* tight—and hot to the touch. When I eased off, he jerked with pain.

"How long you been sick, Josué?"

His head fell away, groping for an answer. "A day or two," he muttered.

Mick was back at my side now. "*Four* days," he corrected, holding up his fingers. "I don't take him for help, Zé, because ..." He shrugged his big shoulders and looked completely lost. "I don't know the way."

"Do you have any money?" I asked.

"A little," Mick said.

"Okay." I looked past him, caught Ana's eye, and shouted her over. "Put the fish down and get over here! You too, Nina!"

"What are you going to do?" Mick asked.

"Get help," I said. "I know a woman who's good with herbs and remedies. She lives up the island a ways. Maybe she would come."

Ana was standing across from us now, with little Nina at her side, still clutching the bananas.

"I'm going down to Alzira's place," I said. "I want you and Nina to stay here and bathe this man with water. You understand? Try to pull his fever down."

"*Wait*," said Josué. He reached out and gripped my wrist. "Who are you going for? A doctor?"

"No. We got no doctors here."

"Who then?"

"*Uma curandeira*," I said.

"*Macumbeira?*"

My voice betrayed me a little. "Yes."

He shook his head. "No. No *macumba*. I don't want her here."

I looked him over again and made it plain. "Listen friend, you better take whatever help you can."

"No!" he said firmly. "No witches."

A bolt of lightning struck so close that we all jumped together. Thunder shook the boat, and Nina began to cry. The odor of burnt air and desperation swarmed over us.

"Take the girl and go home," I told Ana.

"What are you going to do?"

I shook my head at her. "Just *go*, woman!"

Nina had already bolted away from her and was halfway up the ladder. Ana followed her up, but stopped at the top and looked back at me. There might have been affection in her eyes, I guess, though it had been so long a stranger that I couldn't say for sure. Then she was gone.

A dead man's plan was hatching in my brain, born out of stubbornness and desperation. I walked forward a ways, then aft, checking the planks along the hull. "Do you have any fuel?" I asked.

"Some," the Irishman responded.

"How much is *some*?"

"I don't know. Twenty-five liters. Maybe thirty."

The plan was hatching fast, as foolishness always does. The closest health clinic was in Mirindá, to the east. But that would take us into the teeth of the storm. *Better to beat for the hospital in São Jorge. It was farther, and against the current, but at least we'd have the wind to our backs and some towns along the way.*

"Does the bilge pump work?" I asked him.

But Mick didn't understand, and Josué had lapsed into sleep.

"The pump!" I yelled, pointing to it and pumping my fist up and down. "Does it work?"

Now he got the idea. "Yes!"

"We'll try for the hospital!" I shouted. "Take the boat. Go to the *hospital*." I gestured off to the west and shaped my hands around an imaginary helm. *"Bora levar ele para o hospital!"*

Mick nodded slowly, grasping the idea, sifting the odds. His soft blue eyes looked me over with such intensity that I had to look away. He knew how strong the storm, how small the boat, how easily a man can drown.

"Okay!" he yelled, *"Vamos!"*

What I hadn't told him, exactly, was that it was ten, maybe twelve hours to São Jorge, and we didn't have enough fuel to get us there. Somewhere along the way, his God would have to provide.

Gently as we could, we moved Josué off the engine and into his hammock. Though the man had lapsed unconscious, Mick kept talking to him, in English I guess, with soft and soothing words.

I went up into the wheelhouse and started the engine. It caught on the first turn and sounded strong. I noticed a long crack in the starboard glass and drops of rain seeping through, dribbling down across the controls. *Not good.* I turned on the searchlight, mounted on the deckhead above, and breathed a little easier. The beam was strong and swiveled smoothly from side to side.

Meantime, Mick had shuttered the starboard windows and battened the doorway aft. With the cabin secured, he went ashore, shielding his face against the rain, waiting for my signal.

I revved the engine, took a long, deep breath, and gave him a thumbs up.

Like a ghost sifting through the rain, he threw off the lines and hurried back up the gangway. Thoroughly drenched now, he heaved the plank back through the railing and made fast the ropes.

I backed the boat out into the river and headed us west-southwest, hugging the shore. With the wind howling at our stern, the boat surged forward, riding the swells.

Straight before the wind! Got to keep us straight! If a big wave should catch us across the beam, there'll be no second chance.

An hour out, Mick brought me a cup of coffee that was old and cold and filled with grounds. With gibberish and wild gestures he tried to communicate something, that there was water in the bilge, I guess, that he was pumping hard. Then turned and disappeared in a hurry.

Night was full upon us now. I struggled at the helm, gripping the wheel with both hands. Swinging the searchlight left, I'd spot the shore and try to get my bearings, then swing it forward to light the way ahead. Sheets of rain hammered the little wheelhouse and swirled forward into the darkness.

Heaved up on the shoulders of a massive wave, we hung there like a toy, then pivoted forward on the keel and plunged down the other side. Ploughing into the bottom of the trough, a massive sheet of water broke over the wheelhouse and shattered the starboard window. Torrents of water and glass crashed through, pouring around my feet. The stern pitched sharply up, and up some more, till the prop spun free.

For a long, horrible moment I wasn't sure we'd climb out of it. "Come on up," I begged. *Come on, little boat!*

Somehow, incredibly, the bow righted itself and climbed up through the wave, streaming sheets of water off the deck. When the prop bit into the river again, the driveshaft groaned against the diesel.

We couldn't survive another hit like that.

Rain was blowing through the broken panel now and pooling around my feet, ankle deep, laden with shards of glass.

Mick came topside again, clinging to the rail, splashing into the pilot house. "He wants to talk with you!" he shouted.

"What?!"

"Josué wants to talk to you!"

56

"*What?*! No! Not now!"

Mick peered out onto the river, tracking the searchlight. "I'll take the wheel for a minute," he said calmly. "Go talk to him. *Please*. He's asking for you."

This was madness heaped upon madness. What did the foreigner know of the river? And yet, something nudged me into going. "Okay then. Keep her bearing at two-sixty." I tapped the compass to make sure he understood me. "Two-sixty. Okay? *Two, six, zero*. I'll be fast!"

The Irishman took the wheel.

Grabbing the rail, I scrambled down the hatch and secured the door behind me. The cabin was a scene from hell, filled with riotous shadows and diesel fumes. The deck pitched and rolled with such violence that I could barely keep my balance, made worse by the clutter of pots and pans and other gear that clattered underfoot.

The Irishman had tied off his friend's hammock so it wouldn't buck around. Even so, the man was wailing with pain.

I leaned over him and gave him all the cheer I could. "We're making good time!" I shouted. "Headed straightway to the hospital!"

He peered up at me from the depths of his hammock, pushing back the pain. "I want you to look after Mick," he uttered.

"*Como?*"

Drawing what little strength he had, he reached out and took my hand. "He and I were a team, you know? For Jesus ..."

"*Eu sei.*"

"Without me, he won't be able to—"

"Listen friend," I cut him off, "you just need to *rest* here, that's all, and let us get you to the clinic. "*Tá bem?*"

"I want you to look after him," he repeated. "Help him along."

I was wild with fear and too exhausted for kindness. "Listen, Josué, I'll tell you straight. I'm *not* going to look after him. He's *not* my problem. Neither is he my answer."

How strangely calm he smiled back. "I know you will," he said. And *died*. Just like that. Closed his eyes, with his hand still wrapped in mine, and died.

Twice I checked his pulse, first at his wrist—gone limp now—then at the artery on his neck.

The man was gone. And suddenly, though I hardly knew him, I began to cry.

I sat down on the bench beside him, exhausted. *How had we come to this sad and terrifying hour? And how dare he put such a weight upon me! A perfect stranger ...*

"*Meu Deus,*" I muttered. "What was he thinking?"

The answer seemed apparent: *It was madness. That's what it was. The last dim thought of a failing mind.*

I decided then and there, that should I live out the night, I'd mention none of this to the Irishman, or anyone else. *Ever.*

We found an inlet to the south, protected from the wind, and tied off the boat for the night.

Refusing any help, Mick wrapped Josué's body in his hammock and carried him topside, so the stink might leave the cabin.

We had a short, silent meal—the dried fish and bananas I'd brought —then lay down, exhausted. I was grateful the Irishman had found me an extra hammock, which I strung high across the beams.

There in the darkness, after a time, I heard him crying. Had I not known better, I'd have guessed him a child, for who but a child could weep so freely and unashamed? After a while, his tears dissolved into a most extraordinary prayer. Understanding not a word of it, I still perceived its meaning. No regrets or recriminations spoke he. Neither was there any bitterness or anger in his voice. Against all odds and circumstance, the man was giving thanks.

It was late morning, under a clearing sky, when we brought the boat back into Jacaré. We had traveled for hours in silence, like soldiers slogging home from battle.

I wanted nothing more than to find my house, my hammock, my bottle, and put the wretched night behind me.

But Mick cut me off at the gangway and pointed aft, to the place he'd left the body. "You help me?" he pleaded.

I am not very good at hiding my feelings, especially when it's aggravation.

He saw the look and opened his hands to me. "No shovel, Zé. Don't know where to dig."

What could I tell the man? Go dump your friend in the river?

So I helped him carry the body out to the graveyard, about a half kilometer east of the village.

We picked up some followers along the way, kids mostly, and idle women, who trailed us along with their curiosity. I summoned one of the boys and sent him to my house to fetch us a pair of shovels.

Am I the only man on the island who knows how to dig? Why shouldn't the gringo pick himself a good Catholic to help him here, someone who knows how to sanctify the shovels and bless a dirty hole?

Pushing through the gate to the cemetery, we laid the body down and waited for the shovels to come.

The Irishman looked out over the yard, where hundreds of graves were spread. "Where?" he wondered aloud.

"Well, over there we got the Catholics," I said, pointing off to my left. "On the other side there, running back to the fence, are the spiritists and the undecideds. Neither one thing nor the other, you know what I mean?"

Mick stood there in a daze. He'd probably not understood me.

"So, what was your friend here?" I asked. "What's his religion?"

He hesitated a moment, then said, "A follower of Jesus."

"Would that be Catholic?"

"No."

"Well, I don't know where then," I admitted.

"Back there," he said. "Beyond the trees."

"Looks good to me, friend, if he doesn't mind being alone."

"He won't be alone," the Irishman said.

We dug the grave just deep enough to keep the urubus out, left the hammock wrapped around the body, and shoveled him under.

Mick stayed by the grave for a while, praying I guess. But there were no more tears.

I waited for him at the gate, with the shovels braced over my shoulder. I had to admit that the man had a fair amount of steel inside him.

Presently, he came up to join me and we left the cemetery together. "Thank you, Zé," he said. "You been a friend."

I stopped him on the path and took hold of his arm. "Why don't you go back home now, Mick? There's nothing here but ignorance and corruption."

He shook his head at me.

I pressed him a little further. "Look Mick, you don't know how to fish. You don't know how to hunt, do you? Or crop the land?"

"No."

"So what are you going to do here, without your friend?"

He shrugged at me.

"You think these people are going to support you with their offerings?" I said. "*Porra*, we're so poor here we have to buy one shoe at a time."

"I'll be all right," he said. "I got friends in Ireland who can help. And Canada ..."

We walked along in silence for a while, till we came to the place where the path split off to the river. "Go back to the land of plenty," I urged him. "You'll do better there."

He shook his head again, wincing at the thought. "It is not like you think, Zé."

"No? Then what? What's your Ireland like?"

"Like the rest of the world," he said. "Beautiful and rotten."

With that in my pot to simmer, we parted ways, he to his lonely boat and I to my loveless house.

If I should ever get an interview with God, I'll put it to him blunt: *If you truly sent this fool here to deliver some kind of blessing, what a mean damn trick it was to let his partner die!*

CHAPTER EIGHT

THERE IS AN EVIL ON OUR ISLAND THAT NEVER SLEEPS, AND ITS NAME is Gossip.

Unknown to me at the time, and also to the luckless Irishman, Nina had started to gab about her adventures on the gringo's boat.

When she saw how great the story played among her friends, she began to embroider the tale and add little bits of sparkle. So enticing did her adventures become that some of the older kids and adults began to listen in.

Not only had she been aboard the gringos' mystery boat, Nina told them, but she had *personally* carried in boxes of vital supplies, in that horrible terrible storm, trying to save the gringo's life. She described in breathless detail how his belly had looked, puffed up like a pregnant lady. Course he wasn't pregnant, she'd giggle, 'cause *that* would have been pretty strange! No, she lamented, it was *cancer*, 'cause his belly split open when he died and there was all them yucky cancer worms inside. That's why they wrapped him in his hammock and never showed the body. But one thing was certain and forever sure, Nina announced: "The gringos *hate* witches!" She'd heard them say it with her own two ears—that witches was bad and Alzira the worst! Never in a million thousand years would they ever ask her for help, even if she was the lastest person on earth and they were dying of complicated measles and lucrative diarrhea. That's what the red-haired gringo said. And when he spoke them words, cursing Alzira with his strange, gringo curses, a bolt of lightning struck the boat and—

Like any good storyteller, Nina would take her listeners to the edge of the cliff and leave them dangling. "Have to go now," she'd say. "But tomorrow I will tell you more. A *lot* more, and even *better*. But you have to bring me candy, okay?"

Never mind that Mick had never uttered a word about witches or mentioned Alzira's name. Never mind that the dead man, who'd refused her help, was a Brazilian. The Father of Lies was happily at work, with Gossip, his nasty little dog, running here and there and everywhere, *yelp, yelp, yelping* ...

Within a few days, some darkly twisted version of the story had reached Alzira herself. She suffered the slander very poorly, for she was immensely proud of her art and extremely sensitive to how people addressed her. She preferred, above all, to be called "Mother of Saints" or "Benevolent Healer." If those didn't find a voice, then simply "herbalist" would do.

To be labeled a "witch," though a witch in fact she was, put her in a raw damned mood, and quick. When she learned that the man on the other end of the slander was a redheaded foreigner who couldn't even get the language right, it peeved her even more.

In hindsight, it was predictable that she would send her young disciple, Tatianni, to exact revenge. To the men on the island, she was known as "Tatianni the Shape," or sometimes "Pleasure Girl." But the women called her what she was.

For the moment, Mick lived in blessed ignorance of all this, organizing his first big show for Jesus.

On the Tuesday prior, I saw the first of his colorful posters, nailed to a palm tree next to Chico's beer shack.

**A Party for Jesus!
4 O'clock Sunday
On the Beach
See the Red-Haired Juggler!
*Free Candy for All!***

It was an irresistible pitch, written—it seemed to me—by an over-grown elf.

Similar handbills appeared, as if by magic, in various and far-flung corners of the island: taped to the wall of the Flamengo Soccer Club; nailed to a mango tree near Tuma's well; tacked, with real audacity, to a hitching post beside the Catholic Church.

Some of Mick's posters dissolved in the rain; others were torn down by competing philosophies. Either way, a fresh poster would always take its place.

When I walked down to the beach that Sunday afternoon, I found the place swarming with people. Thanks to the colorful posters and the even-more-colorful gossip, everyone who breathed knew that a red-haired giant had landed on the island and was about to put on a show for free.

Mick, who was nowhere to be seen, had placed a small wooden table on the shore, about fifteen meters from his boat. Atop the table sat a Bible, an old cigar box, and a blue ceramic bowl filled with goose eggs. On the ground below lay a small brown knapsack.

The stage had been carefully set to fire our curiosity.

A swarm of chattering kids pressed in close around the table, bursting with anticipation. Behind them swirled a crowd of older kids and adults—a couple hundred or more—engaged in wild speculations about the foreigner's origins and intent. Some said he was a criminal, running from the law. Others, a spy. Everything pointed to the moment at hand—something *big* was about to happen.

I found myself a quiet spot in the shade, well back from the beach, where I could watch and hear everything without getting involved. There were quite a few others of similar mind, souls timid and leery, weaving around the fringes of the crowd. Some were well-established drunks and sluggards who would never, on any occasion, approach anything that hinted of sobriety, edification, or work. Others were men of good standing who couldn't resist the lure of a circus but weren't quite bold enough to go up front. I noticed Duba, our famous-for-nothing president, winding his way along the edge of the crowd. More surprising still was the quiet arrival of Padre Xabrega, who, judging by the painful look on his face, had caught a splinter in his butt.

Suddenly, the Irishman appeared on the forward deck of his boat, at once a tremendously imposing figure and wholly ridiculous.

Silence fell. Every eye swung 'round to look.

At almost two meters tall, Mick was quite the biggest man they'd ever seen. He was barefoot, dressed in loose green shorts, a bright green muscle shirt, and a little green derby, which nested in his curly red hair at an impossible tilt.

He stood there for a full minute, his eyes solemnly closed, as if to summon every possible ounce of mental and physical energy for the impossible feats he was about to try.

Despite myself, I had to smile. It felt, in some strange fashion, like he was tickling me in the ribs.

Finally, sensing that the crowd was primed, he bounded down the gangway, veered right, broke into a full run, and did a double cartwheel across the beach that landed him perfectly beside the table.

There was a split second of astonished silence from the crowd, then a great gush of delight and applause. The giant was nimble as a monkey! His little green derby had moved not a bit! His eyes twinkled with laughter.

The kids broke into hysterics and pushed in closer to the table; the teens were in awe; the grown-ups, flabbergasted.

Now Mick put his finger to his lips—waiting, waiting, waiting—till silence returned.

When it was his, he extended his big arms, as though to embrace the whole island. "Bless you all for come!" he declared loudly. "No greater peoples is there, in all the world, than are you Brazilians. Except, of course, we Irish."

He let the thought percolate among us for a few seconds. We were sure, almost, that he had complimented us.

"My name is Michael Taron O'Hannon," he said. "But everyone calls me *Mick*. Or *Micky* ... like the mouse.

"I am a true Irishman, yes! If you not know where Ireland is, it be *way* over there." He pointed off to the north and east. "Three-thousand kilometers, if you flies like a parrot." Here he flapped his huge, long arms and waved his ludicrous hands, looking *nothing* like a parrot.

This brought another round of laughter, especially from the kids.

"I was born in Ireland," he said, "and always assume that I should die there too. Now I live on that little boat over there and don't assume nothing, except that God loves me."

I was impressed with his Portuguese. Though his accent was rough and plainly foreign, I could understand most every word. He must have written the thing out and practiced it for days.

"I want you to know that God loves you," his voice swelled up. "That you are *precious* in his eyes."

He reached forward, took one of the goose eggs from the bowl, and began to toss it up and down in his hand, easy as you please, just up and down.

"You there," he said, pointing with his other hand. "What is your name?"

The boy gawked from one side to the other, incredulous that the giant had singled him out, and cupped his hands over his mouth to hold in all the giggles.

"Tell me you name," Mick persisted.

"Kiko," the boy mumbled.

"You are precious in God's sight," Mick said. "And you, *senhora*, what is your name?" He was pointing off to his left now, deeper into the crowd. And all the while the egg went up and down, up and down.

"Luiza," she answered timidly. "Luiza Valadão."

"You are precious in his eyes, Luiza. Your soul is worth more than all the gold in the Brazilian treasury."

"There *is* no gold in the Brazilian treasury!" someone spouted. "It's full of paper!"

Mick thought it over a second. "Okay then, worth more than all the geese in all the world." He tossed his egg up high and caught it cleanly coming down. "And all their eggs!" he added brightly.

Out of all the faces in the crowd that he might have chosen next, out of the hundreds of eyes that were fixed upon him, he suddenly looked at me. "You there, in the shadows, did you know that God loves you?"

I bristled at the words. What did *he* know of my misery and frustration? I wanted to step forward and yell back at him: *If we're so precious in God's sight, why do we live like dogs? Can't you see that half the kids in front of you are pot-bellied with worms? Don't you know that we die young here, before our hair turns gray, of malaria and tuberculosis? Don't you realize that most of the folks in front of you can't read your stupid posters or count to fifty?*

He must have sensed the anger boiling off me. And yet, he persisted. "God knew your name, amigo, while you were still inside your mama." He held up his thumb and wiggled it at me. "*Deste tamanho.*" Which galled me even more.

Keep it up, big man, and I'll shout you down. I don't care how many people hear me!

His face grew pensive, held fast a second more, then moved gently off.

"I was a violent and rebellious man!" he said. "In rebellion against my family. In rebellion against my government. In rebellion against my God. From my rebellion came every evil thing that a man can do or think."

Up and down went the egg. Up and down. Like some sort of peculiar clock.

"All of it, even *murder,* was forgiven," he went on. "By the blood of Christ I am pardoned. For in him all things are made new. Even *me.*"

With his free hand he opened his Bible, found his place, and read boldly, "'God demonstrates his love for us in this: while we were still sinners, Jesus died for us, taking the punishment that we deserve upon himself.'"

The sun had settled over his shoulder now, and seemed—with supernatural splendor—to frame him in gold and scarlet.

"I *must* have another egg," he said. "Kiko, would you help me?"

The boy put his hand on his chest, startled by the invitation. "*Eu?*"

"*Tu mesmo!*"

Kiko rose to his feet, stepped shyly up to the table and plucked an egg from the bowl.

"Now you must do this *just* as I say," said Mick. "So you can become my official assistant, okay?"

The lad nodded, shaking with excitement.

Mick gestured with his free hand. "Come over here beside me. That's it. A little closer. Good. Now hold the egg up ... that's it ... just flat on your hand. No fingers, okay? Higher ... right next to mine ... a little more ..."

In a flash Mick grabbed the egg and sent it into orbit, juggling both now with a single hand.

"Very good!" he said. "Now stay there, okay, because I will need you again?"

Mick looked out upon the hundreds of sunset faces before him, bathed now in marmalade light. "Some of you will say, 'I am a drunk. God could never love me.' But he does! Kiko, *por favor*, another egg."

The boy rounded the table, fetched an egg, and positioned himself as before.

With one slick move Mick snatched it off his palm and tossed it up. Now he was using both hands, juggling three eggs in an easy, steady rhythm.

"'I am a loose woman,' you say. 'God could not love me.' But he *does*!" Mick nodded to his young assistant.

Kiko grabbed a fourth egg and sprang back to his post.

Without missing a beat, the Irishman launched it into space. "'I am a thief,' you say. 'And a liar. God could never love me.' But he *does*! More than we can ever know."

Again, Mick nodded to his helper. "Please now, open the box and bring to me my friend, Alfredo."

Seeing how fast the giant's hands were moving and how high the eggs were flying, Kiko hesitated.

"We can do this," Mick assured him. "*You* can do it!"

The boy edged his way around the table, lifted the lid on the cigar box and cautiously peeked inside. He looked puzzled at first, then delighted.

"Bring him over," Mick said. "He won't hurt you."

At a distance, I couldn't quite see what Kiko carried in his hand. Then realized it was a little turtle, painted blue with yellow spots.

The crowd, already on tiptoes, pushed closer.

"Hold him up a little higher," Mick said. "That's it. So he can say hello to everyone."

The boy was no fool. He handled the turtle from above, gripping the edges of its shell.

The turtle was no fool either. He took one nervous look at the crowd, pulled back into his shell and unloaded his little bladder.

Kiko stepped quickly back, so the tinkle wouldn't catch his feet.

The crowd roared.

"Better now than later," Mick laughed. "Don't worry, Kiko. He's done now. Hold him up here for me."

The boy moved fast, placing the turtle on his palm and lifting him up.

"This is an *Irish* turtle," Mick said. "Come from far away, from Shannon."

The crowd grew silent.

"Are you ready, Alfredo?"

The turtle probably had an opinion, but had run out of urine.

"Count with me now, *everyone!*"

I had to smile, despite my irritation. If nothing else, the man was making us laugh.

"Ready everyone! *Um ... dois ... três e já!*"

Mick whisked the turtle off the boy's hand and lofted him up. But his rhythm faltered and suddenly he was losing it, losing it, staggering off to his right.

Higher and higher he tossed the eggs, trying to gain some space, while the turtle tumbled wildly out of control.

"Hold on, Alfredo! Hold on!"

On the brink of calamity, he somehow regained his timing and brought the whirling fantasy into order.

A cheer went up from the crowd. Applause broke out, including mine. I'm not sure that I have ever seen the equal of that moment: Mick shifting like a dancer across the cooling sand, his eyes fixed upon his art, his hands a blur of indescribable motion. It was poetry at play, cast against the setting sun. There are shows in São Paulo and New York, I'm sure, with much finer clientele, and circuses in Paris and Vienna with more and varied acts. But none will you ever see that are more beautifully lighted, more energetically performed, or more fully appreciated.

"Okay!" the Irishman shouted. "We're coming down! You ready, Kiko?"

The boy was set.

"Here it comes!"

And *zam!* An egg appeared in his hand.

"Give it to a friend!" Mick urged him. "Quick! Another one's coming!"

Kiko lurched into the fringe of the crowd, gave it to the nearest taker, and was back on his spot in three quick steps.

Pow! Another egg came safely home.

"Give it away, boy!" Mick shouted. "Give it away!"

Thus they brought the whole thing down, egg by careful egg, till only the little turtle remained, nestled gently in Mick's hand. "Let's hear some applause for Alfredo, the incredible flying turtle!"

We cheered him wildly.

"Applause for Jesus, the lover of your soul!"

And Jesus too they applauded.

Mick put Alfredo back in his cigar box and picked up the knapsack at the foot of the table. Out came a notebook, a pencil and a jumbo-sized bag of candy. "Kiko, my wonderful assistant, will pass among you, giving candy. *Please* do not mug him."

He held up his hand, trying to silence the crowd. "If you want to repent of your sins and give your life to Jesus, to know his love so wonderful and his discipline so good, please come forward."

And so it ended, with candy and prayers.

Mick stood by the table, greeting those who came, praying with each person in turn, jotting down their names in his little notebook. He was in no special hurry to leave. When the last of the daylight failed him, he turned on his flashlight and continued.

Neither was I in any hurry to leave. I waited under the trees, watching him, until the last of the kids—pressing for more candy—finally gave up and went home.

I walked down to the shore and stopped in front of the table. Mick had his knapsack opened in front of him, packing away his things. He looked up at me and smiled. "Hey, Mister Zé! How are you?"

"Well enough," I allowed.

"This is for you," he said, pulling a piece of candy from his pocket. "The last one."

I unwrapped it and ate it on the spot. "Where did you learn how to juggle like that?"

He snapped an elastic band around the cigar box and slipped it into his pack. "In jail," he said. His voice sounded so cold to the question that I let the subject go.

"You've become a clown for Jesus," I said. Whether he took this as an innocent remark or realized that I was mocking him, I couldn't tell.

"Yes," he said. "A clown." Then added softly, "I do anything for the Gospel. Even be *serious* if I have to."

He waited a moment for the thought to sink in, then added playfully, "But that not be much fun, right Zé?" Mick shouldered his knapsack and picked up the little table.

"So, you've decided to stay?" I said.

"Yes. Till God shows me another where."

"It was a good crowd," I admitted. "A lot more people than the Padre gets."

The flashlight threw a halo up across his face. Beneath the silly green hat, his eyes were deeply grateful. "Fifty-three kids give their lives to Jesus today. And thirty-one adults. God is *very* good."

I shook my head and sneered at the thought. "These people will tell you anything you want as long as the show goes on and the candy holds out. You *understand?* Anything to please you, so long as it doesn't cost them anything."

Mick stood perfectly still for a moment, weighing the thought, then turned slowly toward his boat. "Yes," he said. "I am sure that is true."

Whether it was true or not, I wished I hadn't said it.

CHAPTER NINE

I KNOW NOW, LOVING RAFAEL THE WAY I HAVE, THAT LOVE GIVES birth to dreams. Or in my case, resurrects them from the dead. And more, if you will grant me this, that no love in all the world is more pure and persistent than a father's for his son.

Day and night, the iron cage hung under the cinnamon tree, swinging on its chain. Day and night the Colonel's hand lay prisoner there, groping for the rest of him. Was it only by wind and imagination that his bones seemed to creep around the cage? Or was something else at work of which we dared not speak?

Witch Alzira knew the answer. But who had the courage to ask?

Life, when you puzzle things out, is all about fear and dreaming. The soldiers may have hung the cage from the branch of a cinnamon tree, but their deeper mission was to hang it in our hearts. In order to discourage men from revolution, one must first discourage them from dreaming. It's not armed revolt the dictator fears most, but the poets and the singers, who spur our imagination. *That's* why they murdered The Voice. *That's* why they had me bury him under the cinnamon tree, where everyone could see, where everyone would remember.

Be evil as it may, love will never stop dreaming. I learned this from a curly-haired boy who thought me God, yet must have seen the sadness in my eyes, who blessed me with a thousand easy smiles, like water bubbling up from a spring.

As Rafael grew older, I realized that my little bit of learning was not going to be enough. I could teach him reading and writing, since I was strong in that, but where would the math come from? And the music?

Thus, when he turned eight, I found myself down at the old school lot, machete in hand, cutting back the jungle.

People would gawk at me as they passed. Some would stop and ask, "What are you doing here, Zé?"

"Preparing the land for our new school," I told them.

They'd laugh at me and shake their puzzled heads. The school was one of the oldest jokes around, along with the joke of clean water, and the joke of a health post, and the joke of electricity.

All jokes.

Profoundly funny.

Funny to the point of death.

I remember when Duba's rude little brother came for a visit. He was sitting up at the beer shack one night, making fun of our poor estate. He was from Brasília, you know, where everything was just *ultra-modern* and completely *civilized*. "You poor dogs," he remarked. "You don't even have power."

"That's not true!" Chico challenged him. And suddenly he was right in the man's face. "We got oil for our lamps and batteries for our flash-lights!" he snapped. "Plus all that hot gas you brought in from Brasília!"

Though Chico was two-thirds nuts, he sometimes came up brilliant.

After I'd finished clearing off the land, I went directly to Padre Xabrega's. I'd already composed the letter in my mind. All I needed now was the proper name and address, a fountain pen, and a couple sheets of decent stationery.

Padre Xabrega, just that week, had completed his third year as our village priest. If he wasn't always wise, at least he was sober. If not truly a man of letters, at least literate. Whatever his shortcomings, they were overwhelmed by his irrepressible kindness. It was always Xabrega, and often him alone, who showed up in the middle of the night with aspirin and prayers. It was he, chief among the faithful, who believed it possible to make a silk purse out of a sow's ear. That is to say, to birth a proper Christian out of sheer corruption.

The Padre lived in the back end of the church, in a pair of narrow rooms above the vestry. Though his quarters were small and simple, they looked out over a walled courtyard that was perhaps the most beautiful spot on the island, made so by his time and benevolent care.

It was late afternoon when I arrived at the church, Our Lady of Perpetual Help. I rounded the building to the east and knocked at the stout wooden door that gave entrance to the courtyard. It dawned on me, standing there, that I was still in my work clothes, still had my machete in hand, and smelled—sniffing quickly at my armpits—like a wild goat. What a poor way to come asking favors of the Father, who barely knew me, except for our common interest in burying the dead. But the door had already swung open upon my embarrassment and there stood the Padre's altar boy.

I recognized him immediately. "Silent Fernando" we called him, for he could spend hours, even days, without uttering a word. If memory serves, Fernando is my mother's oldest sister's youngest stepson by her third husband. I wondered vaguely if that made him a cousin of some variety. Second cousin? Third? Step cousin? Who can keep *track* of such complicated lines? At any rate, coming from the Catholic wing of my family, Fernando had become an altar boy at fourteen and, over time, assumed responsibilities as the Padre's houseboy and faithful understudy.

"Forgive me the poor clothes," I said. "But I need a word with the Father. If that is possible?"

I found something wonderfully calm and unassuming in the way Silent Fernando looked me over. Without a word he waved me into the courtyard, pushed the door closed behind us, and shoved the heavy bolt into place.

"Wait here," was all he said. Silent as a mist, Fernando climbed the open stairs that ran up the back wall of the church. He stopped on the landing above, clapped three or four times to announce his presence, then disappeared into the upper room.

I'm not the sort of man who waits very well, especially when there is a garden set before me and a path to be explored. Its entrance was guarded by a large jambo tree that had carpeted the ground with bright pink petals. I meandered inward, following the little trail through a wonderful tunnel of ferns and blooming bushes. The courtyard wall vanished behind a luxurious hedge of bougainvilleas, draped with purple and scarlet flowers. Beyond the bougainvilleas stood a fine guava tree, and beyond the guava a mango, spreading its deep cool shade over the courtyard wall. So carefully and cleverly did the little path wind its way along, with every twist unveiling a flower, a pool, a songbird, the garden began to trick me in time and space.

Coming out the other end I couldn't be sure whether five minutes had passed or fifty, whether the length of the path had been a mere hundred paces or a thousand. Later, looking back at it from the street outside, I marveled at how much beauty the Padre had packed into thirty meters square.

Underneath the Padre's balcony grew a beautiful mimosa tree with five or six orchids suspended in its arms. In its shade sat a rough wooden table and a pair of facing chairs. The table held a large chessboard with a set of finely carved pieces. I'd never understood the game, but could see that a match was in progress and that several pieces had already been taken off the board.

"You didn't *move* anything, did you?" Fernando whispered. He had come up behind me and caught me snooping.

"No, *no*," I assured him, though half a second before I'd been handling one of the pieces, admiring its workmanship.

"The Padre's finicky about his chess," he said.

"Of course he is," I agreed. Then added stupidly, "We're all finicky about our chess."

Fernando looked at me oddly. "You play?"

"Ahh ... *no*." I suddenly remembered Aunt Leona's little tale about the fool who couldn't stop talking. Blundermouth was his name ... "But if I *did* play," I prattled on, "I'm sure I'd be finicky too."

If there is a silence *beyond* silence—a sort of *super* silence—that was Fernando's response.

I hurried to fill the void: "Who's he playing?"

Fernando cracked a little smile. "Since no one else on the island plays ... the Padre plays himself."

"Huh? How can he do that?"

The whole thing seemed perfectly obvious to Fernando. "Well, first he sits here ..." He pointed to the chair on the right. "... and moves the white pieces. Then he gets up and moves over there ..." He swung his hand methodically to the left. "... and plays the black."

"Well who *wins*?"

"Xabrega *always* wins," came a voice from heaven, followed by a boisterous laugh.

I walked out from under the tree and looked up. There, on the narrow balcony above, stood Padre Xabrega. He was naked to the waist, gripping the railing with one hand and grasping his hard little belly with the other. "Senhor Zé, the undertaker," he said. "Welcome!"

I was pleased that he called me "undertaker" instead of "gravedigger." Though the pay's the same, the dignity's somehow better. "Good afternoon, Padre. How are you?"

"I myself am fine, Senhor Zé. But my stomach's not." As though to punctuate the remark, he belched loudly and rubbed his belly. Then belched again. "Wooo ..."

There was not a pinch of fat on the man, except maybe his hands, which were large and plump. *The hands of a musician*, I thought, *or ... more obviously ... a priest.* Whether he was thirty years old or forty depended on where you focused. His eyes looked sharp and bright and filled with vigor, but the bags underneath them were dark and puffy. His ancestors had provided him a fine German nose, still strong and youthful, but his skin was weathered like an old leaf. Out at the cemetery, and on other occasions, I'd seen him in his big Panama hat and long-sleeved shirts, doing battle with the sun. Even so, he was splattered everywhere with liver spots and freckles.

"I trust you haven't come looking for *work*," he laughed. "*Ahh ha ha ha ...*"

"No, Padre."

He patted his stomach, as though to calm an unruly dog. "Just a bit of gastritis," he said. "Or maybe worms. Nothing to get *buried* about! *Ahh ha ha ha ...*"

"Yes sir. I mean *no*, sir ... Padre."

"How do you like my garden, Senhor Zé?"

"It's beautiful."

"The mangos are coming in nice, eh?"

"Yes, Padre. I like mangos."

"Well then, you should know that we have a *policy* regarding the fruit."

"You do?"

His hand came off the railing, with a finger raised. "Whatever falls outside the wall belongs to whoever finds it. Whatever falls inside the wall belongs to me and Fernando. And whatever God wants for himself, he can catch on the way down." He waited a second for me to get it, then let go another salvo of laughter. "*Ahh ha ha ha ...*"

When finally he'd settled, I took a step forward and presented my petition. "I've come to ask you a favor, Father. Help, that is, with something I'm working on."

"Is it *legal* ?" he wondered severely. But his smile was toying with me.

"Yes sir. All very legal."

"Is it something God would smile upon?"

There he had me. "I don't know, Padre. I'm asking the government for a new school. I intend to write them a letter."

"A new school, eh?" His eyes rose gently and rested on the garden for a moment, then swung out over the wall and onto the village. From his vantage there on the balcony he must have been able to see forever. "Well, I'm certainly in favor of that!" he declared. His eyes vaulted back over the wall and landed squarely upon me. "And so, we might surmise, is God. Though you would do well to ask him yourself."

"Yes, Father."

"So what do you want from me?"

"Some writing paper. A pen. A name and address in Belém to send it to."

He nodded and pointed at Fernando. "Take this good man into my office and provide him everything he needs. Give him my best pen. And don't be *stingy* with the paper."

Fernando was already on the move, and I right behind him.

Xabrega waved and gave me an encouraging smile. "Write good," he said, "and pray for these testy bowels of mine."

The Padre's office wasn't nearly as pleasant or well organized as his garden. It did, however, boast an Underwood typewriter—useless to most everyone, including me—and a small library.

Fernando wiped the dust off the Padre's desk, seated me there, and provided me everything I needed, including a cool glass of water. But it took him a long time to find the *State Directory of Public Offices* and dig out the name I needed: *Ivanildo Abreu Bonfim*.

In my very best hand, slowly, meticulously, I wrote out the letter:

Senhor Ivanildo Bonfim
Vice-Minister of Education
Construction and Maintenance Section
31 Jardim dos Palhaços
Belém, Pará

Estimado Sr. Bonfim,

Here on the Isle of Fair Winds, in the community of Jacaré, we are in desperate need of a school, so that our children can have a better life.

We have a good plot of land reserved for the school. It lies beside the soccer field, measuring fifty-four meters across and forty meters deep (except for a little corner that's in dispute, where old man Braga and his family illegally put their latrine, and are squatting there).

The land has been sitting idle now for twenty-two years, since it was first set aside by the Ministry of Education. I think you will agree, Sr. Bonfim, that twenty-two years is a <u>long</u> time to wait. While we have waited for our school, a whole generation of children, including me, has grown up ignorant.

Please, with all speed, liberate the money we need to build our new school. We have little hope without it.

I worked last Saturday and most of today preparing the site. I cleared away the brush and carted off the trash. We are ready to start work on the foundation the very hour that you liberate the money for cement, rebar and bricks.

God will smile upon you for doing this. So will my young son, Rafael, who needs teachers and books.

Respectfully,
Zemário Luan Vasconcelos dos Santos Licata
Former Soldier, Fisherman, and Community Undertaker

Bursting with hope, I sealed the letter in its envelope, placed the stamps that Fernando gave me, and kissed it for good luck. That was as far as my faith would take me.

Time slogged by and my letter remained unanswered. The jungle gradually took back the land I'd cleared, except for the southwest corner, where old man Braga and his family kept squatting.

Rafael was growing up fast. Sometimes I'd take him over to the lot with me and show him where the new school would be, where he'd learn mathematics and music.

"I already know a lot!" he'd tell me.

"I know you do. You impress me all the time."

"Do you know what runs all day and never gets tired?" he riddled me.

"That would be *you!*" I laughed.

He shook his head. "*Não Pai.*"

"Then what? I give up."

"The river!" he beamed. "*Corre e corre e nunca se cansa.*"

It was during those long months of waiting that Chico made history by bringing in the island's first television set. The thing came with a thirteen-inch black-and-white screen, a full array of knobs and dials, an instruction manual printed in English, Spanish and French, and the potential, on a cloudy night, to receive one or two channels, more or less.

By virtue of his sacred meteor and the fact that he owned the only generator on the island, Chico was already a man of some renown. Now—*Ta-dah!*—he had a television set!

When I heard the news, I couldn't wait to tell Aunt Leona, so she could record the event in her encyclopedic brain.

"What's it for?" she wanted to know.

"For entertainment." I told her.

"Like dominoes?"

"Come along and see, Auntie. Just come along."

An hour later, the oldest human being on the river shuffled into Chico's beer shack to get her first-ever look at television. Reverence, like a wave, preceded her into the bar and brought all conversation to a halt. Two of the boys, seated up front, hustled to their feet and gave up their chairs to us.

The little screen winked and blinked and played us a bossa nova. We had arrived just in time to catch the opening scene of a popular *novela*:

There we met Antônia, a bitter old woman, and her beautiful daughter, Gabriela. Gabriela, we learn, is married to wealthy Júlio, who is a little too slick for comfort.

Antônia suspects that Nilda, the housekeeper, is stealing from the family and determines to put an end to it. Hiding herself in a closet, the old woman looks smugly on—ah-ha!—as Nilda sneaks into the office, takes a handful of cash from the drawer and quietly slips out. But before Antônia can remove herself from her hiding place and denounce the thief, in comes slick Júlio, arm in arm with beautiful young Mera Petre, who is Gabriela's oldest and dearest friend. Antônia, unable to escape from the closet, is forced to look on—shocked and revolted —as slick Júlio closes the office door and takes beautiful young Mera into his arms ...

The screen went blank for an instant, then burst into a string of noisy advertisements, urging us to buy cars (though we had no roads), to purchase laundry detergent (though we had no washing machines), and to invest in health insurance (though we had no doctors).

"What stuff!" Leona spouted. "It's for the pleasure of idiots!"

But the show was back now, demanding our attention.

Driven by greed and resentment, Antônia decides to blackmail her son-in-law rather than expose his steamy affair with Mera. She considers Júlio a stingy and arrogant man who has never shared his wealth the way he ought, leaving her, a lonely widow, to fend for herself.

As Antônia puts the finishing touches on her blackmail note, snipping and pasting letters from a magazine, Gabriela bursts into the room, with tears in her eyes. "I must talk with you, Mamãe! You are the only one who can help me ..."

Antônia moves quickly to cover up the bits and pieces of her dark project. "What is it, my darling?"

"I'm pregnant, Mamãe!" she sobs. "I just got word from the doctor!"

Antônia clutches her startled breast. "But why the tears, sweet daughter? Surely Júlio will be happy for the news. He's wanted children."

"Yes, Mamãe, but the baby's not—" Now the tears were rushing down her cheeks. "The baby's—"

Again the screen went dark, as though judgment had fallen on them all, then whisked us into a world of happy music and brilliant, smiling teeth. Apparently, if I got the message straight, we needed lots of toothpaste to make us happy. So said all the handsome, healthy people who danced and sang before us, displaying their perfect, gleaming teeth.

"I have *never* seen teeth like that," Leona groused. "It's a shameless lie!"

"I have," I told her. "When I was in the army I met a little girl who had teeth like that."

But Gabriela was back on the screen now, agonizing over her situation.

"The baby's not Júlio's, Mamãe!" she cries out. "It's Pedro's!"

"The gardener!" Antônia shrieks. "Nilda's husband!"

Gabriela is in the throes of misery now, biting her lovely red lip with her lovely white teeth. "Yes Mamãe ..." She wipes her tears with a hanky and confesses yet another fear. "And Nilda knows about it, Mamãe! The way she looks at me, with that treacherous smile ..."

"Easy, honey, easy."

"What if she should tell Júlio, Mãe? Or decide to blackmail me? What then?"

Antônia realizes now that hell's full blast has come upon her and the whole family is coming unraveled. Wringing her hands in desperation, she asks, "Who else have you told about this, daughter?"

"Only Mera," she answers, "You know how loyal she is to me, how we share everything …"

And there the episode ended, with an interlude of music and another barrage of advertisements.

Leona shook her head, disgusted. "They're supposed to be *city* people," she said. "Intelligent … rich … educated …" She stood up and looked us over as though we were a bunch of howler monkeys. "*Deus me livre,* they're worse than we are!"

With that, she cranked her walking stick into motion and sidled out of the shack. In her wake there was nothing but silence and beer gone flat.

"It *was* pretty stupid," one of the boys admitted.

Some of the others murmured along with him.

Chico, sensing that his investment was failing, got up fast and tried to tune in the sometimes-channel from Manaus. Fiddling with the V-shaped wires on top of the set, he pulled in a scratchy image of dancing girls, dressed in ostrich feathers and not much else. Though the girls were smallish and fuzzy, and the music sounded tinny, the boys found them a lot more interesting than Gabriela and her miserable family.

Beer sales rose steadily.

Time kept slogging along and finally stopped on me, with no word from Belém.

Confused and frustrated, I went back to the church and imposed myself again on Padre Xabrega's good humor.

With real cordiality, he invited me into his office and heard my complaint.

"Why haven't they answered my letter, Father? It's been *nine months.*"

The Padre was seated at his desk and I in a chair alongside him. At his elbow sat a Bible, a pair of scratched-up reading glasses, and his big, black-and-silver Underwood writing machine. "Well, what exactly did you say to him?" he asked. "Can you tell me?"

So often had I run the letter through my mind, I was able to recite it to him word for word. When I came to the end of it, to the part that said, "God will smile upon you for doing this," the Padre's eyebrow shot up and a little smile rippled across his lips. "I didn't think you believed in God, Senhor Zé."

"I don't, really, but I thought it might help to mention him."

He scratched his head and smoothed back the lonely strands of hair. "It's a fine letter, actually. Where did you learn how to write like that?"

"In the army."

"Hmmm ..." he mused. "I don't usually associate the army with fine writing." His voice was pleading for more details, which I had no intention of giving.

"Well, the only thing it lacks," he went on, "is more *sugar*. Sugar and flowers."

Without explaining himself any further, he swung around in his chair, inserted a fresh piece of paper in his machine and began to click-clack away.

Padre Xabrega is the only person on the whole island who knows how to use the Underwood writing machine, the only person on the island who speaks Latin, and the only person who understands the dark art of turning a perfectly good cabbage into a stringy, inedible mess called sauerkraut. He also eats little silver fish packed in sour mustard sauce, which come to him in sterile little tins all the way from Germany. Since no right-minded man with a healthy stomach would ever choose a diet of sauerkraut and pickled fish, people assumed Padre was doing some sort of penance, perhaps for sins related to gluttony.

I sat there for half an hour while he click-clacked away on his Underwood. When he was satisfied, he scrolled the paper out, along with a carbon, and handed it over to me. I decided to read it aloud:

"Most esteemed and highly venerated Vice-Minister of Education:

"With all due respect, humility, and our vast appreciation, we bring this petition before you and your most excellent office, this day of our

Lord, July 21ˢᵗ, 1976, confident that you will address our situation with wisdom and understanding, if not promptness, because the great State of Pará has so prudently appointed you the task, recognizing your talents, your extraordinary accomplishments, your tireless energy and your compassionate heart in all such matters as this.

"If it pleases you, Senhor, and you find occasion in your busy schedule to consider us, please know that our community, called Jacaré, located on the Isle of Fair Winds, finds itself at a loss for any sort of educational institution, and also at a loss for teachers.

"Through the graciousness of your office, we have a piece of land available, which was—"

I stumbled over the next word.

"Sequestered," the Padre supplied.

"... sequestered in 1953, without any recompense to our community.

"While many people in Jacaré have since passed away, those who are still alive and able to remember the occasion recall that a new grade school was promised us, to have been completed within two years.

"Clearly, the timetable has slipped a little. For this we assign no blame whatsoever, understanding that various circumstances and competing needs—and even acts of God—often work against the timely completion of public works.

"With all of these, ah—"

"Mitigating," Padre put in.

"... mitigating factors and considerations in mind, we beseech you to consider us and our humble request, whenever the occasion proves convenient."

I rested the letter on my lap and cleared my throat, trying to get the sugar out of my windpipe.

The Padre leaned anxiously forward. "Well? What do you think?"

"This should *spur* him into action," I remarked.

Xabrega caught the sarcasm in my voice. "You don't like it."

"It's ah ... very *sweet*, Padre."

"It *needs* to be sweet," he insisted. "These are *bureaucrats* we are dealing with. Trust me, I *know* about bureaucracy."

"Yes Padre, but this ... *this you could grind into sugar and make pastries.*"

He sagged in his chair and stared hard at the typewriter. "I'll rewrite it then."

"No, no, Padre. I was only joking. It's just that ... ah ... I have no ear for this kind of thing. No sensibility."

He opened the drawer to his right, plucked out a fresh envelope, and handed it to me. "You'll sign it, then?"

"Absolutely. We'll send it on the first boat."

When I got home I took out the letter and read it again. I had to make sure that somewhere in there—midst all the flattery and fluff—we'd actually asked the bureaucrat to build us a school.

CHAPTER TEN

IN THE END, NEITHER PLAIN LETTERS NOR FANCY HAD ANY IMPACT in Belém. The only thing accomplished over nineteen months of waiting was to teach me patience, and in that I mostly failed. When I realized finally that no answer was going to come, and the neighbors started jabbing me—"What ever happened to that big *school* of yours, Zé?"—"Hey *teacher*, when the classes going to start?"—the frustration turned bitter, and the bitterness to anger.

For no good reason I took it out on Ana one night. Because she was there, I guess. And I'd been drinking.

"Maybe it wasn't meant to be," she whispered.

"What the hell does that mean, woman?! *Meant* to be."

She opened her hands to me, as if our whole sad history might be gathered in her arms. "Into this life we were born, Zé. And—"

"This is how we'll die, is that it? *Is that what you think!?*"

"I never said that, Zé. Maybe God will provide a—"

"Let's leave God out of it, shall we?" I hated the way she patronized me, how quickly she had sided with the hecklers and naysayers who surrounded me. Even her voice I hated, like salt pressing into an open wound.

"No, Zé! Please ..."

But nothing could check the fire inside me or hold my angry fist.

"Don't, Zé! I beg you!"

What a wretched man I was, consumed with rage … stupid with liquor …

Ana cried out and cupped her hand over her mouth. Blood oozed between the fingers and splashed down across her belly, where a tiny life was clinging.

I stepped back in horror and nearly fell over Rafael, who'd slipped in through the door behind me.

He uttered a single word, "*Mae!*" and bolted back into the kitchen.

I chased him into the yard, caught him by the gate and spun him around.

He looked at me with stark, unblinking terror. "Don't hit me, *Pai!*"

"*Calma.* I'm not going to hit you."

He slumped to his knees and looked up at me, horrified, as if an *onça* had leapt out of the shadows.

"What did you see in there, *Filho?*"

"Please don't hit me."

"What did you *see?*"

"Mama bleeding."

"Your mama fell, boy. That's all."

He shook his head at me, disbelieving.

"You go up to the shack and ask your Tio Chico for some ice. You hear me? Tell him your mama fell."

"She only falls when *you're* in the room," he said. "Yelling at her."

I looked down at my hand, still clinched and trembling, and forced it slowly open. "Go do what I say."

Rafael gathered himself up, wiped his eyes, and pushed out through the gate. It wasn't from love or respect that the boy obeyed me, but cold-blooded fear.

I suspected the mail service was somehow to blame, that my letters had never even arrived at the ministry door. They were notorious bumblers, weren't they? Didn't people make *jokes* about the mail?

How long does it take to send a letter from Bahia to Rio de Janeiro?
Well, that depends on whether you choose incompetence or corruption ...

Or maybe my letters had arrived, but were shuffled off into some remote corner of the bureaucracy from which they'd never emerge.

Whatever the case, I was sure that if I could just meet Senhor Bonfim face to face and describe our situation to him, appeal to the man in person, we would soon have our school.

So, out of stubbornness and naiveté I determined to go to Belém, for the sake of Rafael and his friends, who were growing up ignorant.

It's very telling, in hindsight, that no one but Chico showed any interest in accompanying me on the trip. He, on the other hand, leaped at the idea and went rushing off to pack his stuff before I'd even mentioned a departure date.

"Don't you want to think it over?" I called after him. "Work out the details?"

"I'm with you, Primo," he shouted back. "*Vamos!*"

It wasn't so much the educational benefits that excited Chico—in fact he didn't have any children to profit from a school. Rather, he saw in the plan a chance for entrepreneurial glory, the chance to be first again with something that was indisputably important. It was his love for anything new that had pushed him to install the island's first electric generator, to introduce chilled beer and fireworks, and to bless our unsuspecting lives with television.

Beyond the immortality that came with being first, Chico imagined he could use the new school as a political tool, to embarrass and unseat our long-time community president, Duba Escobar. Or as Chico *affectionately* called him, "Duba Do Nothing."

Duba, out of sheer orneriness and a streak of jealousy, had opposed Chico at every turn. He opposed the generator, opposed the chilled beer, opposed the fireworks, and opposed the television set. Had Duba been clever enough to pull it off, he would have opposed Chico's meteor, declaring it an "illegal import" and insisting Chico pay taxes on it.

Hoping to raise money for my passage, I promoted the trip to anyone who'd listen. I painted dreams of our children learning how to read and write, of a future where they might work with something other than fishing nets and hoes.

Confronted by slugs and skeptics, I'd sometimes lose my patience. *No, our kids aren't stupid! Given a chance, they can learn most anything they want. To do numbers and read music and find their country on a map!*

"It's a *long way* to Belém," they'd always say. Usually this was followed by a yawn or a clearing of the throat, then a pointed repetition: "A *very* long way."

I could tell by their look—that dead fish gawk—that distance wasn't the issue. Rather, they suffered from a hereditary disease called *hopelessness*, passed down from our mothers and fathers. Had it not been for a little girl named Esmeralda and an old man named José Nery, I might never have recognized the disease and determined to fight it.

When we get the school finished, I thought, *we'll find us some teachers— maybe get Padre Xabrega involved—to recover all the precious words we've lost and teach them to our children!*

Already a list of verbs was forming in my mind. *To dream ... to imagine ... to invent.* Words infused with power. *To dare ... to change ... to hope!*

Those six words alone, implanted in the heart, stirring the mind, could revolutionize our lives. I had to smile at the thought. After all this time I was yet a rebel, inciting revolution.

In the end, only a handful of people came 'round to support me. Among them were Padre Xabrega and Domingos, the old *gaúcho*. And Little Aparecida, who never lost faith.

As a final preparation for the trip, I wrote a letter to my cousin, Ozias, who lived in Belém with his wife, Jamela. Though four years had passed since I'd seen them last, they responded quickly, giving me directions to their house and a promise to welcome us there.

The morning of our grand departure fell on the 9th of May 1977. Never, I think, came a dawn so bright and filled with promise. Chico and I were like crusaders breaking camp, fresh to the journey ahead, anticipating glorious results.

Waiting at the dock was the *Botafogo*, bound for Santarém, Monte Alegre, and Belém. The boat was rated for forty-four passengers (though always accommodating more) and might hit fifteen knots with a following wind. Her cargo deck was laden with pineapples and hardwoods, which put her a little lower in the water than an honest captain would have liked.

A stout little band of supporters had come down to the dock to see us off. Not many, really, but enthusiastic.

Padre Xabrega and Silent Fernando were there. Somehow, the Padre had scraped together twenty-six cruzeiros for the cause—a lot of money by his economy. The good Padre had further provisioned us with a half dozen papayas, two kilos each of rice and beans, four packages of soda crackers, and—here a very personal sacrifice—six little tins of pickled fish.

Close by the Padre stood Domingos the cattleman, who had given me sixty cruzeiros and—for some odd reason—a fine set of handkerchiefs. I had never owned a gentleman's handkerchief in all my life and had to wonder what Domingos was anticipating with his gift, whether sweat or snot or tears, or maybe a miraculous conversion to gentility. In any case, he was plenty old enough to remember the original promise the government had given us back in 1953, and he meant to hold them to it.

At the cattleman's right elbow was Little Aparecida, bursting with excitement. Her father, my cousin Geraldo, who was sympathetic to our cause but too poor to help, had shown her the land where the school would go and drawn her a picture in the sand. Insulated from the pessimism that surrounded her, Little Aparecida believed in the dream and had personally encouraged me with three hugs and a kiss on the cheek.

Ana was there also, with Rafael. But neither of them brought me smiles. There was no use pretending that things were good at home. We imposed upon one another long days of silence, punctuated by violent quarrels. As I shouldered my bag and turned toward the gangway, Ana gave me a little wave. Had her eyes been able to speak, they might have said, "I would love you better if I weren't so badly wounded."

At the last possible moment, Duba "Do Nothing" Escobar came hurrying along the dock to see us off. Giving Chico all the room he could, he slipped in among us and smiled (sort of), wished us good luck (sort of), and quietly pressed some coins into my hand. If our mission succeeded, he wanted to be firmly attached to it, the way a leech fixes itself to your heel.

Chico scowled at the man and puckered his lips, preparing something tart.

Duba could see it coming and was surely thinking, *How can I escape this lunatic?*

But Chico was inescapable. He snagged Duba by the arm, pulled him out before us, and grinned him into submission. "What can I say about this man's timely arrival and *surprising* generosity? With *this* ..." He gestured majestically to the coins that Duba had given us. "... we can buy a *whole entire Coca-Cola* and borrow a couple straws."

Awkwardness waddled in among us like a dirty hog.

I felt compelled to smooth things over. Duba was, after all, the community president. "Thank you for coming down to see us off, Senhor Duba, and for your contribution. I'm sure Chico didn't mean to offend you."

"Yes I did," Chico blurted.

I have never felt any finer, any truer to my course, than when our boat cast off her lines and headed down the Amazon. Chico and I were like birds rising up at first light, compelled to sing.

I am sure there were other people on board that morning with dreams and destinations all their own. *But none,* thought I, *so grand as ours.*

Beside me at the railing, Chico kept waving, waving, waving, till the island vanished in our wake. "This is going to take us to the heights," he said.

"*Como?*"

"The new school."

"Right."

"I can see it standing there, all fresh and painted. Dignitaries in dignitary dress. Speeches being spoke and pictures being took. Lots of fireworks and beer. Can you *see* it, Zé?"

"I can see it, Little Cousin. I've been seeing it for a long, long time."

"Maybe a band," Chico went on. "With a horn and a clarinet. Maybe even one of those trombones. I hear there's a man over in Óbidos plays trombone. We could bring him over special for the day."

"Yes."

"Can you hear it, Zé?"

"Hear what?"

"The *band*?"

"Yes, I can hear it."

Chico danced along the railing a few steps, then back again. "The way I see it, your boy goes first in line, Zé. The first-ever student to be enrolled in our first-ever school."

"I'm not so sure about that Chico."

"... on account of all you've done," he rambled on, "pushing through the project for us, being a war hero and all."

"I'm not a war hero," I put in.

But he was sailing on his own now, across his private sea. "When the campaign starts," he mused, "we'll play it up big."

Though I'd never expressed the least interest in politics, Chico was determined that I should become president of the community, and after that, I guess, governor, and after that ... well ... *king of the world*. Without any consultation or approval from me, he'd made himself my campaign manager, campaign coordinator, campaign consultant, campaign publicity manager, and campaign treasurer.

"*You* are a decorated soldier," he reminded me. "That's worth a *lot* of votes."

"Yeah, I'm *decorated* all right." I ran my hand down the side of my cheek, from one pockmark to the next, where Gasolina's shotgun had peppered me. "I got five decorations right here. And eleven more down here ..."

"*Escuta, cara*, I got the perfect slogan," he said. "Duba Don't Do Dung!" He chuckled over his cleverness and clapped his hands. "What do you think?"

It is, in the end, impossible to discourage the plans of a lunatic. Especially a lunatic you are fond of. Nor is it possible to outwit him, because he's not committed to rational thought or constrained by the things that go with good judgment. Like most people, I tend to think in sequence, moving from thought A to thought B to thought C, arriving at conclusion D. But Chico's mind works in wild circles and unpredictable spirals, leaping from Q to B to 23, pumping out hummingbirds and strings of Chico-brand baloney.

I discovered, over the course of our trip, that it was *indeed* a long way to Belém. I also discovered, along with my fellow passengers, that it's possible for a man to talk incessantly for three-and-a-half days without spraining his tongue.

It never once occurred to Chico that he was annoying the people around him, particularly the salesman who was trying to sleep in the hammock alongside him.

By the time we docked in Belém the poor salesman had scarcely enough strength to gather his things and stagger to the gangway. Realizing that Chico was impervious to criticism and that I was his friend, the man aimed his parting remark at me:

"Too bad the boat don't run on jabber," he said. "... or we'd *all* be traveling free."

CHAPTER 11

"I NEVER SEEN ANYTHING LIKE *THIS*!" CHICO EXCLAIMED. HE KEPT saying it over and over again, all the way from the boat to the Ministry of Education. "Have *you* ever seen anything like this?"

"Never, Little Cousin. Not like this."

The entire city was whirling around on wheels. Honking, fuming, speeding. Giant wheels and pigmy wheels. Shiny wheels and rusty. Wheels that were reckless and rude, roaring past us like an angry wind. Popcorn wagons and buses. Bicycles and motorbikes. Tiny little cars for two and trucks that were twenty-five meters long!

"I never seen anything like this!" Chico said. "Have *you* ever seen anything like this?"

We were maybe twenty blocks up from the docks and walking hard when we came across something that would change Chico's life forever. It was sitting smack in the middle of the sidewalk—where it had no business—placed there, I guess, by the Devil himself. It was a brand new, sparkling-in-the-sun, impossible-to-resist, cherry red motorbike. On the side of it, in stout white letters, it said: **Honda 50**.

Chico was love-struck. He sat his bag on the sidewalk and circled the scooter, oblivious to the people who were bumping and jostling to get around him.

"Come on, Chico. We got to go."

But the man was struck helpless, except to lick his lips and utter his heart's desire. "Someday, I will get me one of these, Zé. Just like this ..."

Twice I took him by the arm and tried to pull him away. But the machine had become a giant magnet to him, and he the hapless nail.

Unable to restrain himself, Chico knelt down and ran his hand over the long chrome muffler, which reflected his adoring little face.

At that very instant the owner appeared, with plenty of muscle and no patience at all. "*Eh, seu cachorro!*" he barked. "Get away from there!" The man moved in fast, pumping his fist. "You touch my *moto*, I'll punch your face!"

Poor Chico! Never has a man been so rudely parted from his love.

"*Nos perdoe, senhor,*" I apologized, then latched hold of my cousin's arm and steered him quickly off.

It was an hour more before we found the Ministry of Education and pushed our way through its big front doors.

Inside, we found ourselves in a crowded foyer that must have been thirty meters round and ten high. Rising from its center was a majestic old staircase that narrowed as it climbed, opening onto the restricted balconies above. Its white marble steps must have been brilliant in their youth, but were cracked now and grayed from a million passing shoes.

To the right of the stairs sat a little newsstand that was so heavily faced with newspapers and magazines that I could barely see the vendor, tucked back in the shadows of his cave, smoking a morning cigar.

Out of the crowd appeared a scruffy young man, who introduced himself with a flourish. "Good morning, senhores!" he said. "I'm Paix-ante." He bowed slightly from the waist and snapped his ready fingers. "They call me 'The Knack.' How can I help you gentlemen?"

Judging by his clothes, the man had no formal ties with the ministry, but was some kind of parasite that roamed the halls. He wore a bright orange baseball cap with the bill turned back and a sleeveless T-shirt that was clean and freshly ironed. Tattooed across his bicep was a pair of bright red lips with a rude little tongue protruding. Whenever he flexed his muscle, the lips would curl up and the tongue come wagging out. Underneath it said:

Smile While You Can!

Chico was fascinated. "*Eita! Que legal!*" he said, moving closer. "Can you do that again? Just flex them muscles?"

The Knack was happy to show his stuff. He elevated his arm and worked his big biceps for us. The lips grinned ... the tongue wagged lewdly out ... the lips grinned ...

I thought it was strange and vaguely repulsive.

But Chico loved it. "Someday, I'll get me one of them," he vowed.

"We need to get on with our business," I said. "Come on, Chico."

"So what *is* your business?" the man pressed. "Let me help."

I hadn't liked him from the start and didn't like him now. He reminded me of the street punks who used to hang out around the base in Manaus, selling marijuana and pimping their little sisters.

I turned and walked away from him, but Chico hung back.

The Knack hustled after me and latched hold of my elbow. "Hey, *mano*, just tell me what you need."

I studied his face for a moment. Though it was clever and salted with experience, there was nothing in the mix that suggested honesty.

"We're here to see Senhor Ivanildo," Chico piped up.

The Knack looked us back and forth, and finally settled on me.

"That's right," I said. "Ivanildo Bonfim."

He adjusted his baseball cap and let out a long low whistle. "The Bonfim himself, huh?" He reflected on it a moment. "That would be the deep office with the fine bourbon, beyond the dragon lady and the armed beef. It's *complicated*, amigos. But ..." He raised a confident finger. "I could do it for you."

"We'll find our own way in," I said, backing off.

But the man latched hold of me again and raised his voice. "*I'm* The

Knack here," he said, thumping himself on the chest. "No one gets to the big man *except* through me."

With that he turned and swaggered off, confident that we'd follow.

"Come on," said Chico. "We *need* him."

With no better plan in mind, we tagged after him, down a marbled corridor that tunneled straight back into the building. Every twenty paces or so, staggered left and right, we passed a wooden door. Each of these was identical to the next, except for the letters stenciled on the glass:

> Administration
> Personnel
> Accounting
> Mimeograph
> Record Keeping
> Drafting

At the seventh door, marked "Construction," The Knack abruptly stopped. "It's here."

Opening the door, we found ourselves in a large, windowless room that was crowded with people—mostly men—seated on dark wooden benches. These were arranged in parallel, like the pews of a church, with an aisle running down the middle. At the far end of the room sat a gray metal desk, with a gray metal lamp, occupied by a gray metal functionary. Behind him was the only other door—the gateway, apparently, to Ivanildo Bonfim.

The occupants of this cheerless room were in various states of boredom and resignation, as though they were waiting for a ship that had already gone down. Here and there I spotted signs of life: a wisp of cigarette smoke swirling up; a folded newspaper fanning a tired face; a tedious foot tapping out the minutes.

The place reminded me of my old army barracks, reeking of stale smoke and fungus. Overhead, only one of the half dozen ceiling fans was actually spinning with any effect. The others paddled lazily around or moved not at all, clogged with dust and cobwebs.

From off the nearest bench sprang a little black kid with bloodshot eyes and a mouthful of bad teeth. He was quick to meet us, smiling broadly, waving a fistful of little white papers that were printed with bright red numbers.

The Knack cuffed him fondly on the arm and introduced him with great affection. "This here's my associate, Pega-Ficha. He's got the most excellent numbers for you, don't you, Pega?"

"*Tem, sim,*" said the kid, brandishing his slips. "Look here! I got a big number *three* for you, just twenty cruzeiros, or an eight for fifteen. Or, if you don't got fifteen, then I can sell you a twelve for ten. Much over that, you're not getting through today, less Mother Mary comes down and walks you in."

Chico tugged at my sleeve and whispered anxiously, "Did you understand that, Primo?"

Pega was looking us up and down, measuring the possibilities. "What's with the bags?" he laughed. "You *caras* planning on spending the night?"

We didn't quite get the joke, though we were destined to get it later.

"No," said Chico. "We just got off the boat."

The kid gawked us up and down. "*That* I believe." Now he'd seen the pockmarks on my cheek and was peering in close to investigate. "Shotgun?"

I didn't feel like saying. It was none of his business.

He pointed to his ear and drew his finger along the scar where the lobe had been severed. "Knife," he said. "The *moleque* mostly missed me. Didn't mess my hearing any."

"Look," I told him. "We're not buying any numbers from you. You guys don't work for the ministry."

The Knack found this enormously amusing. "Course we don't work here," he said. "That's how we get things done." He stuck his face up close to me, taunting me a little. "Look, fresh-off-the-boat, you *wanna* deal with the ministry? See that guy up there?" He pointed to the functionary seated at the metal desk. "*He* works for the ministry. You go talk to him." He gave me a little push. "Go on now. Go talk to him. Get things done. *Rápido ...*"

And so I did. Striding right forward, sure of my cause, I presented myself before the big metal desk. The functionary looked up from his work, twiddling a rubber band between his fingers.

"We are here to see Senhor Ivanildo Bonfim," I said. "I have a carbon here of the letter I sent him, about the new school in Jacaré, on the Isle of Fair Winds. As you can see, it's a matter of real and special importance that we get in to see him, having come such a long way, at such great expense, on such *important* business."

I thought the speech was pretty good, actually.

The functionary seemed amused by my appeal and tempted, almost, to do something original. Then he remembered his bureaucratic roots and his bureaucratic sustenance, from which there was no escape. "Take a number," he said. "Find a seat." He pointed me to a large round dispenser that sat upright on the corner of his desk. It was designed to feed little slips of paper to a hungry world.

"You'll tell him I'm here then?" I said. "Tell him it's important?"

"Take a number. Find a seat."

I took a slip from the dispenser and stuffed it in my pocket. "You tell him we're here," I persisted.

But the man had returned to his twiddling.

Old Aunt Leona once told me that a lot can be learned from waiting. I can't imagine what that might be, unless it's learning how to wait. The first hour on the bench *did* remind me of something important that I'd learned in the army: *that wood is five times harder than rump.*

The number I'd pulled from the dispenser was 62, which Chico declared "extremely lucky."

I, on the other hand, thought it strange to be holding number 62 when there were only forty or fifty people in the room. *Had some of them already been called in to their appointments? Had some given up hope and left?*

"I think it's going pretty good, don't you?" said Chico happily.

"Well, we're lined up in the line," I said.

I'd been watching the functionary with growing interest, trying to imagine how a human being could possibly sit still so long. He might have died in his chair and no one would have noticed the difference.

Proving me wrong, he picked up his telephone, nodded dutifully, returned the phone to its cradle, and shouted out across the room, "Number five!"

Lucky number five, a tall man in his late thirties, got quickly up, stopped briefly at the desk to receive an admittance slip, and disappeared through the mysterious door beyond.

I found this very discouraging. Half the morning was gone and we were only to number six. "Look," I said. "I'm no good at this waiting thing, Chico. It makes me crazy."

"I can see that," he agreed. "Why don't you go out in the lobby and get yourself one of those newspapers to read. I'll stay here and move us along."

Though Chico is three bananas short of a bunch, he knows my strong points and weak, and treats me twice better than I deserve.

I left my bag with him, walked back into the lobby, and after much dibbling and dabbling around the newsstand bought myself a *Jornal do Brasil*. Like a kid with fresh candy, I took it outside and found a shady spot on the steps where I could sit and read.

There in my hands, a dozen new worlds unfolded. Worlds that had nothing to do with us and our school. Or did they, maybe, in ways I couldn't imagine?

I read that our dictator was "pleased" with the way his military planners were handling Brazil's economy and that things were "destined" to get better. I liked the word "*destinado*" and circled it with my pen.

Next came a story explaining why the Americans had lost the war in Vietnam, a place I'd never heard of. Then a report from "Johannesburg"—somewhere in Africa—where black people were fighting white people for racial equality. On the next page, I learned that microwave ovens were revolutionizing the way people cooked, but noted that the new machine needed *electricity* to work. Not much future there. Not in Jacaré.

I read the whole first section of the newspaper, ads and everything, without looking up. I circled dozens of new words that I'd never heard before and dozens more that I wasn't sure about. Had it not started raining, I'd have read on till nightfall, I guess, but remembered suddenly that I'd left poor Chico stranded on the bench. *What if they had called our number? What if we'd missed our chance?*

Rushing back, I found Chico exactly where I'd left him, whistling softly to himself. The room, almost empty now, was strewn with little slips of paper that had been abandoned by their holders. "How we doing?" I asked.

"We're up to number nine," Chico said, putting on a smile. But his shoulders were slumping.

I sat down beside him, with the newspaper on my lap.

"I got us a better number," he added, showing me the slip. "See here, number *eighteen*."

"Picked it off the floor, did you?"

"Sure did. I mean, eighteen's about half of sixty-two, right? So *twice* as good."

Up front, the functionary glanced at his weary watch and considered the handful of weary people who still clung to their benches.

"I think we're done for today," I said. "Don't think we're going to make it."

"Me neither. So how was the newspaper?"

"Full of *news*," I laughed. "And advertisements. And words I never heard of." I spread the paper out across my lap so he could get a look.

Chico pored over it, from one curiosity to the next, then singled out a photo with his finger. "What's this?"

"People fighting," I explained. "A revolution it says. Somewhere in Africa."

"And this here, this word you circled?"

"*Apartheid*," I read. "A brand new word, I think. At least it's new to me."

"Lots of words, huh?"

I whacked the paper with the back of my hand. "There's a whole ocean of words that we never even heard of, Chico. We just splash around in the shallows."

"Hey, you're the best reader I know!" he said. "Best writer, too. That's going to be a powerful big help when the election comes."

"Come on, Little Cousin. Let's get out of here."

Chico pulled our bags out from under the bench, muttering under his breath. "*Puxa,* Duba don't even know how to make his mark."

With our bags in hand, we pushed out through the door and into the hall.

There, leaning against the far wall, cool as the marble, was Pega-Ficha. He rolled his bloodshot eyes at us and let his toothpick swing scornfully from one corner of his mouth to the other. "*Malucos!*" he said.

Chico stopped short and dropped his bag. "Oh yeah! Well I got *this* readied for tomorrow!" He held up the slip of paper that he'd scavenged off the floor.

Judging by the kid's face, he had never suffered such stupidity before. "You morons," he said. "Tomorrow they'll change the color and start new numbers. That thing's worthless."

My cousin took a quick step forward, clenching his fist.

I grabbed him by the elbow and held him back. "It's okay, Chico. Come on. Here, pick up your bag."

Bitter as a pair of limes, we shouldered our bags and slogged off down the corridor.

"*Malucos!*" the kid called after us. "I am not afraid of you, you fat little man. Come on back here and I'll give you something to remember."

"*Vá pro inferno!*" Chico muttered.

"Tomorrow we'll come early," I said. "Be up with the owls and in here fast. Grab ourselves that *first* little piece of paper."

I was glad now that I'd written my cousin, Ozias, securing us a place to stay for the night. His response had been warm and inviting. Included with his letter was a rough little map that he'd drawn by hand. It steered us to the central bus terminal, onto bus 241.

The ride was long and winding, out to the city limits, to a street called Rua da Felicidade. There we got off, alone at the stop, and tried to get our bearings. The only direction on his map said, "Go west from the stop."

Putting the moon to our backs, we followed a tough little road that ran out across the top of the ridge. Left and right we passed shacks and shanties of the poorest sort, heaped one upon the other. Some were dimly lighted with oil lamps or candles. Others sat in complete darkness. Now we could see the full extent of the *favela*—a squatters' town really—spilling down the flanks of a vast ravine.

With no street names or numbers to help us, we wandered down through the slum asking one person after the next if they'd ever heard of Ozias or his wife, Jamela. When finally we got a "yes," it turned out that we were standing almost on his doorstep.

"Right there," the neighbor said. "Right there he lives." He pointed to a squalid little shack raised on stubby poles, set in a yard about the size of a postage stamp. There were no trees or bushes to break the awful harshness of the place, no flowers to sweeten the air.

This was worse than Jacaré!

We walked into the yard, stopped at the foot of the steps, and clapped to announce our presence. I could see a sheet of slimy gray water percolating down the slope and running under the house. Back in the corner, the latrine had overrun its hole and filled the air with a stench that made me want to breathe shallow, or better yet, not to breathe at all.

Suddenly Ozias appeared in the doorway, naked to the waist. Jamela came up beside him, plump and fatigued, holding a small oil lamp.

"What we got here?" Ozias said, squinting into the darkness.

"Two cousins for the price of one," I said. "It's Zé, from the island! And this here is Chico."

They poured out of the door to greet us, followed by a passel of kids and a dog that insisted on sniffing everybody's crotch. Their words were sweet and plenty, especially from Jamela, who gave out hugs and kisses. But once the pleasantries were over, they cut off our path to the door.

"We got your letter," I said hopefully. "And the map. We just got off the boat this morning."

Ozias had moved back into the doorway and stood there with his arms crossed. He looked like he'd swallowed a mouthful of bad water. "Look Zé, I know I said yes, but now I got to say no."

"What?"

"I got *eleven* people here now," he pleaded, "including a new baby, Jamela's diabetic mother, and two kids with the *gripe*. *Puxa*, I haven't got room to fart."

We could see it was true.

His hands opened sadly out. "I'm sorry, Zé. Truly I am."

"Wait a minute!" Chico broke in. "I got *beer*." With the zeal of a traveling salesman he knelt beside his bag, unzipped it fast, and pulled out one ... two ... three ... *four,* quart bottles of beer! He set these on the ground in a perfect file, like soldiers on parade. "*See?*"

Before anyone could answer, he plunged deeper into his satchel. "And look here! I got my *meteor* with me!" he announced. "And my *pickled toes!*"

These produced an incredible stir in the household, which spread quickly to the neighbors. Kids poured in from every quarter, straining for a peek. "Don't touch it," Chico warned. "No one touches the meteor!"

Once again, my little cousin had looped me into his madness and struck me dumb. Who in his right mind, I have to ask, would pack a bag full of warm beer and meteorites?

Even so, the man was irresistible, proving once again that tripe will sell just fine as long as the gravy's thickened with charm.

Whether it was the promise of free beer, the meteor, or his pickled toes that persuaded them, I'll never know. But Ozias's face began to soften, and Jamela's too.

I took up my bag and moved a little closer. "We can see you're really pinched here, Ozias. But *any* place will do ..." I showed him my bag and patted it gently on the side. "I got rice and beans here. Lots of crackers. Enough for everyone."

He was nodding now, taking it all in. "Well," he allowed. "Maybe you could stay in the bus."

"Yes, the bus," I said. "That would be *perfect*." So will desperation nod its head to anything. "Ah, what exactly *is* the bus?"

"On down the slope there," he pointed. "It's mostly dry. You'll have to put up with the rats, though."

What choice did we have? There was no money in our plan for hotels or *pousadas*.

"It'll be fine," I said, lowering my voice. "Just don't tell Chico about the rats."

Down the slope a ways lay the carcass of an old city bus that had been stripped of its wheels and left there to rust. Scavengers had removed all its windows and doors, ripped off the mirrors and chrome, and taken everything off the engine that could be unscrewed or pried loose. Only the rusty old block remained, with little pools of water welling inside the cylinder holes.

I made it a point to climb up into the old hulk first and stamp my feet around. Under the beam of my flashlight I could see the rats scatter back along the aisle.

Chico had caught up with me now and was peering up through the stairwell where the door had been. "What you doing?"

"Just shooing away the crickets."

"I don't hear no crickets. Don't care anyway."

"Hand me up the hammocks," I told him.

"Huh?"

"I'll hang them for us. High and dry."

"I can hang my own."

"I want you to take the bags and go back up to the house," I said. "Keep Ozias and Jamela company. We'll leave our things up there tonight. They'll be safer that way."

Now his suspicions were roused. "Safer from *what*?"

"Go on now," I told him. "Find a little corner up there where the bags will be safe. I'll be up in a minute."

That night, the little shack filled up with people old and young, family and friends, curious strangers and too many kids to count. Those who couldn't squeeze their way into the front room were left standing in the doorways. Others craned their heads through the open windows or peeped through cracks in the rough board walls. Wherever I looked there were faces pressing in and eyeballs peering back. Here was a one-ring circus that'd come all the way from Jacaré.

Though Chico's beer was a welcome gift, no one could imagine drinking it hot. "It'd be heresy!" one man joked. "An offense to Santa Cerveja."

Thus, against Chico's ardent protests, did Ozias send the beer off down the road, entrusted to some friend of a friend who owned a kerosene-fired refrigerator. This violated the eleventh commandment, which I'd learned in the army: *Never ship beer without an armed escort.* So disappeared our beer into someone else's belly.

Jamela cooked up the rice and beans, served from a large black kettle, with bowls of farinha and fresh papaya. Next came Padre Xabrega's little silver fish, packed like bullets in their little tin boxes, marinated in mustard sauce.

These were an instant and hilarious failure. Some folks gagged and others guffawed, twisting their noses into horrible shapes. "Why would anyone *do* such a thing to a fish?"

Once the plates were cleared, we were ready for the evening's special show.

With barely a word, Chico stilled the crowd and brought forth his jar full of picked toes, holding it up in the lamplight so that everyone could see. First with wonder, then horror, folks realized that those nasty little balls of flesh bobbing around inside the jar were the self-same toes that Chico was missing from his feet. Some of the kids, being kids, pushed in close so they could examine his stubs, visible through the open ends of his sandals.

With a tart little smile, Chico set the jar aside and threw out his favorite riddle: "How do you turn a brown man blue?"

No one could imagine.

So Chico told them his story, shortened a bit and prettified a lot.

But the blunter version is this:

If some babies are born wealthy and others wise, let us say with all kindness that Chico was born weird.

When he was only eleven, his parents felt compelled to take him to Manaus for psychiatric treatment. In that day, a certain Dr. Blu was all the rage, flouting a doctorate from the Institute of Wholesome Health & Full Recovery in Buenos Aires, plus a long list of prominent Argentines and Chileans who had experienced "miraculous cures."

By placing his patients in a special bathtub, packing them up to their necks in ice for twenty-six minutes, and filling their ears with an odd selection of Paraguayan polkas and Rachmaninoff, Dr. Blu claimed extraordinary results in treating every sort of mental and nervous disorder. But more, he applied his "special ice" to the treatment of arteriosclerosis, high blood pressure, arthritis, ulcers, gallbladder disease, gout, warts, and iron-poor blood.

No one knows exactly how long little Chico was left in the tub that afternoon when things went wrong. Apparently, Dr. Blu had stepped out of the room to meet with a local entrepreneur, who was trying to persuade the good doctor— one of the largest consumers of ice in the city—to invest in his own ice plant. Dr. Blu became so distracted by the conversation and enamored with the idea of becoming an ice baron, that he forgot all about little Chico.

By the time the boy was plucked out of the ice, he had turned a frosty blue and suffered frostbite on four toes, three of which withered into sad little peanuts and had to be surgically removed. Thus, Chico became the only human being in history to suffer frostbite in the Amazon.

Not long after, there came the sad revelation that there was no such place as the Institute of Wholesome Health & Full Recovery, that no one in Argentina or Chile had really experienced miraculous cures, and that the closest Dr. Blu had ever come to the world of medicine was a five-month stint as a veterinary assistant. Not to be deterred (or arrested), Dr. Blu hastily shut down his clinic, moved himself to safer quarters, retooled his reputation, and made a vast fortune producing ice.

The great irony in all this is that Chico actually got *better*. Having left home as a full-blown nut case, he returned only half a nut. That is to say, on a good day he would tune into reality seventy or eighty percent of the time, which is about normal, isn't it?

Years later, when Chico opened his beer shack, an odd little jar found its place alongside the cachaça bottles and wine. Inside it, pickled in formaldehyde, were the sad little toes that he'd lost to frostbite.

While others might have grown bitter over the experience, Chico turned it into a riddle, which he never tired of telling.

Now he'd finished his story and was leading us to the climax. "So let's try it again!" he exclaimed. "How do you turn a brown man blue?"

Choking with laughter, he himself sprung the answer: "Pack him in ice and play him a polka!"

Everyone roared with laughter. Though I'd heard the story a hundred times, I couldn't help but laugh again. Such was the man's gift and the delightful effect he had on those around him.

Now, close upon midnight, the main attraction was at hand. Not a word was heard as Chico reached into his bag and pulled out the sacred leather pouch. Solemnly, in a reverent whisper, he warned us: "No one is to touch it, or attempt to touch it, except for me. *Understood?*"

Yes, yes, we all agreed.

With great delicacy and drama he untied the pouch, removed the meteor, and sat it softly on the flat of his palm. He held it high and showed it around, so that everyone could see.

"I remember the very *day*, the very *hour*, the very *minute* it ripped through my roof," he said.

Amazing, thought I, *considering you were asleep at the time.* But who was I to spoil a good man's yarn?

Chico raised the meteor a little higher. "... the streak of fire ... the blast when it hit the floor ... the odious smell. And there it was, lying at the foot of my hammock."

Some of the kids, and maybe some grown-ups too, were so enthralled with his tale that they'd apparently stopped breathing.

"It traveled forever through time and endless space to find me," Chico concluded. "It carries still the *sacred essence of outer space.*"

He knelt down and extended his hand so the kids could have a better look. "You can smell it if you want," he announced. "But no fingers."

One after the other they craned forward, astonished, to take a little whiff.

From that elevated place, where we were celebrated and adored, we descended to the bus, which stank of old hobo fires and urine, and was overrun with rats.

Never have two men climbed so swiftly into their hammocks or been so glad to separate themselves from the ground.

We hung there in the dark for a while, sleepless and silent, while the rats mustered underneath us. The thought crossed my mind: *bold as they are, and cunning, the little devils might try climbing.*

"You lied to me about the crickets," said Chico.

"Yes."

"They're *rats*, aren't they?"

"A few."

"A few, *eh*? I saw a *big* one down there, Primo. *Deste tamanho!*" His hands spread out in the darkness, describing a rat the size of a pig.

"Relax," I said. "We're strung up high and safe."

He rolled over in his hammock and took a deep breath. "Above the rats and bureaucrats," he said. "All I need now is a dream."

"Dream about the new school then," I suggested. "Tomorrow, we see our man."

The night was filled with noises: a wild dog, yapping at the moon; a baby crying for its supper; and the rats, clattering across the floor beneath us.

"Why did you bring all that stuff with you, Chico?"

"What stuff?"

"The meteor," I said. "The toes ..."

"I couldn't leave them home, Primo. Someone might break in and steal them."

"You think people want to steal your toes, Chico? Is *that* what you think?"

He was strangely silent. Then suddenly announced, "I forgot my underwear."

"What?"

"I just remembered."

I didn't know whether to laugh at the man or scold him. "How is it possible for you to bring a meteor and a jar full of pickled toes and a bag full of beer and *forget your underwear?*"

There was no answer.

Time passed.

I figured he'd lapsed into sleep.

Then, from out of the darkness, he said, "Can you loan me some?"

We were up at four and glad to be gone. The downtown bus came through the stop at five—almost empty—and took us into the city without any traffic.

"Where'd all the wheels go?" Chico wondered, peering out the window. "Don't roll much at night I guess."

By dawn, we were off the bus and walking toward the Ministry. Chico was whistling merrily along. Hope was rising strong.

But 'round the last corner we got a rude surprise. There before us, running down the steps from the Ministry, was a long line of people waiting for the doors to open. Thirty ... forty ... maybe fifty of them! Whatever their true number, it was crushing.

Chico stopped whistling. His mouth gaped open. "*Puxa vida,* I'm not believing this!"

Moving closer, we could see how the game was rigged. At the front of the line stood Pega-Ficha, with his cocky toothpick. Behind him, in shadowy disarray, followed a long line of street kids and drunks, gang punks and frustrated hookers—creatures of the night—paid to stand in line and grab a number as soon as the doors were opened. Thus would Pega again, as every morning, end up with a fist full of choice numbers, ready to sell.

We gravitated toward the end of the line and took a spot, standing there like a pair of empty bottles.

Just before seven, The Knack showed up to encourage his little mafia. He walked along the line with smooth authority, shaking hands, greeting some of his minions by name. When he came finally to Chico and me, he stopped short and looked us strangely over. So far as it's possible for a weasel to express sympathy, that's what he showed us.

"This is just frustrating as hell, isn't it?" he said. "I *hate* the damned place."

Oddly enough, I believed him.

"Me too," Chico grumbled.

The Knack rubbed his hands together. "You know, I could get you number four, in about fifteen minutes, for just thirty cruzeiros. You'd get in for certain."

I hated the man, hated the scam, and hated the idea of paying him. But what other choice did we have? Go home empty? "Since we're talking numbers," I said. "Why not get us number one?"

He shrugged. "Cause that crooked asshole in there—you remember the ass at the desk, don't you? *The Twiddler?*"

I nodded.

"He always grabs the first couple tickets for himself, to pass along to his friends."

"I see."

"So what do you think? Number four for thirty?"

"Yesterday you offered us number three for twenty."

"It's inflation, amigo," he said. "It's pinching us everywhere." He pointed down at his red tennis shoes. "You know how much these shoes here cost me?"

I shook my head.

"A hundred and forty cruzeiros. *That's* how much. Tomorrow they'll be a hundred and fifty!"

Chico threw up his hands. Thirty cruzeiros was about all we had left. There'd be nothing for food on the long trip home.

"All right," I surrendered. "Get it for us."

Number four was magic! It propelled us right past The Twiddler, up a flight of stairs, and into Bonfim's private reception area. This was a much smaller room, with only a dozen chairs, and no one waiting. The only thing now that stood between us and our man was his secretary, a chubby little woman with honey red hair. She sat at her desk the way a queen possesses her throne, stiff-necked and vain, confident that nothing should occur in the kingdom without her approval.

I would like to say that we approached her with confidence and courage. But the truth is, we were bone tired and penniless, conditions that can't be easily masked. Our clothes—plain enough to begin with—were two days dirty now, as we'd had no place to wash. More, I think we offended her majesty's sensibilities by lugging our dusty bags into the middle of her court.

"What are you doing in here?" she said. Her brows, which were heavily plucked and painted, flapped up like the wings of a vulture.

"We're number *four*," I said. "Just called out." I handed her the admittance slip that The Twiddler had given me and kept right on talking. "I'm Zemário Licata. From the Isle of Fair Winds. I'm the one who wrote those letters to Senhor Bonfim. About the school." I handed her the carbon, wrinkled now from too much travel.

"That's right," Chico put in. "Fancy letters, and nicely wrote."

She set aside the carbon, unread, since her opinion was already cast. "You can't just walk in here and expect to see this great man," she said. "He has enormous responsibilities with *important* people. He can't take time for mar—"

Though the word hadn't quite spilled out, Chico and I understood it.

"*Marginais*," Chico supplied. "*That's* what you're thinking."

She didn't bother to deny it.

"Well, we *are* marginals!" Chico erupted. "We live in a *marginal* village filled with *marginal* people who think *marginal* thoughts. That's why we're here, you see, 'cause we need a *school*!"

I thought it was a fine little speech, but it moved her not at all. I could see now that she was made out of cowhide and that her favorite color would be khaki.

"Maybe you could come back next month," she said.

We smiled at her joke, then realized horribly that she wasn't joking.

I craned forward across her desk and put on my old sergeant's face. "We traveled three and a half days to get here, senhora. We mean to *see* him."

Thus did my sergeant's eyes do battle with the queen's, till finally she looked away. "Take a seat over there and wait," she snapped.

We retreated into a pair of chairs directly in front of her.

"That lady is not here to help us," Chico whispered.

An hour passed that seemed like three. Twice Chico got up to examine the little air conditioner that was set in the window beside us. With a curious grin, he'd place his big brown hands before the grille, washing them, as it were, in the stream of cool air. "*Rapaz, que coisa boa!*" he marveled. "I have to get me one of these."

A door at the far end of the room swung open and in walked a well-dressed man, about thirty-five, toting a handsome leather briefcase. He strode up to the desk, smiled, and trumpeted his name for all to hear, "Antonio Cabrera."

The queen rose and greeted him with that special deference that nobles reserve for nobles. "Of course, Senhor Cabrera, please ..." She opened the door for him and bowed ever so slightly. "The vice-minister is expecting you."

And in he went.

"I thought *we* were next," I said.

She gave me a weary look, reserved for paupers and idiots. "Can't you see he's a man of *importance*?"

A few minutes later, the prince emerged from the inner sanctum, smiling broadly, his business completed. On the way out he looked back over his shoulder at me with a peculiar mix of wonderment and fear. *What now? Peasants in the courtyard?*

Even as he closed the door another man came in, of similar thread and bearing. "Hélio Alves Bianchi," he announced.

Again the queen rose and curtsied and ushered him in.

Now I understood the way things worked. While the outer room, where we'd waited yesterday, was a numbers racket, the inner room was an aristocracy. Here it mattered not what number you held or how long you'd been waiting, or even how important your business was, but who exactly you knew and how well dressed you came.

"If I should die here," Chico said, "I want you to bury me, okay? Because you know all about burying people, right?"

"I guess."

"Just put a little sign over the grave," he went on. "Here lies Chico. Still waiting."

As noon approached, the last of the nobles departed through their special door, followed shortly by three or four other people who looked to be ministry employees. I noticed with great interest that the inner door was left ajar.

A minute later the queen herself arose, pocketbook in hand, and departed.

"This is it!" said Chico. "Our big chance. She has gone to the outhouse."

"They don't have outhouses here, you moron."

He was up out of his seat now, tugging at me. "Come on, Primo! Let's go!"

I snatched my letter off her desk and followed him into the room beyond. A row of small offices ran down the left-hand side, partitioned with half walls of frosted glass. All of them were empty. The right side of the room was spacious and open, dominated by a large wall map of Pará, marked with dozens of little map pins—green and orange and blue. Above it, written in proud letters, the sign said:

New Schools Today for a Better Tomorrow!

I stepped in closer, found the mouth of the Amazon and traced its long course west across the map. "Look here, Chico. The Isle of Fair Winds. Right *here* ..."

Chico leaned in beside me. "So that's where we live, huh? Right there?"

"That's it."

"A blue pin!" he exclaimed, jabbing his finger next to mine. "We're going to get a school!"

"No, Chico."

I took a deep breath and double-checked the key. "Blue means we already *have* a school."

He stood there for long moment, scratching his wooly head, then whacked me on the arm. "Come on, Primo. Let's talk to him!"

Rushing ahead of me, Chico homed in on a large, impressive door that seemed to command the whole office. He stopped short, gathered himself up, and was about to knock when suddenly the door swung open. There in the threshold stood a tall, fair-skinned man dressed in an immaculate suit and bright orange tie. *Ivanildo Bonfim!*

"*Oi!*" Chico squeaked. His hand was stalled in mid-air, positioned to knock on the man's chest.

I came up fast beside him, smiling hard.

Bonfim was now twice surprised and doubly confused. "Who are you?"

My first impression of him was *big*, though not so much in height as he was in belly. Everything about him—his feeble chin, his sunken chest, his spindly arms and legs—seemed to pay tribute to his belly, which bulged out over his belt like a watermelon. The cut of his suit was rich and finely sewn, but the tailor must have struggled with the fit.

"I'm Zemário Licata," I said, offering my hand. "From Jacaré, on the Isle of Fair Winds. I'm the one who wrote you about the school, *remember?*"

He frowned as he took my hand, then looked past me into the empty room. "Where's Cassilda? How did you get in here?"

"She went to the outhouse," Chico blurted.

I stepped in closer. "We would just for a moment like to talk with you, sir. To tell you about our community. About the kids. So you might know how desperately we need a school."

"Jacaré," he said. His memory had found the name now. His frown deepened.

"Yes. On the Amazon," I said. "I wrote you about it, sir. About the land that was set aside for the school and how eager we are to get started. I sent the first letter more than a year ago. Then last July, this second letter ..." I held out the carbon, so he could have a look.

His eyes fell away, as though he were regarding something hidden in the carpet. He'd remembered the name now, and somehow it troubled him. "We are of course very anxious to help you," he said politely. "But there is a certain *process* that must be followed."

"We followed the process," Chico said. "All day yesterday and today we followed the process."

Bonfim stepped past me and looked at his watch. It was solid gold, like the rings that bejeweled his hands and the crowns of his teeth. The metal seemed even to have colored his skin and yellowed the whites of his eyes.

Now the queen came marching into the room behind us, infuriated. "What are you doing?" she shrieked. "You're not permitted in here!"

I ignored her and confronted the man again. "You should be aware, sir, that the map over there is wrong. Maybe *that's* the problem?"

Quick as a fox, he glanced over at the map and back. "There's nothing wrong with our map," he said calmly. "It's perfectly accurate."

The queen was shouting at me now. "I want you *out* of here!"

But I stayed on him, like a dog on the hunt. "With all due respect, sir, there *is* a problem. Someone's stuck a blue pin into Jacaré, to mark a completed school. But we have no school, Senhor Bonfim. No building. No teachers. No books. Your map is *wrong.*"

It was his lips that betrayed him, curling at the corners, quietly gloating over his cleverness. I knew then, with all certainty, that the man had eaten the money for our school and digested it into fat and gold.

Chico had spotted it too. "That's a pretty lie you tell!" He said it with such exuberance and sincerity that it almost sounded like a compliment.

The great man cocked his head at a peculiar angle and smiled stiffly. With narrowing eyes he looked past us to his secretary. "Go get Jarbas," he told her.

Red-faced and rumpled, she turned happily to the task and hurried out the door.

"You should leave now," Bonfim said. "Before Jarbas comes."

"You ate the money for our school, didn't you?"

He blinked at me three or four times, as though I were a cockroach that had somehow squirmed its way in. "Why don't you go back home, little man. You have no sway in the city. No future here but to get yourself hurt."

"How many others have you cheated over the years?" I said. "How many kids without a school?"

He smiled again, fearless and condescending. "My word settles everything," he said. "Including your departure."

In came the little queen, pounding the war drums, pointing us out with her finger. Behind her stormed a creature that inspired immediate fear—half ox, I guessed him, and the other part troll—dressed up to look like a security guard.

Bonfim beckoned him forward. "These gentlemen are leaving the hard way, Mr. Jarbas. Handle it as you will."

"Trespassing!" the queen charged. "And the little one there—" She pointed a trembling finger at Chico. "... was *ogling* me!"

Chico was stunned. "Lady, you're twenty kilos past sexy."

Jarbas lurched forward and blinked his stupid eyes. *I'm gonna break something now.* He threw his arm around Chico's waist, lifted him right off his feet, and ran him stumbling through the door.

I was fast on their heels. "Let him go!" Twice I punched the man in his kidney, to no effect at all.

Out through the special door we stormed and onto the balcony, overlooking the crowded foyer below. Chico bucked like a wild calf, jabbing his elbows, wheezing for breath.

Jarbas ran him to the top of the white marble stairs, abruptly stopped, and pitched him out over the staircase. Had I not seen the launch with my own astonished eyes I would never have believed a human being could fly so far and land so hard. Had I not heard it with my own incredulous ears, I would not have believed that bones could break so loud.

I rounded on the man and tried to kick him in the crotch. He slammed me in the chest with his giant hands, one for each lung. And I too went sailing, backwards flailing, down the same hard path that Chico had followed. In this alone there was mercy: I landed on my feet.

Scrambling across the steps, I found Chico sprawled out on his back with his head cocked oddly down. There was blood splattered across the marble. Blood also in his hair, slick and red.

How strange that I should reach so fast for my handkerchief, as though I'd always carried one, and find it there in my pocket—*right where it needed to be!* My thoughts whirled back to that funny little moment by the dock when Senhor Domingos had given them to me. Fancy handkerchiefs for a gravedigger. A gift out of time and place, but *perfect* now in both. Not for sweat or tears or snot were they given to me, but to sop the blood off my friend's head.

In the midst of this wild nightmare a second guard appeared, come up from the foyer to investigate. I sensed him standing there on the step beside me, tapping his big black shoe. Down below, at the foot of the stairs, a crowd was gathering, excited by the blood.

Now our bags came tumbling down the steps behind us. I heard the sound of glass breaking, then caught the unmistakable scent of formaldehyde.

Chico came slowly up, clutching his shoulder.

I braced him with my arm till he found his balance. "You'll be fine, Little Cousin. You'll see ..."

"You boys are going to have to move on," the guard said. "You can't be staying here on the stairs."

I looked up at him, unbelieving. "*Meu Deus,* can't you see the man's bleeding?!"

The guard nodded his wooden head and issued his wooden orders. "Well, he'll have to go bleed somewhere else. Because this here is a *restricted* area."

The wound to Chico's scalp was nothing much to worry about, but his shoulder was bad. Bad enough that I had to carry his bags down to the boat for him. Bad enough that he couldn't sleep in his hammock, or anywhere else on board, but would sit for hours in the galley, or stand idly at the railing, so that he wouldn't have to move it.

We would discover later—too late to be of much help—that the fall had fractured his left shoulder. The fool procrastinated a long time in finding a doctor, then fell victim to the slow, backward medicine that has always been our lot. There was confusion over his X-rays, confusion over the diagnosis, confusion over the treatment, confusion over the confusion. Thus, Chico's shoulder never really healed, but earned him a nickname that would stick forever: *Chico Lists to Port*.

Over time, my little cousin would turn his wounds into jokes and funny stories, because that's how he dealt with things that hurt him. But some things are too sad to be laughed away. Where in all the time and money we'd spent was there anything but failure?

When Chico saw how angry and depressed I was, he tried to cheer me up. "Look at the better side," he said. "We got to see Ozias and Jamela, didn't we? Got to ride the bus and see the city. And how about that shiny red scooter? How about *that?*"

"I plan to go back there and knock the fire out of that man," I said.

Chico raised his good right hand, as though to push the thought away. "You go back there again, and that man will break you in half. He and that ape-boy of his."

"Not if I break him first."

"He's not worth it, Primo. You *hear* me?"

But the thought kept pushing me. *I'm going to kill that man!*

"Think how lucky we are," said Chico. "I bet no one on the whole island—even the old gaúcho—has ever seen the things we did."

But bitterness has no ear for consolation, even from the lips of a friend. "Why don't you shut up for a while," I told him. "You chatter like a parrot."

And he did shut up. All the way home and longer. On top of his cuts and bruises and busted shoulder, I had managed to hurt his feelings.

Our boat got into Jacaré on the fourth day.

The sky was full of sweat and thunder.

There was no one at the dock to meet us, except for Little Aparecida, who gave us flowers and hugs.

I had no heart to return her smile. The quest had failed. The heroes fallen.

We would learn later that Aparecida had met every boat for the past three days, to make sure she didn't miss us.

Oh to borrow a little of her faith or a sliver of her smile. It might have saved me a world of misery.

CHAPTER 12

ON THE FIFTH DAY BACK, OLD AUNT LEONA CAME POKING AROUND to see how I was. Or more aptly put, how I *wasn't*.

Auntie knew that I'd not been eating and not been fishing and not been out to crop the manioc. She knew all this because everybody in the village knows everything.

With full Auntie authority she sidled into our yard, ignored the lie I'd put in Ana's mouth, that I was ill, and barged right into the room where I was hiding. "I hear you've been moping around here like a sloth," she said.

I shrugged and scratched my armpit.

"That *there* is exactly what I'm saying!" she snorted. "And *that* too." She threw a scornful look at my friend Cachaça, half empty now, sitting on the floor beneath my hammock. "Listen to me, Zé. You got to put that damned bottle away, get out of your hammock and do something useful. *Anything*. Pick the nits out of your boy's hair for God's sake!"

"Maybe tomorrow," I said.

She was exasperated now, and it sounded in her voice. "What did you expect, Zé? Did you think he was going to give you a bag full of money and a bulldozer? Is *that* what you thought?"

"It was a waste, Auntie. A complete waste."

"There's *no such thing* as a complete waste," she said. "Tell me something you learned!"

"I didn't learn anything."

"*Tell* me something, boy." She lifted her walking stick a bit and waved it vaguely in my direction, as though she might smack me on the butt.

I sifted through the memories, grasping for something to say. "That I'd rather be poor in the country than in the city," I said.

"That's worth knowing," she agreed. "What else?"

Since she wanted the truth, I told her. "I learned that evil wears a three-piece suit, wraps itself in gold, and devours our dreams for lunch. *That's* what I learned, Auntie."

"It's that government man, isn't it, that's soured you so?"

I nodded. "I *hate* him, Auntie. I hate him for his arrogance and greed. I'd like to set him on fire."

She took a couple steps forward and planted her walking stick at the foot of my hammock. Her dark old eyes were only inches away. "You better let go of that, boy. That will eat you alive."

But I couldn't let go of it. Hour after hour I lay brooding in my hammock, wanting nothing of Ana, nothing of Leona, nothing even of Rafael.

Day after day the bitterness grew, till the root sprouted branches and the branches grew thorns. It was bitterness Bonfim had planted in me, and it was bitterness the man should reap.

I reckoned the simplest way to kill him was to take my Colt back to Belém and wait for him in the parking lot. Over and over I plotted it through, arranging and rearranging the details. I must have pulled the trigger on him a hundred times before I finally gave up on the plan. Though the "great man" would surely have ended up dead, I just as surely would have ended up caught. The thought of sitting out the rest of my days in some hellhole prison made my hands turn cold. Thus did fear shove me onto a very different path, which, though slower and less certain, seemed safer at the time.

On the eleventh night, under cover of darkness and a light rain, I slipped out of the house and walked the long trail west to Witch Alzira's house.

It was after midnight when I arrived, yet the place was glowing with light. Every window, though closed against the rain, showed streaks of lamplight through the shutters.

The house had five or six rooms to it, with a fine tile roof and real glass windows. *If evil doesn't pay,* I thought, *why does Alzira own the richest place on the island?*

There by the gate, clapping for her, I felt I'd made a horrible mistake, that I should turn around and run. *But what then? Swallow my bitterness? Leave that fat bastard to his game?!* Even now I could see the gold sparkling in his teeth, his belly lurching forward like a weapon. *"Go home little man!"* That's what he'd said. *Go home and let me screw you some more ...*

Out of the shadows the witch's dog suddenly appeared and padded silently up to the gate. He was big as a small horse and black as coal, except for a streak of reddish-brown fur that raced along his spine. Alzira had bred him to be a nightmare and named him so: *Pesadelo*. By all accounts, he was one-third Doberman, one-third wolf, and one-third damnation. It would have been better to have faced a jaguar in the open jungle.

Slowly, the animal bared its teeth at me, then barked so sharply that I peed down the leg of my pants. I turned to run but had not got three steps when Alzira called after me. "Please don't go, Senhor Zé. *Please!* He's really just a pup ..."

I stopped on the path and turned. She was at the gate, gripping the dog by its collar.

"Here, let me chain him up," she said. "Just give me a minute."

It would be awkward now to run off into the night. What would the woman think?

A moment later she was back. "Now then, come on in and let's have a talk," she said. "I have been expecting you." She pushed the gate open and ushered me through.

"*Expecting* me?" I said. "How's that?"

She bustled about in the darkness, latching the gate behind us. "Oh, you know how it is, *meu amor*. Bad news runs like a rabbit from ear to ear. I probably heard about your problems before you did." She laughed wildly at the thought, and louder still when she saw how strange it made me feel.

"Please sit down," she said, beckoning me onto the patio. "I'll put some fire to these candles." She indicated a white wicker table and some chairs, where I quietly took a seat.

The patio was roofed with large sheets of corrugated tin that rattled under the rain. The floor, set with dark green tiles, was crowded with flowerpots and herb pots and vines that twisted up the posts and leafed into the open framing.

Alzira fetched up a long blue candle, set a match to it, and moved around the patio like an altar boy, lighting one candle after the other till a dozen or more were flaming, high and low and everywhere, flickering in the wind.

In the dancing light, she showed herself an attractive woman, maybe forty-five, with the shape and agility of a twenty-year-old. Her dress, a swirl of orange and white flowers, hung loosely on her bronze-colored skin. Had it not been for some odd damage or disease that had struck her left eye, she would have been quite beautiful.

Alzira took a seat across from me and smiled pleasantly. She was careful in the way she positioned herself—out of vanity I guess—to keep the fair side of her face inclined towards me. Her hair flowed back across her head in tight little curls, very black in front, fading to gray across the top, turning strangely yellow down the nape of her neck. Very strange it was, but not unattractive.

"You're Zé the gravedigger," she said, declaring the obvious. Then leaned forward a bit and sniffed at me, the way a dog sniffs out a tree. "I remember your father. He wore the same lotion."

"I'm not wearing any lotion," I said.

"Cachaça I mean."

The woman was blunt as a hammer.

"No offense intended, *meu bem*. Just an observation."

"My father never mentioned that he knew you."

She smiled playfully and winked at me. "I never said that he knew me, Senhor Zé. Only that I knew *him*."

"Oh ..." The woman was like a ball of mercury sliding around a dish.

"Tell me why you're here, *meu amor*."

So intensely did I hate Bonfim and wish him dead—*worse* than dead, if that were possible—I had no words to say it. Did she expect me to pour lava into polite little cups and place them on the table?

Alzira leaned forward and patted me sweetly on the hand. "I can see the struggle here," she said. "Take your time, Senhor Zé. We have no hurries here."

I tested some words in silence, to see how they sounded: *I'm here to arrange the death of my enemy. I want him killed in secret, the way that he's been killing us ...*

I took a deep breath and tried it. "I'm here to arrange the ... that is, to ask ... ah—" But couldn't get it out. *What if she found me repulsive or dangerous? What if she turned me over to the law?* Finally I asked, "What is it you do, exactly, Dona Alzira? We rarely see you in the village."

She looked at me coyly, almost flirtatiously. "What is it *exactly* that you want me to do, Senhor Zé?"

I was wringing my hands now, cracking my knuckles.

"Would you like a drink?" she said.

"Yes. Very much."

"And maybe some chocolates?"

"All right."

She promptly rose from the table, disappeared into the house and returned a moment later with a small wooden tray. Upon it set two hefty glasses, filled to the brim, and a plate loaded with dark round chocolates.

"Cachaça for you," she said, handing me the glass. "Something else for me."

We sat and drank for a moment in silence. A queer little breeze played around us, tickling the candles.

Her soft brown eye lay upon me, inviting confidence. "I do many things for many people, Senhor Zé. One thing I do very well is chocolates." She pushed the plate a little forward.

I tried one and found it indescribable.

"When I was a little girl, I was always at my grandma Jaci's hip," she said. "Trailing her around the kitchen like a puppy. I knew the scent of cocoa butter and fresh vanilla years before I took any interest in perfumes."

"It's the best chocolate I ever tasted," I said. "It's what the tongue would dream of if the tongue could dream."

"Then have another, *meu amor*." She nudged the plate forward. "*Please*. Take all you want."

While I savored a second chocolate, and then a third, she wandered into the past.

"We were living in Bahia in those days," she said. "One morning a stranger came by the house and offered my grandmother a hundred Swiss francs for her recipe. He'd tasted some of her chocolates in the Praça de Tiradentes, where my family ran a little barraca selling sweets and pastries.

"I remember the look on Dona Jaci's face when she took that banknote from him. Like a child she was, delighted by the game. Front side and back she examined the bill, testing it with her fingers. Then sniffed it with her sharp, inquisitive nose—she was *always* sniffing things, you know?—and gave it back to him. 'I would rather own the secret,' she told him.

"Two days later the man returned and upped his offer to three hundred francs, a fortune to a family as poor as ours.

"Again, she turned him down, a decision that would cause grumbling in my family for weeks to come. 'Still, I would rather own the secret,' she said.

"So the man bought every last chocolate she had, wrapped them neatly in his bag, and left for parts unknown.

"Many months went by, till finally he returned. 'I am willing now to give you four thousand francs for your recipe,' he offered.

"'Where did you take my chocolates?' Jaci asked him. 'Far away you took them, didn't you? Across the ocean.'

"The man was caught off guard by her question but answered truthfully. 'Yes,' he said. 'To Switzerland.'

"'And what did you learn?'

"'That your chocolate contains some sort of exotic plant oil, and a wonderful aromatic, neither of which could be identified by our chemists.'

"I remember the way she laughed at him, like a bird chortling over a berry. '*Chemists?*' she giggled. 'What does chemistry know of confectionary? You should spend your time in the kitchen, Senhor— ah, what was your name again?"

"'Lutz,' he said.

"'Senhor Lutz,' she repeated. 'Well, I admire your honesty. You might have lied to me.'

"'My company is interested in making the world's best chocolate,' he told her. 'And *very* interested, Dona Jaci, in partnering with you.' He pulled a bouquet of francs from his pocket—more money than any of us had ever seen—and waved them gently about, as though to perfume the air. 'This is only the *beginning*,' he said. 'As the business prospers I'm sure there'll be additional payments. You should become a very wealthy woman, Dona Jaci.'

"'I'm sorry,' she said. 'But if I sell you my secrets, what would distinguish me then from a Swiss franc? They're printed by the millions, aren't they? Available to everyone from the king to the shoeshine boys?'

"An odd little smile—like bittersweet chocolate—puckered his lips. 'Yes,' he conceded. 'Widely available.'

"'So you understand me then?'

"'Yes.'

"She winked at him in her mischievous way. 'What would we be without our *secrets*, Senhor Lutz?'

"He bowed gently from the waist, did his best to smile, and placed his little bowler on his head. 'We shall continue then to make the *second* best chocolate in the world,' he said.

"What Dona Jaci hadn't told him—though maybe he suspected— was that she possessed secrets a thousand times more valuable than a mere recipe for chocolate. You see, Jaci was the greatest *mãe de santo* that Brazil has ever known, except for her special apprentice, who surpassed her in *macumba* and the secret arts of *candomblé*, who acquired powers that she'd never even dreamed."

"And who would that be?" I asked, though the answer sat plainly before me.

Alzira placed her hand over her breast and tipped her head. "I've never been inclined to modesty, Senhor Zé. The truth is true regardless how it's robed. So why not present it naked and unashamed?"

In that telling moment, when she laughed and reached for her drink, she inadvertently showed me the other side of her face. I had never before, and have never since, seen a person with one eye brown and the other green. Yet it wasn't the difference in their color that rattled me so, as it was their warring personalities. The green one, fierce and probing, looked like a raptor descending on its prey. I wanted not to look but couldn't really stop myself. How such a popeyed horror could live in tandem with the other eye, so soft and reassuring, I dared not guess.

She looked up suddenly, caught me staring, and turned her fat eye into the shadows. Apart from her embarrassment, she was plainly annoyed. "But you didn't come here to eat chocolates, did you Zé?"

"No, Dona Alzira. I came to curse my enemy. To buy a *maldição*."

Her annoyance lingered. "I'd rather not use that word," she said. "It's from an older and less enlightened time."

"How then would I say it?"

She rested her hands on the table and took a long quiet moment to compose herself. "To right a wrong, perhaps."

"All right."

"When providence fails us, when the judges are corrupt, I offer alternative forms of justice."

"I see."

"Especially to the *little* man I offer them," she explained. "You *are* a little man, aren't you?"

"So I've been told."

"Who is it we're talking about?" she asked.

"His name is Ivanildo Bonfim. He lives in Belém. I want him killed in secret, the way that he's been killing us."

The word "kill" pushed her back in her chair and left her silent for a while. Then she asked, "What is it he's done to you, *meu amor*?"

"Humiliated me!" I blurted. "And *robbed* me."

She seemed strangely unimpressed, tapping her slender fingers on the table, waiting for further indictments. "Is that all?" she said.

I shrugged. The words were eluding me again.

"*Credo,*" she said, "I wish I had a centavo for everyone who's been humiliated in the last week, and another centavo for everyone who's been robbed." She waved me off toward the village. "Why don't you go home and kick your dog a couple times. Get over it."

But my anger was boiling to the surface now, like lava from the depths. "He robs me of my dreams! Rapes us in broad daylight and has us paying for the privilege!"

The lights came up in her eyes. "*Us?*"

"My boy," I said. "My family. *The whole village!*"

"Ah, now I see it plainly," she whispered. "It's about your boy, isn't it? About the *school*?"

"Yes," I said. "The school that never will be."

A malicious little smile played across her lips. "We'll have to bake the man a *cake*, won't we?"

"You make fun of me."

"Not at all."

"A cake?"

"Something enticing, I mean."

"You have an idea then?"

She shook her head. "This is not so easy what you're asking me. It will take time. It will take a great deal of prayer and fasting. Also a lot of money. Do you have money, Senhor Zé?"

I dug down into my pocket and came up with a fistful of coins and small bills. I piled the coins on the edge of the table, then stacked the bills alongside it.

She watched me patiently, counting with her eyes. "That's it?"

"It's all I got."

I'm not sure which disparaged me more, her dismissive look or the flip of her hand. "For this," she said, "I could fart in a bottle for you and send it floating down the river to him."

"I can get more!" I pleaded. "Over time I can get more."

"Over time," she mused.

"How much would you want?"

"Everything you own and a little more."

I assumed she was joking. But her face was humorless and calculating. With nothing left to say, I settled back in the chair and finished my drink.

"We would need special materials," she said finally. "From Belém. Perhaps from Salvador. But I have friends in Belém and family in Salvador. Everything is possible."

"You'll do it then?"

"I will think about it," she allowed. "If the answer is yes, you will pay me over time until everything in time is paid."

"What?"

"You *are* trustworthy, aren't you? A man of your word?"

"Yes."

"You would have to go to Belém," she said. "At least once. Maybe more. You'd have to join me in prayer and sacrifice. Are you willing to do that?"

"Yes. Whatever you say."

She seemed pleased at that. "Return here a week from tonight, at this same hour. Bring sweet words and presents for me, as though you were courting a virgin. For you ask me a great favor and I need to be *persuaded*."

"All right."

"And here, take the rest of these to Rafael. Tell him they're the best chocolates in the whole world, *including* Switzerland." From out of her pocket she produced a small paper bag, placed the remaining chocolates in it, and gave it to me.

I was almost home before it occurred to me that I had never mentioned Rafael's name to her. Yet she'd used it so casually. That, and the thought of her vicious dog, were enough to ruin my sleep.

CHAPTER 13

I PITCHED IN THE LAST BIT OF DIRT AND TURNED MY BACK ON IT, resting the shovel against the papaya tree. Truly, there wasn't much grief in the moment. We had never met the baby or given it a name, and I'd already laid some others in the ground beside it.

"It wasn't your fault," said Ana. She had come up behind me with a cup of water.

"Whose then?"

"Maybe it's mine," she whispered. "Maybe something's wrong with me."

"Maybe something's wrong with both of us."

She stepped closer and held out the cup. "Have some water."

I shook my head. "I'm going up to the shack."

Her eyes fell away, first to the shovel, then to the empty bottle that lay beside it. "I wish you'd stay."

"Why? So we can be sad together? Count our losses?"

With that I left her there. Cup in hand. Staring blankly at the ground.

"I'm not selling you any more cachaça," said Chico. "Because you're drinking yourself worthless, Primo."

"A beer, then."

"No. No beer neither. You need to get home and sober yourself out."

"Go to hell!" I told him. Loaded with bluster and fury I stomped out of the shack, then turned and shouted—so everyone could hear—"I'm going to take my business elsewhere!" (Though in fact there was no place else to take it.) "And all my friends with me!" I threatened. "And never coming back. *Ever!*"

One of the great lies that drunks like to entertain (you might say it's packaged in every bottle) is that their foolishness is somehow charming and their lives abound with friends. The truth is, at that moment I had but three true friends in all the world: Ana, Aunt Leona, and the little curly-haired man I'd just consigned to hell.

On the very day I was going to see Alzira again, who should come clapping at my gate—way too early and way too loud—but Padre Xabrega.

I rolled out of my hammock, shuffled to the door, and peeked out into the yard. It was the Padre all right, gripping a book in one hand and his big Panama hat in the other.

After a long moment of grumbling and indecision, I threw on some pants and walked out to meet him.

Xabrega drew back from the gate, appalled, as if he'd come upon a corpse. "*Bom dia, Zé. Está bem?*"

"I am as you see me, Padre." I opened the gate for him and stood there like a post, pretending hospitality. "You want to come in?"

"No, no," he said hastily. "I just came by to ... ah ... Well, to say how *sorry* I am that you lost the baby."

"The baby?" Thoughts like languid fish began to surface, swimming through pools of mashed bananas.

"That Ana lost the baby," he repeated softly.

Now it was clearing. Of *course* the Padre would know of it. By now everyone would know.

"Yes, the baby," I said. "We lost the baby."

"Ana's not here, then?"

"Gone down to the river with the others. To do the wash."

He put his big straw hat on his head and stepped through the gate, just far enough to rest his hand on my shoulder. "I'm sorry, Zé. I truly am. Sorry, too, that the school didn't work out."

"Me too, Padre. Me too."

With great tenderness, he tried to catch me with his eyes.

With great elusiveness, I managed to avoid them.

"I've been praying for you, Zé."

"That's good," I mumbled. "Everyone should have someone praying for them. And since it's not me, it might as well be you."

He shook his head in frustration. "You can't be carrying on like this," he said. "The drinking and all. It's doing damage, Zé. *Real* damage."

I looked at the man in his beautiful ignorance and his do-goody-ness, and thought suddenly of Alzira. What would the good Padre say if he knew I was conspiring with a witch, that I was going to meet her that very night, that more than anything in all the world I wanted to pour hellfire on my enemy's head? What then would *His Holiness* think? Out of that nasty little thought Alzira's eyes came swimming, first the brown one, winking softly at me ... alluring and tender ... then the hideous other, peering greenly down ... so hot and persistent in its stare that my hands began to sweat.

"Did you hear what I said?"

"No, Padre. I'm not feeling so good."

He took his hand off my shoulder and adjusted his hat. "That you *can't* go on like this, Zé."

"I plan to do worse," I blurted.

"What?"

"Nothing Padre. Only joking. It's just as you say, I need Jesus."

"I didn't say that."

"Whatever you say or didn't say is all right with me, Padre. Is there something *else*?"

"Yes," he said. "I brought you this." From under his arm he handed me a large, hardbound book. Across its dark green cover, in worn gold letters, it said:

Bettencourt's
Complete Portuguese Dictionary
47,000 Entries · Finely Illustrated · 5th Edition

I took it in my hands and opened it to a random page ... *descuidado* ... *descuidar* ... *descuidista* ... then flipped further on, into the Ls and Ms ... *malquerente* ... *malquistar* ... *malquisto*. My eyes raced up and down the columns of type, from treasure to treasure, from mystery to mystery, from key to key. Not since the Colonel's private library had I held such a book in my hands. "For *me?*"

"For you and your boy," Padre said. "I know you've been teaching Rafael how to read and write. A worthy project. *Very* worthy."

"I *was* teaching him. Before I went to Belém."

"Well, it's time you started up again, don't you think?"

Never in my life was a present given me with more kindness, nor delivered in such a queer and dangerous hour.

That night I made good on my appointment with Alzira, carrying with me a pair of live chickens, thirty-two cruzeiros, and a bottle half gone. Though I'd promised myself to come sober, Cachaça had not agreed. Resolve can flex all the muscle it wants in the freshness of the morning, then dissolve into fish farts when the sun goes down. Now I found myself weaving up to her gate, ignoring the voice of caution—that poor, half-drowned spirit, speaking through the buzz—that might have steered me away from her.

I was relieved to find her gate left open and Pesadelo nowhere in sight. I stashed my bottle by the trail, in the cradle of a root, and whispered my instructions, "Wait here, amigo ..."

Alzira was sitting at the wicker table, waiting for me, with an oil lamp burning dimly beside her and some papers spread across the table. *"Entre, meu amor,"* she called out, when she heard me clapping. *"Estou te esperando ..."*

I walked into the yard and onto the patio, and felt compelled to remove my cap, as though in deference to a priest.

"As well you should," she affirmed, "for I *am* a priest."

"Como?" How in God's name did the woman respond to my silent thoughts?

"What have you brought me?" she said.

I set the chickens at her feet. "Good layers. Two of my best."

She aimed her nose at them and sniffed. Judging from her empty look, they might have been a pair of rocks.

"And *this*," I added quickly, digging into my pocket. "Thirty-two cruzeiros." I set the money on the edge of the table and stood there feeling small.

"You *are* small," she said. "But I like you, Zé, and have decided to help you. Here, take a seat."

I sat in the chair across from her and placed my cap on the table. In the lamplight, with her better side toward me, she looked younger than before and very pretty indeed. Her dress was a swirl of bluest water and deepest night, which seemed, through my wondering eyes, to flow around her.

"You stare, Senhor Zé. What are you staring at?"

"I had remembered you older," I said. "Quite a *bit* older."

This flattered her and brought forth a sensual smile. "I move around in age," she said. "I can be a little older for you tomorrow, if you want. Or younger still ..."

The thought fluttered through my head like a hummingbird. Could it be the actual truth she spoke, expressed in innocence? That somehow she played hopscotch with the years, leaping to and fro? I dared not believe it, lest it crack my mind. Yet there she sat, the living proof.

"Where's my poetry?" she asked, heaping confusion upon my confusion.

"Como?"

"I had expected a poem from you, Senhor Zé. Something romantic. Something to court a virgin, *remember?*"

"I didn't bring any poems. I don't write poetry."

She folded her hands together and placed them on the table. "You are a man of *words*, aren't you? Yet don't write poetry?"

"No."

Her head wilted forward, like a flower severed from its roots. "The world's gone dull," she lamented. "Given over to clerks and accountants. Why should I expect anything better from you, a *gravedigger?*"

This landed hard against my feelings and inspired the appetite she wanted.

"Never mind the poetry," she said. "It's a drink you want, isn't it?"

Before I could answer, her head was already rising, already turning, already calling for her servant. "*Dalvina!*"

Out of the house came a big-boned creature that might have been either man or woman, or some odd combination of the two. Its close-cut hair and rough brown garb did nothing to clarify its gender. Only the name—Dalvina—suggested a female was hiding underneath.

Up to the table she came, ignoring me entirely, fixing her huge brown eyes upon her mistress. The girl's head was quite the largest and roundest I have ever seen, so smooth and round in fact that it might have rolled down hill like a soccer ball. Her skin was black as a bat's wing and seemed freshly oiled. Indeed, she smelled of andiroba oil and something else—*unha-de-gato* maybe—that made me sneeze. Here was a woman whose bloodline stemmed not from the Portuguese or the Indians, but from the slaves brought over from Africa.

"A double shot of cachaça for my friend here," Alzira said. "Acerola for me ..."

Dalvina bowed slightly from the waist and lumbered off. She wasn't the sort of woman who would ever be swift or graceful at her work, but I would have staked a lot on her determination.

Alzira gathered up the papers before her, bunched them together and handed them across the table to me. "This is the contract by which we go, Senhor Zé. You will need to sign it on the first page, there at the bottom, and also on the third. Then the carbons." She pulled a ballpoint pen from behind her ear, clicked it with her thumb, and handed it across the table to me.

It is the fate of drunks and morons to be easily confused, and in their confusion to be easily duped. Gripping the papers, gazing down

at the words, I was overwhelmed by their complexity. The contract
was three pages long, written in a small, immaculate script, loaded with
Latin and big-city legalese. Most incredible and confusing of all was
the name at the bottom of the page:

Zemário Luan Vasconcelos dos Santos Licata

"How could you know my full name?" I said. "No one knows my
full name."

"Oh sure they do," she laughed. "I could tell you also the full name
of your wife, each of your six brothers, and the Peruvian prostitute
who birthed your son, Rafael ..." She paused a moment for emphasis.
"Who is actually your *nephew*, isn't he?"

Run from her, you fool!

Though the lamp had begun to flicker and dim, she saw no need to
trim it.

I drew the papers closer, struggling to read. The words looked like
columns of ants marching across the page, which scattered suddenly
whenever I tried to read them. How fuzzy I was with liquor and hotly
thirsting more! Where was that sluggish servant of hers?

"She will be here directly," Alzira promised. Her soft brown eye was
like a shepherd, coaxing me along. Her plush red lips were smiling and
full of promise. "It's all very straightforward, Senhor Zé. No need to
worry the details. I'm hoping yet to show you something *very* special
tonight."

Dalvina finally reappeared with our drinks: a polite little juice for
Alzira and a large, glistening tumbler for me. I took the glass and
threw it back in one great shot. Like liquid fire it swirled down and
landed in my belly, oh mellow friend and happy, how careless do we
wander!

So did the stupors overwhelm my brain. So did the flickering lamp
and her winsome smile induce me to sign I knew not what nor cared,
so long as it inflicted pain upon my enemy.

With quick, efficient hands she took the papers back, and then her
pen. "Done," she announced. "Now to have Dalvina sign it."

"Dalvina?"

Alzira beckoned her servant forward, squared the papers around, and gave her the pen. "Our perfect witness, Senhor Zé. From birth she's been a mute. Can't read or write either. But makes her mark just fine. *Don't* you, Dalvina?"

The girl nodded and obediently took up the pen.

Alzira pointed her to the spot.

But the pen refused to write.

Twice more Dalvina tried it, testing the thing on her palm. Twice more the pen refused her.

Alzira leaped out of her chair, snatched the pen from her servant's hand and snapped it like a twig. "The goddamned thing only has *one* purpose in life!" she shouted. "So why won't it write?!" Her bad left eye swung into view, like a troll storming out of its cave.

I pushed away from the table and held my breath.

She threw the pieces out across the floor. "Go get another one!" she shrieked. "*Rápido!*"

Dalvina shuffled away in a hurry.

I picked up my cap and started to leave.

"Please, Senhor Zé. *Relax* ... " She settled back into her chair and calmed me with her hand. "It's just a little *peeve* I have. With pens and such."

I looked on, incredulous, as her troll eye retreated slowly into its cave. Now her better face was returning to the light, her soft brown eye repossessing. "You mustn't be afraid of anger, Senhor Zé. It's a fine and potent friend."

"*Pode ser.*"

A few seconds more and she'd become her charming self again. I could scarcely trust my eyes for what they'd seen. What trick of boozy brain and flickering lamp had produced that awful hag before me, shrieking like a hawk, then reversed itself in half a wink to produce this comely shepherd girl?!

"In fact, it's anger that's brought us here, isn't it, Senhor Zé? That we might take your feelings—honest, *legitimate* feelings—and turn them to something useful. The way that iron's smelted hot and hammered, to make a blade."

"So how do you plan to kill him?" I blurted.

She shook her woeful head at me. "You are such a crude man, Zé. Either that or you are a sensitive man, made crude with too much drink."

"Do I get to choose?" I asked.

"Yes. You can choose."

"Then I'll choose another one of those tumblers."

"No more drinks," she decided. She stood up and beckoned me with her hand. "Follow me now and I'll show you something special. Dalvina can finish here. She knows what to do."

Alzira led me off the patio and onto a catwalk that trailed alongside the house. It was built with stout wood planks and sturdy railings, just wide enough for two. Beyond the railing, the bluff fell sharply away, descending into the river. To the west and north, the Amazon spread out like a vast black sea—almost twenty kilometers across. Only a thread of it flowed along the southern side of the island, forming the narrow channel that cut us off from the mainland.

We walked a ways farther and came to a broad landing that opened onto two flights of steps. One led sharply down the face of the cliff, zigzagging from landing to landing, arriving finally at the water's edge some fifty or sixty meters below. The other steps twisted up the slope behind us and disappeared.

I was surprised, looking down into the angry boil of waves and current, to see a dock built of steel and concrete. We stood there at the railing and watched the river surge around it, chewing away at the shoreline. "It's very loud!" I shouted. "Like an animal roaring over its prey."

Her eyes narrowed upon it, the way a hunter draws a bead. "Yes," she said. "Loud and hungry. Eating all the time ..."

Indeed, the bluff was under attack. Big chunks of earth had let go and crumbled into the water. Others seemed ready to go at any moment.

"This is my *third dock*," she said. "I've given up using wood. We'll see now how the river likes the taste of concrete and steel."

"Why have it at all?" I said. "Why not use the dock in Jacaré?"

She smiled over her secrets and gave me a hint. "Boats put in here

from everywhere, Senhor Zé. Private boats and yachts—seaplanes even
—with celebrities and *manda-chuvas* on board. *Gente boa, sabe? Gente rica
e poderosa.* They come here to right their wrongs and fill their pockets,
to heal their diseases and change their fates. Like you, Senhor Zé, they
prefer to come in secret."

I was focused still on the wild, growling water. "It does what it will,
this river," I mused. "It has no masters."

"The whiskey's made you weak," she laughed. She extended her
long, proud arm out over the railing and shook her fist. "I have eleven
years and five months before it threatens my door!" she crowed.
"Plenty of time to make plans and provisions." She giggled then like a
little girl who'd just thought of something naughty. "Maybe I'll send it
running back to the Andes and turn it into snow."

*What wild strain of woman was this, railing against the river and proph-
esying her future?* I could have told her some things that fishermen learn
by night and gravediggers see by day that might have humbled her a
little. Yes, I'd peed in the river and vomited in the river and
complained to the river when the fishing was poor. But never in a
thousand years would I mock it.

"Now come with me to the high place," she said, "and we'll seal this
thing between us."

She led me across the landing and up the steps, ascending the rocky
knoll behind her house. The way grew steeper. The wooden steps gradually narrowed and passed through yet another landing. Here the railings fell away, where most we needed them. I dared look neither up
nor down, but only at the step before me.

"It's a damned poor place for drunks," she said. "Watch your step
here or you'll die on the rocks down there."

I dropped to all fours and crawled up the last few steps like a turtle.
Gasping for breath, I cleared the edge and sprawled out onto a large
smooth rock.

Alzira was just a step away, looming over me. "You mustn't pass out
yet," she said. "Get up, Zé! Get up on your knees."

Boozy and exhausted, I pushed myself up. Now a pale green moon
was breaking through the clouds, shading her face and lips with a
strange, voluptuous light.

"I want you to pray with me now," she said. "Repeat exactly what I say."

I nodded dimly. The wind blew fast across my cheek and slipped its chilly fingers down the collar of my shirt.

"Xangô, you are the fountain of all my favors ..." she began.

"Xangô, you are the fountain of all my favors," I repeated.

Suddenly, I was trembling. A company of eerie shadows leapt up and danced across the smooth gray rock. It was *me*, of course, silhouetted in the moonlight. *But what of all those other shadows that mingled there with mine?!*

"You alone are my satisfaction and my consolation," she went on.

"You alone are my satisfaction and my consolation."

And on I prayed, exactly as she led me: "I declare and plead that the injuries inflicted upon me by Ivanildo Abreu Bonfim shall be avenged in full and six and twenty! That he shall become the refuse of my intestines, an object of wrath! That he shall be plundered by your many hands and several, O Xangô, through *Desânimo* and *Depressão*, empowered by our prayers, our faithful service, and the blood of those you crave.

"I, Zemário Luan Vasconcelos dos Santos Licata, declare that I am your apparatus in this work, given wholly this night and complete."

"Now place your hands on the altar," she said. "*Here.*" She pointed me to a large white tile embedded in the rock, painted with strange-looking figures and dark blue runes.

I crawled forward on my knees and placed my hands upon it.

"Worship him," she urged me. "Worship the one who comes."

Only half conscious, I lay in a netherworld of dreadful hallucinations. For some spell of time—whether minutes or hours I couldn't say—Alzira walked in tight little circles around me, and sometimes danced, speaking a foreign tongue. Waves of heat poured off her, as if a torch were circling around me.

In the hour before dawn, she spoke again, this time in Portuguese and directly in my ear. "We will lessen him and lessen him and lessen him some more. Then encourage him, through whispers and sacrifice, to lessen himself. Why should we kill him, Senhor Zé, when we can persuade him to do the job himself?"

I sat up and looked around in the darkness, straining to see her. If indeed she was there, she was nothing but shadow. "Is it sure?" I asked. "Is it guaranteed?"

Alzira found this enormously funny and me incredibly stupid. Never had I been so punished by a single laugh.

"Xangô will ride you like a horse," she said. "With an iron bit and six-point spurs he will ride you."

"But is it *guaranteed*?"

"What you dish out to your enemy will return to your own plate," she said. "*That's* your guarantee."

To the east the sun's first light was glowing. In the west the moon looked like a slice of cherry floating on the river.

"It's time for us to go," she whispered. "The sun does us no favors."

I looked over my shoulder to find her. Then left and right and everywhere around me. With that first touch of sunlight she had fled the altar, leaving nothing but a whisper.

I sat there for a long while, trying to remember who I was. Then hoisted myself up and edged backwards down the steps onto the landing below. Encouraged there by the railing and the better light, I turned and descended face forward, clinging to the rail. I have no name or reference for the terror that seized me at the bottom. Beyond the fear of snakes and storms and illness this demon rose, pushing me along the boardwalk and across the patio ... driving me through the open gate like a horse brought under the whip.

Not since the army had I run like that, dashing along the path, twice stumbling to my knees.

Now the fear took form. *Her dog was coming after me, howling like a wolf.* I lost a sandal in my recklessness, threw off the other and raced barefoot on. The hound was closing—its very breath upon my neck!

Rounding a bend, I came upon Lula the Shrimper and one of his boys, coming up the path toward me. Frantically, I tried to brake myself, to veer around them, but plowed headlong into poor Lula and knocked him flat.

"It's the dog!" I shouted. "The witch's dog is loose!"

Lula hustled to his feet. "*Nossa Senhora!*"

"You got a machete?" I screamed. "A *knife*?"

His boy yanked a slingshot out of his pocket and then a rock, about the size of a guinea egg. He loaded the sling, drew the elastic back, and aimed it down the path.

Lula and I fell back in fear. But the boy stood firm, his eyes fixed upon their task.

"I don't hear nothing," Lula muttered.

"Like a wolf, it howls," I said. "Can't you *hear* it?!"

Lula cocked his ear. "I don't hear nothing, Zé. Do you hear anything, Mário?"

The boy eased off his sling and listened for a moment. "*Não, Pai. Nada.*"

"Probably a UFO," said Lula. He was not joking in this. He had long been a student of UFOs and the island's self-appointed expert. "They use all kinds of tricks, you know? Clever alien tricks. To suck the happiness out of us."

But the boy was not as understanding as his father. He lowered his sling to one side and gave me that exasperated look that people reserve for lunatics and drunks.

"Looks like they clipped you a little," Lula observed.

"What?"

He pointed to the nape of my neck. "There ..."

I ran my fingers through my hair and found it moist and sticky. Then brought my hand around to look, first with curiosity and then with horror.

It was *blood*—from one of the chickens maybe, or something else—smeared across my head, my soul, in the secret hours of the night.

Later that morning, after I'd slept and sobered up, Ana approached me at the table.

"Two of the chickens are gone," she said softly. "Two of the best."

"I should know, woman. I got up in the night and took them."

Her eyes were fixed on the ground, as if something helpful might be hidden there. "We'll be missing the eggs."

"I hadn't *thought* of that," I mocked her. "I thought it was the *dogs* that laid them."

My sarcasm humbled her further. "Yes, Zé. I just thought—"

"Look woman, I will do with my chickens what I want! You understand?"

"Yes, Zé." Though she could see that my fist was clenched, she still found nerve to speak. "You were out all night," she whispered. "Are you seeing another woman?"

"You were up checking on me, were you?"

"No, Zé. It wasn't that. Rafael was sick in the night. We were needing you."

"And *now*? Is he better?"

"Yes."

"Listen to me, Ana, and fix this in your head. What I do with my nights is exactly what I choose. *Entende?*"

"Yes, Zé." She was backing up into the doorway now, nodding her head.

"Wait!" I called after her. "Just tell me *this*. If I were out hunting women, would I bait them with chickens? Is *that* what you think?"

"There are some who would do it for less," she retorted. Her glance was quick and searing, shot full of tears.

"Ah, *there* you got me," I said. "Next time I'll take some *eggs* and see what the market bears."

CHAPTER 14

RAFAEL WAS THE GREATEST KID THE ISLAND'S EVER SEEN. CUTE AS A button. Quick and strong. Smarter by twice than his closest rival.

If you think me boastful in saying this, or prejudiced by a father's love, just ask his friends and family. Or even strangers passing through.

"That boy's a striker!" they'd say. "He'll become a very great man ..."
Never mind what they said about his father.

To have a boy in the house—especially a boy like Rafael—is to have a memory ever before you of the things you've lost and the things you're busy losing.

In the face of my bitterness and bad temper, Rafael filled the house with laughter.

In the face of my lethargy, he was a comet streaking through the yard, off to have some fun. Though it's painfully difficult for a comet to halt itself in orbit, sometimes he'd do it for me. Sometimes he'd linger by the door or by the gate, looking back at me. *Come on!* his sparkling eyes implored. *Let's go have some fun. Be a comet with me!*

No, my worried face would answer. *I've become an utter adult with utterly grown-up problems, so serious they can't even be uttered. In fact, I'm so overcome with utterness that I've forgotten how to play.*

He'd stand there as long as he could, my little comet, pleading with his eyes. Then burst away, as comets must.

Wait! my heart would call after him. *Show me how!*

When Rafael turned nine, it was all about butterflies. With no encouragement or help from anyone, he fashioned a fine little catch net out of bamboo and muslin. Roaming through the brush, he'd snare the insects live, bring them gently home, suffocate them in his killing jar so their wings wouldn't be damaged, then pin them neatly onto scraps of foam board that he'd scavenged off the beach.

All told, Rafael collected fifty-one kinds of butterflies and moths, some so rare we'd scarcely seen them. To each he gave a special name: *Purple Dreams and Cotton*; *Lady Tangerine*; *Fast and Seldom Seen* ...

From where this fascination came or where it went a few months later, I couldn't tell you. Perhaps it bubbled up from the fountain of youth. Then bubbled down again.

When he turned ten, it was all about stars. Out of his fantastic imagination came a whole new universe of constellations: *The Pink Dolphin. Spear Man Angry.* And *River of Endless Pearls.* Night after night he'd sit on the beach and map the stars, using a little notebook that Aunt Leona had given him.

Sometimes, out of curiosity, I'd plop myself down beside him just to see what he was doing. I tell you plainly that he knew the phases of the moon as well as any fisherman alive, the difference between planets and stars, and how they moved in season.

"Ever wonder where they go?" he asked me early one morning.

I was sitting alongside him on the riverbank. The first stripes of dawn were playing across the sand before us. "What?"

"Where the stars go," he said. "When the sun comes out."

I considered the sky and tried to imagine it his way. "No boy. I never really thought about it."

"They're still there, you know."

Off to the west, the last of the stars were disappearing. They looked like bits of ice dissolving into a pool of light. "I see what you mean. They're just hiding out, really. Waiting for night."

Rafael smiled at me. "That's right. Waiting for a chance to shine."

His notebook, opened on his lap, was covered with big dots and small, drawn with a careful pencil. Some of the dots were numbered. Others had names. "So what's this?" I said, tapping the paper.

"I'm counting the stars."

"Uh-huh."

"That part," he said, pointing to the northern sky.

"How do you keep track?"

"With my hand," he said. Squaring himself up, he extended his arm —rigid as a pole—and positioned his hand against the sky. "Tonight, I counted four hands left, from the rock there, out on the point, then three hands up. That's my square." He turned his notebook sideways and held it up for me. "It works good. So long as I don't move."

"Ah, now I see why you always sit right here, in the same spot." I tickled him in the ribs. "*Puxa*, I thought you were staking a claim."

He laughed at me. "*Não, Pai.*"

"So how many are there?"

Rafael gazed up into the heavens. Perhaps he loved the question as much as he wanted the answer. "It depends on the moonlight," he said. "On how much mist is in the air. On how good your eyes are."

"*Claro que sim.* But right now, tonight, how many are there?"

"Two hundred and seven in that part there," he said. "Counting the ghosts."

"Ghosts?"

"The ones that come and go," he explained. "The ones so dim that you can only catch them in the corner of your eye."

"Ah, I see. *É mesmo.* Some of them come and go."

Rafael closed his notebook and stuck the pencil in his pocket.

"So how long you plan to stay with it?" I asked. "You going to count them all?"

"Tonight is the end."

This surprised me, and also saddened me. "Why is that?"

"Because some things are impossible," he said.

Beyond the butterflies and stars the boy was dreaming big. In his eleventh year he would build the most amazing *papagaio* that anyone had ever seen, earning him a forever page in Aunt Leona's encyclopedic brain.

He began with popsicle sticks and paper clips, bamboo splints and paper, building strange little models that mostly failed.

Sometimes, when I glimpsed one of his odd little prototypes, I'd pump him for information. "What is it?" I'd ask.

"It's nothing yet."

"Well what is it *going* to be?"

"However it turns out."

"Well when will that be?"

"On the day it's finished."

Thus he kept me carefully informed.

On the first of September, after months of mysterious activity, Rafael invited a small group of friends and family to Aunt Leona's house. Ana and I were there, and Leona of course, with Chico, Leo the Boatman, and Leo's youngest boy, Nonato.

Gathering in the lean-to behind Leona's chicken coop, we formed a little circle around the whatever-it-was, which was cloaked under a bunch of old onion sacks.

With a proud little smile and not much ceremony, Rafael pulled the sacks away and showed us the full expression of his creativity. Words fail me here in describing the elegant contraption that sat before us. To call it a "kite" would never do, unless rainbows resemble rags. Nor was it much like an airplane, for it had no prop, no wheels, no tail. All in all it looked like something an elf king would build to fly himself to the moon.

"It's wonderful!" Ana exclaimed. "And *big* ..."

Indeed it was. Though I never actually measured the thing, it was more than two meters long and a fat meter wide. The frame was built from long, stout splints of bamboo that were cleverly braced with old bicycle spokes and nylon fishing line.

Looking closer, I was amazed at the workmanship. Every joint was cross-braided with line—five turns this way and five turns that—doped with cobbler's glue to keep the ends from unraveling. Suspended within the frame, and cantilevered outside it, were eleven small sails— triangles mostly—cut from scraps of nylon—yellow, red, and black— that were double-stitched along the seams.

Who but Leo the Boatman, who was into his third childhood, could have provided the boy with such rich materials? Who but Aunt Leona, a fine seamstress, could have helped him stitch the sails? And who but Chico could have supplied the lunatic element, goosing him on?

While the three of them never really admitted their involvement, their eyes were bright with complicity, their smiles confessing all. "I can see your fingers have been dabbling in the pudding," I said. "And *quite* a pudding it is!"

Ana circled 'round and 'round the thing, then knelt beside it and traced her hand along the outermost sail. *"Can it really fly?"*

Here on the river the questions have always been simple and the answers familiar. Will the rains come early? Will the rains stay late? Was the catch any good? Can Fulana survive her tuberculosis? How's the manioc coming in? Will Pelé go another season with Santos?

Though our family has been forever poor and uneducated, we've managed from time to time to burst a new question upon the village.

Can Zé really get us a school?

For two-and-a-half years the question had tickled our ears and wagged our tongues, till my failure became obvious.

Now it was Rafael who was doing the tickling.

Chico, being Chico, insisted that we carry the contraption up to the beer shack and put it on public display till the following Sunday, when the thing was scheduled to launch. "No one is to touch it," he insisted, "since it carries the essence of aeronautical research. And don't forget too," he added importantly, "that it is protected by patents pending, particularly where they apply." He'd heard all about "patents" from a salesman in Manaus, who'd sold him his Yanmar diesel-powered generator.

Now, the boys up at the shack aren't noted much for their quick wits or subtle speech, especially when it's inspired by alcohol. "What the hell is it?" they wondered. Some voiced the question aloud, using real words. Others just grunted and scratched.

"It's a *sky sailor*," Chico said. "*O Veleiro do Céu!*" Though he had just invented the name, without really thinking, he liked the way it sounded. "*O Veleiro do Céu*," he repeated, his voice rising like a trumpet. "Graceful as an eagle!" He lifted his hand and described a glorious path across the heavens. "Come Sunday morning, she's going to soar right out of here!"

"If that thing flies I'll eat my shorts," said Chocolate, my old friend from the rebel days. To him, the sky was never blue unless you somehow proved it. "I got five cruzeiros here says it never clears the trees."

This was an unfortunate thing to say, for it opened the door to that rancorous old foolishness—a kind of hysteria really—that seizes men in the midst of their beer, provoking them to boast and ridicule, and finally to bet their money.

"*Puxa*, the thing don't even have a tail," Chocolate put in. "It's clumsy as a Monday goose."

Chico and I, and later Leo the Boatman, were to take these remarks personally, as though our manhood was somehow staked to the thing's success. Thus we agreed to take all bets, which ran about nine to one against us.

Only Chico, who kept the books, knew the full extent of our foolishness. On Saturday night, mere hours before the maiden flight, he called me and Leo over to the bar for a little whisper. His notebook, which had heretofore been dedicated to soccer bets, lay open upon the bar. He clutched a little pencil in his hand, which was shaking noticeably. "If that thing don't fly tomorrow," he whispered, "*we'll* have to fly."

This produced a very long and sobering silence.

"Well, what are we into it for?" Leo asked.

Chico glanced down at his notes. "About three lifetimes, if they don't charge us interest."

Thus does a man go home at night and sit in his lonely hammock, pondering his own stupidity. Thus does he calculate, in lonely desperation, how much his dog might be worth if folly made him pay.

September 16th, 1979 broke sunny and excited upon our village. A steady east wind coursed across the soccer field and rustled the palm trees along its western edge. It was a day splendid made for kites and carnivals, and for foolish gamblers to hold their breath.

People came from every which way, walking, running, riding oxcarts and horses, paddling their canoes. Old man Dalvo, who'd fractured his hip a couple weeks back, was carried up to the field on a homemade stretcher.

We are, if nothing else, a curious people. And nothing was more curious than the colorful whatever-it-was that sat in the middle of the soccer field. Everyone and his baby had a feisty opinion as to whether or not the thing could fly, with cynics overwhelming the optimists about twenty to one.

Rafael had been at the field since sunrise, assisted by his little squad of helpers. They'd positioned *O Veleiro* right at midfield and posted Nonato there to guard it. He was to allow no touching or tampering of any kind. No premature launch.

Leo took charge of the line, the knots, and the anchors, insisting that no one—not even Rafael—mess with his command. Using a sledge hammer, he drove a pair of metal spikes into the ground at the eastern end of the field. The first, which was driven in at an angle, would serve as the ground anchor, to tie off the line. The second, fashioned from an old piece of rebar, was set about three meters behind the first and driven in straight. Leo had bent the top of it into an L-shaped arm, designed to hold a large spool of line that could spin freely. On closer inspection, I realized the spool was wound with high-test nylon, which would have been the envy of any fisherman on the island! Who could argue now, in view of such extravagance, that Leo had not joined the ranks of happy kooks and lunatics?

By ten o'clock, everything was set, and the moment was upon us. Chico and I patrolled the flight line, pushing the crowd back to give the boys some room. The wind, for some unforgivable reason, was beginning to wane.

Rafael stood ten, maybe twelve meters away from his craft, with his eyes fixed hard upon it. He was barefoot and shirtless, gripping the line in one hand and worrying his chin with the other. One might have guessed, from the bent of his smile, that he wasn't half as confident as he pretended. Maybe it had dawned on him, as he spied out friends and family in the crowd, that the flipside of glory—should the thing fail him—wasn't going to be much fun.

For those of us who had bet our souls on the moment, there was no help at all. Poor Leo, who'd run out of things to do, looked like he was having a gas attack. Chico had plopped himself down beside the goal and seemed to be praying.

Rafael waited a long moment for the wind to stiffen. When it refused, and seemed in fact to shift and die, he gave the signal anyway.

The crowd hushed.

Nonato lifted the craft by its keel and held it above his head as far as he could reach.

"*Vira já!*" Rafael shouted.

Nonato turned it full before the wind. The sails filled briefly, then luffed, then filled again.

"*Solta!*" Rafael cried. "Let her go!"

No one, not even Rafael, was prepared for the way the thing shot skyward. It leapt from Nonato's hand like a bird flushed out of its cover—straight up, really—and never quit climbing.

Without blinking or thinking I watched the thing soar, up and away, and with it my heart, overfilled with joy and pride. My boy had proved, against all odds, that something new and very good was possible. That dreams can sometimes fly.

Celebration swept the field and poured off the sidelines.

Rafael was suddenly surrounded with kids, begging to hold the line.

Old Leo danced like a gypsy, whirling and twirling, pumping his fists, like a striker who's just hit the winning goal.

I saw Chico doing a frogwaddle along the goal line, then break into a run, pretending with his wild, outstretched arms that he was a bird.

Never have three grown men—with me rounding out the silly trio —so completely reduced themselves to children. We whooped and hollered till there wasn't any whoop and holler left. We performed hootbellies and rabbit jigs that have never been seen before and will likely never be seen again. Apart from *O Veleiro's* glorious launch and the prestige we'd gained, we could savor now that vast relief that only a winning gambler can know.

"*Ele quer subir mais!*" Leo shouted. "It wants to go higher!" He was forced back to work now, keeping the lines clear and tending the spool. "*Ele quer subir mais!*"

This was to become the great rallying cry of our village, which spread like a smile up and down the river, and even sifted into the Indian lands to the south.

"It wants to go higher!" exclaimed Aunt Leona, jabbing her walking stick into the heavens.

"It wants to go higher!" declared Duba Do Nothing, who was delighted to cheer the thing on so long as no actual work was involved.

Even Chocolate, faced with the prospect of eating his shorts, finally conceded. "It *does* want to go higher," he said. "A *lot* higher."

O Veleiro sailed off the end of the soccer field, easily clearing the great dead boughs of the cinnamon tree. It blew past the three crosses atop the Catholic Church and hovered gently over Domingos' cattle lot. There it waited for an hour—reduced now to the size of a thumb-nail—while Leo ran off to look for more line.

With a fresh spool in place, *O Veleiro* sailed on and on, past the lepers' shacks and the waterfalls beyond. By sunset, it was just a spit and a half from witch Alzira's place.

There it stayed the night, hovering before a gentle east wind, while Leo, Chico and Rafael went out scavenging for more line. Soon the word was out: "We need more line!"

I doubt that any single event in our long and complicated history— back even to the days of the Jesuits and the *Bandeirantes*—so invigorated and united us. From every quarter the river folk brought forth their offerings—balls of twine and used kite string, leftover yarn and strips of *liana,* rusty bailing wire and old boot laces—anything to send the papagaio higher. Unhappily, old Leo—our master of knots and lines —found that most of it was too thin or too thick or too frail to use. This put him in the awkward position of having to turn folks down, friends and neighbors included, who'd come forward with good and generous hearts.

Now there are a lot of different ways to say "No," and Leo must have tried them all. "We're so grateful, Senhora, for what you brought. But we can't use yarn, on account of ... well ..." And here his diplomacy sometimes failed him. "... It's just no damned good for this!"

Despite the large amount of "line" that Leo had to reject, *O Veleiro* climbed steadily higher. By the end of the second day it had cleared the western tip of the island and was sailing out over the open river, just a speck now against the clouds. By noon on the third day it had disappeared completely. Only the tension on the line, tied back to the spike, assured us that our champion was still flying.

On the morning of the fourth day Senhor Domingos showed up with an old brass telescope and tripod. These, he declared, would enable us to track *O Veleiro* into the uttermost reaches of the stratosphere. I could tell by the way he carried the scope and how sweetly he cared for it—all spit and polished for the occasion—that the old gaúcho was mighty proud of it.

"Belonged to my great-great grandfather," he said. "A gunnery sergeant in the *Bateria Mallet* ..."

He searched out a little rise that suited his purpose, back a ways from the anchor, and there erected his fine wooden tripod. "Commanded a battery of Whitworths he did, against the Paraguayans. At *Tres Bocas* and *Tuyuti.* Made the bastards pay, I'll tell you. Though it cost him his arm ..."

With great care he mounted the telescope upon its swivel, cleaned the lenses with his handkerchief, and trained it on the western sky.

But before anyone could get a clean look, the project was overrun with kids, pushing in with their elbows and chins. This made Domingos nervous as a cat in a lightning storm. "Back off now!" he warned them. "Or no one gets a look! You there! Don't touch the lens, *you hear me?*"

It must be conceded, since it's completely obvious, that we river folk aren't much good at forming up lines and waiting our turn. Domingos would have done better, I think, trying to order a bunch of piglets.

Overwhelmed and fearing for the safety of his telescope, the old cattleman packed up his things and headed home. Lucky for us, he spied the ladder and scaffolding that had been erected in front of the Catholic Church, where the plaster was supposed to have been repaired last year, or maybe this year, or possibly next.

Domingos moved in for a closer look. There, five meters off the ground, accessible only by a solitary ladder, was a platform planked out with good stout boards. It was, in a word, *perfect*.

With Padre Xabrega's blessing, he hauled his telescope up into the scaffolding and set up the finest little observatory you've ever seen. In the company of birds, with his old gaúcho hat pulled low to shield him from the sun, Domingos manned his happy post. Half the island must have climbed up there to visit him in the days that followed, to see the unseeable marvel. Truth was, Domingos didn't really mind the kids, so long as they came one at a time and kept their smudgy little hands off his freshly polished brass.

On the fifth day, the Indians began to sift into Jacaré—more Indians actually than any of us had ever seen at a time.

These were the *Sateré-Mawé*, who dwelled on the mainland to our south and east. Culturally and linguistically, they are as different from us as blowfish from bats, and consider themselves, with quiet pride, a country unto themselves.

By ones and twos they used to come across the rope bridge and into our village, especially the one called Índio, a *cacique* among them, who spoke just enough Portuguese to get his trading done. I knew him by sight, and also by reputation, as the finest hunter in any man's camp. His sense of smell and hearing were legendary—so sharp, they said, he could hear a baby burp on the other side of the river. Years later, I would learn his indigenous name, which meant "Light Foot." But in those days everyone just called him Índio.

Whether it was a good thing or bad to have these Indians suddenly in our midst—milling through the streets, poking their curious noses into our kitchens, peeing freely wherever the urge developed—depended on how you felt about Indians.

Truth be told, we "tall, hairy ones," who called ourselves "*brasileiros,*" were not as stingy or grasping or dishonest as the Indians made us out. Nor were they as stupid as we liked to suppose. Actually, for us to call anyone "stupid" is for the mold to insult the mildew.

What had lured the Indians into our village, of course, were the stories spreading up and down the river about a giant kite—*um papagaio gigantesco*—that soared above the hawks and high-flying urubus, a kite that had vanished from the eyes of men.

An hour or so before sunset, I was down at the soccer field taking my turn by the anchor. Rafael was sprawled out on the ground beside me, strangely quiet. I don't know how long Índio had been watching us there before I felt the weight of his eyes and turned around to look.

He was standing directly behind us, alone and very still. His arms were folded lightly across his chest, his bright black eyes filled with wonder. He was a very small man—much shorter than me (and I'm not tall)—but packed with muscle and very finely proportioned. To take him lightly in a fight, on account of his littleness, would have been a big mistake.

Filled with curiosity, he came a few steps closer and lowered his arms. Around his neck, hanging from a leather cord, was a tooth as long as my finger, a hunting trophy that very few men have won. Its story was tattooed down the length of his arm; there, peering through a swirl of dark blue leaves, was the face of a jaguar, its teeth bared, its eyes fixed upon its kill.

Now he had moved right up to the anchor, there to examine the spool and the spikes and the little circle of chairs and stools we'd assembled. But it was the line trailing off into empty sky that captured his unbelieving eyes and would not let go. A peculiar little smile played across his lips, delighted with the mystery. Ever so slowly he reached out and placed his finger on the line, pressing it softly, testing the tension. This he did two or three times, peering into the sky and plucking the line, then peering into the sky again. Finally he turned and looked me straight in the eyes. "You are the big kite man," he said happily.

"No," I shook my head. Then pointed to Rafael. "*He's* the big kite man."

Índio looked briefly at the boy and dismissed the possibility. "You the big kite man," he repeated.

"No, it's *him*," I insisted. "He is the one who built it."

But Índio had already promoted me in his mind and decided to like me. Though I would try again on different occasions to convince him of the truth, he could never be persuaded that a mere boy could accomplish such a thing.

Rafael was up on his haunches now, and then his feet, listening closely, watching the Indian's every move. His eyes sparkled with excitement, no less curious about Índio than Índio was about the papagaio. "You want to go take a look?" Rafael asked him. He pointed over to the church, toward the scaffolding, up to the little observatory that Domingos had mounted.

"Church no," Índio said.

"No, not the church," Rafael said. "The *telescope*. Do you want to go see?" He put his finger to his eye, then pointed at the sky. "Go see the papagaio? Through the big tube?"

Without understanding much of this, Índio followed Rafael over to the church and up the ladder. There, through the big brass tube, he saw the unseeable thing, dancing in the clouds. It was nothing like a papagaio, he realized now, and nothing like the seaplane that sometimes flew low along the river. In fact it was like nothing he'd ever seen before. "*Hee hee me*," he laughed, like a bird chortling over a berry. "*Hee hee me*."

The following morning Índio showed up at my gate with his whole big family in tow.

Quieting the dogs, Ana and I went out to meet them, a little unnerved at the sight.

Índio stood square before the gate, equipped now with a satchel on one hip and a big hunting knife on the other. Behind him, in the shade of the banana trees, was his woman—shorter even than he—with a whole passel of bare-butt kids. Judging from their number and size, they must have popped out of her womb one right after the other, or maybe two at a time.

I opened the gate and offered the man my hand.

He gripped it firmly. "I am Índio."

"I know who you are," I said. "They say you can smell a fart at five kilometers. That you can run through the rain so fast that you don't get wet."

He didn't understand me really, but could sense that I was complimenting him.

"I'm Zé," I said. "This here is Ana, my woman."

He came through the gate, nodding to her, leery of the dogs.

"They won't hurt you," I said. "I spoke to them."

Ana held the gate open and gestured to the woman. "Please come in," she called out. "We got *mingau* from breakfast yet. Some papaya too, and *ingá*."

But the woman held back, quiet as a shadow, with her children gathered close.

"You are the big kite man," Índio said, grinning up at me. His teeth were very white and even, with some gaps here and there.

"Come sit in the shade," I said. "Ana, bring us some maté."

We took up a pair of stools under the mango tree and sat face to face.

Índio leaned forward and sniffed at me, catching the *babaçu* oil that I'd rubbed into my hair that morning.

I likewise sniffed at him, catching the *guaraná* that he was chewing. I was impressed again by the bulk of his muscles, which ran like hawsers up through his chest and shoulders. His ears were like a pair of conches, protruding through a curtain of straight black bangs. The lobe on his left ear was pierced with a small white bone, tied off with a little blue feather. I assumed it was a symbol of rank, for he was greatly respected among his people.

Ana brought us the gourd and metal straw, and a pitcher full of cool water, then left us to our business. We passed the maté back and forth in silence, pouring for one another, enjoying its fresh sweet taste.

Unable to control his curiosity, he leaned forward and gawked at the scars that peppered my cheek. Closer still he bent—with no shame at all—and put his curious finger on the pock that sat closest to my eye. No one—not even Ana—had ever touched me like that.

"You are a *warrior* man," he declared. "Warrior and big kite man."

"*Não*," I said. "*É só conversa, sabe?*"

But he could not be swayed from his flattering opinions, which included the bizarre notion that I was trustworthy. Finally he took his finger off my cheek and reached down into his satchel. "We trade," he said.

Out of his bag came a little jelly jar that was filled with thick white fat and capped with a metal lid. "Fat from turtle," he said. "For skin. Scars. *Muito bom.*"

Without warning, he removed the lid, dabbed some fat on the tip of his finger, and gently applied it to my cheek, moving from one pock-mark to the next. What could I say in the face of such unblushing innocence? This, I reminded myself, is the way their hearts are wound.

When he'd finished, Índio put the jar back in his satchel and described how the trade should work. "One jar turtle fat go your way," he said, holding up his index finger. "Ten aspirin come my way ..." Now he showed me all ten of his fingers and wiggled them like a bunch of worms.

"I don't have any aspirin."

"You *get* aspirin," he insisted.

I poured the last of the water into the gourd and handed it to him. "What happened to your deal with Senhor Duba? Doesn't that go anymore?" Now Duba and his sons had for years been trading with the *Sateré-Mawé*, using Índio as their go-between. As far as we village folk were concerned, it seemed like a natural arrangement. Duba was, after all, our "maximum chief," which gave him clout with the Indians. What's more, Duba's family owned the only real store in Jacaré.

Índio sipped at the straw till the gourd ran dry, then reached into his bag again.

"So what about Duba?" I repeated.

"Duba is lazy man and crooked," he said finally.

"That he is," I agreed.

"You are a *warrior* man," said Índio. "*Honest* being."

This was the nicest thing that anyone had said to me in years. Maybe *ever*. The truth was, Índio considered me a lot better than I considered myself.

Now he'd fetched up a second bottle, and handed it over to me. "*Andiroba* oil," he said. "Also *copaíba*."

Such oils and extracts were greatly prized in the city, I knew, and would bring a good price. I thought suddenly of my enterprising cousins, Ozias and Jamela. *Maybe we could start a little trading venture, moving goods up and down the river.* One thing was sure. I was going to need money to pay Alzira. A lot of money.

"What else do you need besides aspirin?" I said.

"Matches," Índio answered quickly. "Popcorn ..." Now his eyes were starting to twinkle. "... and Marlboros."

Thus it happened, through that peculiar meeting, that I began to trade with the *Sateré-Mawé*, or better said, with Índio, for he was their point man in everything linked to the outside world. If not bound by love, or even true affection, Índio and I always managed to treat one another with respect, to trade honestly, and to tolerate each other's odors. He thought me a great war hero, a big kite man, and world traveler. I thought him an honorable man and the greatest hunter I've ever known. While he was vastly deceived in his opinion of me, I was essentially correct in mine.

On the seventh day, which was Sunday again, Rafael decided to send a message up the kite, to see if God would answer. He wrote it on a little piece of cardboard, in black ink, as neatly as he could. When the message was ready, he brought it to me in my hammock and asked me if the spelling and grammar were okay. It said:

Dear GOD,
Are you there?
Do you see us down here?

Sincerely,
Rafael

"What do you think?" he asked.

The message made me smile. It was more or less what I would have written had I owned the faith to write at all. "It's good," I told him. "Right to the point."

"And the spelling? How is the spelling?"

For some reason the spelling and penmanship were very important to him.

"It's fine," I said. "But you mustn't let Padre Xabrega see this. It'll sour his bowels. You know what a hard time he has with his bowels."

"*Não, Pai.*"

"Well he *does*. So maybe tonight we'll send it. After dark."

"*Sim, Pai.*"

That night, after the moon was up, we went down to the soccer field together to send his message. We found Nonato there, watching over the line.

I helped Rafael cut two little holes in the cardboard, then thread a piece of string through them. We looped the string around the line and carefully tied it, so the cardboard would catch the wind and slide easily up.

Nonato was wild with curiosity, poking his little nose into everything. "What is it?" he pleaded. "What's it say?"

"It's a secret," said Rafael. He didn't bother to hide the message, since Nonato couldn't read it anyway.

"Come on, Rafael," his friend begged. "*Sou teu maior amigo. De que fala?*"

"Sorry, it's still a secret." With that, he pushed the cardboard out the line a ways, to get it going. The wind whipped up and swirled around us, anxious to carry the message.

And up it went. Just a little bit of cardboard with a little bit of hope.

Finally, it disappeared in the moonlight.

Perhaps *O Veleiro* would have sailed on forever, soaring over the Andes and the great ocean that lies beyond, had it not been spotted by the pilot of a Cessna 213 in route from Parintins to the Rio Urubu. So spooked he was by the sudden appearance of the thing that he hysterically radioed the tower in Manaus and reported that he'd just seen a UFO. As it happened this played perfectly into the imagination and ambitions of a nervous Air Force officer, who scrambled up an old T-6 fighter to go investigate. This, in turn, provided a rare chance for adventure and glory to the fighter's twenty-six-year-old pilot, who had never actually fired his machine guns at an airborne target.

Though the battle was pitched, the newspapers said, the pilot managed to down the UFO before it could fire its weapons—probably a death ray of some sort.

The good people of Jacaré knew nothing of this at the time. Only that the line sustaining their champion went suddenly and inexplicably slack.

Severed by a bullet, the line drifted lazily down and down and down, settling across the face of the river, backing up across the tip of the island, catching the eave on Witch Alzira's house, draping itself from treetop to treetop, sagging over the lepers' shacks, settling gently upon the dusty gray backs of the brahmas in Domingos' cattle lot, snagging the center cross atop the Catholic Church, and finally, like a dying animal, laying gently down across the soccer field.

We worked long and hard to salvage what line we could, tracking it through the brush, threading it back through the trees and over the rooftops. Most of it, of course, was lost out over the water, snagged in the depths of the river.

Long after the rest of us had quit and gone home, Rafael sat at the end of the soccer field by himself, gazing into the sky. The day had been clear and blue, the wind still willing. What then had happened to his champion? Could one of the knots have failed? Not likely, he thought, with Leo the Boatman in charge. Could a gust of wind have broken one of the struts, or ripped a sail?

As Rafael was pondering this, Lula the Shrimper happened by the field, saw him sitting there, and felt obliged to offer his opinion. "It's aliens," he said. "They don't like us messing around up there. That's where they live, you know? Up there in the uppersphere."

Other villagers had theories all their own. Some said *O Veleiro* had snagged the tip of the moon and crashed. Others that a meteor had struck it, like the one that burned a hole through Chico's roof a few years back.

Incredibly, Rafael entertained all this with patience and came home smiling that night.

"Are you all right?" Ana asked him.

His face was full of laugher, his eyes with twinkle. "That," he said, "was a *beautiful game*."

CHAPTER 15

BY VIRTUE OF HIS JOLLY WEIRDNESS AND EASY LAUGH—NOT TO mention his juggling, his freckles, and his colorful little turtle—Mick won the affection of every kid on the island. While the rest of us were out fishing or cropping the manioc, he'd play happily with the kids, for as long as they wanted.

They discovered in Mick something that was extraordinarily rare—a grown-up who still knew how to play. Three and four at a time he would let them climb up on his body—like monkeys in a tree—then charge wildly down the beach and twirl into the river, daring them to hang on. Bodies would fly every which way and splash convoluted into the water. (It was, said Rafael, "the most fun thing in the world!") Then off they'd go on a different game, wrestling on the beach (it took about nine of them to bring him down) or shooting marbles along the shady side of the church.

"*Minha nossa Senhora,*" said Aunt Leona. "What we got here is a nine-year-old who weighs a hundred kilos!"

She was right in that. But even as he played—galloping like a horse, laughing up a storm—Mick was always learning, picking up new words and expressions. Where better could a foreigner learn the meaning of *nadar ... mergulhar ... chapinhar*—to swim, to dive, to splash—than by jumping into the river with a bunch of kids?

And how better to absorb the gritty wisdom of our culture than through the riddles and tongue-twisters they taught him? "*O rato roeu a roupa do rei de Roma!*"

Yes indeed! Ever since I was a kid—and long before—*the rat has been rending the Roman ruler's robes!*

When Mick used the wrong word or mangled the pronunciation, which was often, his little amigos would snicker and point, and set cruel little traps that would induce him into further mistakes. It was pure comedy when he confused the word "*cuíca*"—a musical instrument—with the word "*cueca*," which means underwear. Thus, the Irishman would smile that good-natured grin of his and with innocent exuberance tell people that he "loved the underwear and hoped someday to play it!"

You would think that someone in the village—out of simple kindness—would have corrected the poor man on that one. But I'm not sure we ever did.

With his Bible and his glossary set before him, Mick would invest hours and hours preparing his Sunday message. Even so, in the moment of delivery he'd often stumble over the Portuguese, turning verbs into nouns and nouns into clowns, wondering why his jokes should fizzle, and worse, why folks would burst into laughter when they should have been moved to reverence.

One Sunday, a few months after he'd arrived, Mick taught the parable of the lost sheep, using the word "*velha*" over and over again, when the word he really wanted was "*ovelha*." (Oh for the lack of a letter, or a simple word mistaken, how many kingdoms have fallen?)

Out of his innocent, unsuspecting mouth the story went like this:

"Suppose that you had a hundred old ladies and were to lose one of them. Wouldn't you leave the ninety-nine old ladies in the open country and go looking for the one you lost? And when you found her, wouldn't you throw her over your shoulder and go home? Then you would call your friends and neighbors together and say, 'Rejoice with me; I have found my old lady!'"

Though I wasn't much interested in the man's sermons, I happened

to be there that afternoon, positioned at a safe and lazy distance with
Chico standing beside me. I could tell, as the parable unfolded, that
Chico was sinking deeper and deeper into confusion, scratching first
his head, then his elbow, and finally (with real vigor) his private parts.
As Mick's story came to an end, he leaned into me and whispered, "I
guess they do things real different in Ireland."

"Guess so," said I.

My only purpose in being there that afternoon was to scoff and
jeer, and pass the bottle around. I was joined in this boorish pastime by
a bunch of other *malandros* and *moleques* who couldn't imagine anything
better to do with their time.

Mick had closed his Bible now and was praying the thing to an end,
"Dear God, we ask you to quicken our minds, that we might understand your word. And more, dear God, that we might see how wide
and long and high and deep is the love of Christ. In Jesus' name,
Amen."

The more I rolled the story around, the funnier it got. I could see
now—despite Mick's vast confusion—that it was a tale about sheep
and the sacrificial love of a shepherd. Suddenly I wanted to go down
front and tease the man with his error, to watch him squirm. So I left
Chico there in the shade and strode forward, full of vinegar and sass.

As always, Mick was glad to see me. Out came his hand—the size
of a ham—to swallow up my little paw. "Did you like it?" he asked
timidly.

"Well, you got a lot of laughs," I said. "I bet Jesus wasn't half that
funny."

His smile wilted. "Thanks ..."

He was like a chicken with its neck stretched over the block, and I
the ready butcher. "It would be good if you learned the difference
between a sheep and an old lady," I said. "An *ovelha* is an *animal*." With
mocking gestures, I showed him the proportions of a sheep and the
way its wool comes curling out. "*O-vel-ha*," I sounded it out. "*Baa ...
baa*. A *velha* is an old lady, like Aunt Leona."

Mick's chin sagged to his chest. Now his thoughts were rolling
back through the parable he'd taught, verse by ruptured verse.

I can't explain what inspired such meanness in me, such malevolent glee, except to blame it on the whiskey. Why should I gloat over the man's failure or take pleasure in humiliating him? Did I imagine that I somehow grew larger in the balance, or would somehow profit from his loss?

But Mick looked up and smiled at me. Then *laughed* ... so hard that it shook him head to toe and finally brought tears.

I couldn't imagine what was going on inside his head. Was it possible for a man to relish his own foolishness? To somehow delight in his own weakness?

Breathless now, he plopped himself down in the sand. "Oh hallelujah!" he said. "Let's hope the ladies weren't offended ... or the *sheep!*" With that he loosed another round of belly laughs and breathless chuckles.

"I don't get it," I said.

He looked up at me, his eyes glistening. "Our God has a fine sense of humor, Zé."

Here indeed was an *alien*! Stranger even than Lula the Shrimper could imagine.

Mick winked and gave me a stout thumbs up. "You and I are going to be great friends," he said.

I could only scratch my head and wonder. "We *are?*"

Mick's weirdness could not have found a more enthusiastic audience, for we are a curious and gabby people, starved for entertainment. All sorts of wild speculations and theories broke out among us and bubbled through the gossip vine. Some said he was a demon in disguise or a criminal on the run. Some said he was a swindler who'd come to fleece us of our money. Then we remembered, sadly, that we had no money.

From somewhere came the idea that his native land—*Irlanda*—was a province in southern Argentina, till Aunt Leona gently reminded us that the man's native language was English, not Spanish. We'd snap our fingers as the lights came on. *Claro que sim!*

Well if he speaks English, people thought, *he must be an American, and if he's an American he must be rich, and if he's rich we should be very glad he's here!*

But he doesn't *look* rich, someone alertly pointed out, judging by his clothes. Well then, the argument returned, he must have some reason for hiding his wealth. This gave rise to the dark and persistent suspicion that Mick was working for the CIA and had come to spy on us. Once again it was Aunt Leona who tried to light a candle in the darkness. "We don't have any important secrets," she groused. "Unless they're doing a study on *ignorance.*"

Mick might have escaped all this wild speculation and gossip without much harm were it not for Nina the Gab, who twisted the truth into big blue pretzels, sprinkled them with lies, and sold them on every corner.

The little blabber couldn't have known, I guess, how dangerous it was to tell such lies, especially when they involved Alzira.

I was right of course about the direction Mick's church would take, because I understood the fundamental difference between faith and candy.

On that very first Sunday, when he juggled for us and gave out sweets, Mick went back to his boat a happy man. Scribbled inside his little notebook was that long list of names—thirty-one adults and fifty-three children—who had come forward "to give their lives to Jesus."

But we are what we are here in Jacaré—agreeable to a fault and very fond of sugar. To please a stranger or induce him to share more candy we would gladly agree that frogs can fly.

Predictably, the following Sunday was a deep disappointment to him. Only forty or fifty people showed up, half of them kids. And when folks realized that he wasn't going to juggle again or offer them candy, a lot of them went home.

Over the next few weeks, Mick built some wooden benches for the people to sit on and erected a little shelter from saplings and thatch to keep the rain off their heads. All this in the hopes that it would boost attendance. All to no avail.

By the third month his "church" had dwindled to just three steady members: Kiko, who was learning how to juggle; Little Aparecida, who had been faithful from the start; and Ney Let The Fire Go Out, our village idiot. (I would use a kinder word to describe poor Ney if it were consistent with the truth.)

In addition to these faithful three, an odd assortment of misfits and drunks would wander through the Irishman's services, coming and going to no particular clock.

Lula the Shrimper would sometimes swing by, not to hear the word of God but to unmask the Irishman's true character. Never, to his dying day, did Lula abandon the suspicion that Mick was an alien from another planet.

So too would Nina the Gab appear from time to time, hoping for some fresh morsel of gossip to liven up her stories. She was often in the company of her friend and understudy, Alma Viralva, who was one of the island's most promising young gossips.

Lastly and most intrusively was Ajuba Barbosa, one of the few men in Jacaré who could consistently outdrink me. Ajuba, when he happened to be vertical and happened along while the service was in progress, was irresistibly drawn to the music. With all the reverence he could muster, which wasn't much, he'd plop himself down on one of the empty benches and listen—sometimes with misty eyes—as the Irishman sang or played his harmonica.

Altogether, it was the most pathetic little church in the world. And *vastly* entertaining.

Take that Sunday in March, for example, when Ajuba, reeling with drink and forgetting where he was, hoisted himself up in the middle of the service and peed off the end of the bench.

To us creatures of the fringe, who were lounging back under the palm trees, this was the funniest thing ever. From laughter to hilarity we soared as poor Ajuba, relieved now, began to struggle with his fly, which had snagged on his shorts at the worst possible moment. It was inevitable, I guess, that Ney Let The Fire Go Out should involve himself in the drama, for he was supernaturally tuned to always arrive at the worst possible moment and inject himself where least you wanted him.

We roared with delight as Ney leapt up from his bench and scurried over to help Ajuba with his zipper.

Startled and annoyed, Ajuba retreated along the shore, trying to free up his zipper with one desperate hand and fend off the idiot with the other.

Chocolate, who was standing alongside me and in lucky possession of the bottle, had nearly laughed himself hoarse. But he did manage, with wonderful dryness, to lift high the bottle and propose a toast: "To the Church of the Broken Toys!" he declared. "Now duly sprinkled and baptized—*formalmente batizada*—by one of our very own! The illustrious *Ajuba Barbosa!*"

This produced another round of hoots and riotous laughter, which rollicked down the slope and into the Irishman's big pink ears, which looked now to be turning red.

"*Puxa vida!*" someone shrieked. "Here he comes!"

It was true! Mick had left his Bible on the table and was marching across the sand toward us.

Faster than you can shoo flies off a rotten mango, the boys fell out and scattered back into the village, except for me and a couple other laggards who were in too much of a stupor to move.

Now Mick was right in front of me, with his hands on his hips. "*Boa tarde,*" he said softly.

I looked up at him, pushing a smile. "*Boa tarde.*"

"What you guys laughing at?" he said.

"Nothing really. *Só brincando.*"

The last of my pals had vanished now, leaving me there alone. "Hey," I said. "I want to congratulate you on your new barraca. And all those nice benches."

But Mick wasn't to be distracted. "So what were you laughing at? I *like* a good joke."

"Just *things* ..."

"*Us,*" he said. "That's what you were laughing at."

I wiggled and winced and finally decided to tell him. "I want to be honest with you Mick. You're preaching to the wind down there. You realize, I guess, that Little Aparecida there ... well ... she can't hear a thing."

"I know that."

"And Ney? He doesn't know his left hand from his right. When you see him counting his fingers like that—you know, never quite making it to five?—he's *not* tracking your sermon, Mick. It's cause his brain got stuck at three, that's why. So on and on he goes, counting fingers and repeating himself, 'Three more days ... three more days ... three more days ...' It's all he ever says."

"I know he's got problems," Mick said. "So?"

"So ..." I opened my hands to him. "They're not exactly the pick of the litter."

"I'm not exactly the pick of the litter either."

I could see now that there was no explaining anything to the man. "*Olha*, Mick, do whatever you want. Go preach to the river."

"So what were you laughing at?" he pressed. "There at the end."

"I've said enough for one day."

"No, go ahead. I want to hear it."

"Well old Chocolate there, you know, he was just talking through his elbow. He said you folks are—" I was afraid now to tell him. What if he used that big fist to take out some of my teeth?

"What?" he insisted.

"Broken toys," I mumbled. "The Church of Broken Toys."

Mick reared up on his toes, like a thundercloud towering over me.

I fell back in his shadow. "We didn't mean nothing by it, Mick. *Really* ..."

Now his fist was coiled, ready to add some lightning.

I took a fast step back. "*Calma, meu amigo ...*"

But he held his fist, and clamped his tongue, and ever so slightly cocked his head, as if to catch some distant, fleeting sound. Incredibly, a smile appeared, like sunlight breaking through. "It's the perfect name," he said. "You tell Chocolate, when you see him next, that he got it just right."

If such things can be marked in time, I guess that was the moment I really began to like the Irishman. The fact that he was a lunatic didn't dissuade me much. In fact, I'll admit to a certain fondness for lunatics, confirmed by my long and friendly relationships with Chico and Lula the Shrimper. The worst of it is not their weirdness or unpredictability, you know, but the suspicion I sometimes get that they inhabit a better world than mine.

CHAPTER 16

IT HAD RAINED SO LONG AND HARD THAT WHEN IT FINALLY STOPPED the silence woke me. Suddenly the dogs were barking and Ana's voice, frightened, whispered in the dark, "Someone's at the gate!"

It was either very late or very early. Either way, an evil hour for visits.

I slipped out of the hammock and found my clothes, dressing in the dark. I opened the wardrobe, took the Colt out of its holster and freed the safety. Then grabbed hold of my flashlight and walked out front.

The world was everywhere slick and dripping. Off to the west, the thunderclouds were rumbling away, still throwing flashes of lightning through the trees.

Old Rompe was barking furiously, leaping against the gate. Ressaca was pressed in tight beside him, his nose jammed through the slats. He wasn't as loud as his older brother, but his teeth were sharper.

"Who is it?!" I shouted.

No answer.

I switched on the flashlight and trained it forward. The beam was so frail that it barely lighted the gate. "Who's *there*?!"

Beyond the fence, a shadow came forth, cloaked in a dark green slicker. "Call off the dogs," he said.

I walked closer and trained the flashlight on him. "Who are you?!" I demanded. "Shut up, Rompe! *Cala a boca!* What do you want?"

"Leiteiro's my name. Alzira sent me."

Milkman? I wondered. *What kind of name is that?* "Come back in the morning," I told him. "It's late."

"There is no morning," he retorted. "I'm back on the boat in thirty minutes. I got something important for you. Come out and get it."

I shooed the dogs off—"Rompe! *Cala a boca! Passa daí!*"—and walked out through the gate. My hand instinctively tightened around the grip, my finger edging toward the trigger.

The man was close before me now, hunched over in a way that concealed his face. He made no move to offer me his hand, nor was I inclined to offer mine.

"We must be fast," he said, letting his hood slip back.

With a flash of lightning, I caught his face full on and recoiled at the sight. Never had I laid eyes on such an ugly man nor felt at once such sympathy and fear. Here was a nose for the ages—a *snout* really, like a *tamanduá*—with sprigs of dark brown hair jutting out the nostrils. His eyes were tiny and dull, but cunning in the way they studied me. This was not a face that you would ever turn your back on. Nor, for that matter, was it a face that you'd ever want to face.

Now his arms came out from under the slicker, holding a burlap sack in one hand and a crumpled envelope in the other. "Put the gun away," he said. "It *irritates* me."

I sized him up again. A repulsive little weasel, to be sure ... but he hadn't come to harm me. I threw the safety and snugged the Colt down into my pants.

"Fine looking weapon," he observed. "Army?"

My hand still rested lightly on the grip. "*Polícia militar.*"

His lips curled up, revealing a pair of canine teeth that were unusually long and pointed. "If you should get another one," he said, "I'd pay you a happy price for it and ask no questions—"

"There won't be another one," I cut him off. "What's in the sack?"

"It's for your *project*," he said, handing it over. "You must take it to Alzira."

The burlap was moist on the bottom and surprisingly cool. "Iced?"

"Yes."

"All right. I'll take it first thing tomorrow."

"No," he said harshly. "You'll take it tonight."

I bristled at his tone. "Why don't *you* take it?"

"It's *your* project, Senhor Zé. Besides, Alzira doesn't like me."

Small wonder, I thought.

"This, too," he said, handing me the envelope. Then stepped in close and whispered sharply. "You are *not* to open these. *Do you understand?* Under no circumstances do you open them."

I could smell something reeking on his breath—like cheese gone bad. "I understand," I said, backing away.

Now he produced a folded paper from his pocket, and a pen. "Sign this," he said, handing them over. He glanced over his shoulder, then peered left and right, as though he'd heard something rustling in the brush. "Be quick!"

I unfolded the paper and struggled to read it. The letters were small and rough. Parts of it were smeared. My flashlight was almost useless. "I can't make it out," I told him.

"It's all very standard," he said. "Receipt of materials. Date of delivery. Just sign it there, at the bottom."

No, Zé! the warning sounded. *"Don't do this!"* Such a strange and urgent voice it was, as if my heart itself had whispered.

I let go the pen and felt it hit my sandal.

"Droga!" he cursed. In one quick motion he leaned over, snatched the pen off the ground and thrust it back in my hand. *"Sign, Senhor Zé!"* he hissed. "I don't intend to miss my boat."

I wavered a second more, my hand shaking, then scribbled my name across the paper.

Quick and rude he snatched it away—*"Tudo bem!"*—and folded it into his pocket. "My pen, please."

I handed it over. "You must be a figment of my bottle," I muttered. "Something Cachaça's painted in my brain."

"Ha," he laughed it off. "This is only the beginning. I'll see you in Belém."

"What?"

But he had turned now and was hurrying down the path.

"I got no plans to go to Belém," I called after him.

Leiteiro glanced back at me, cloaking his face. "*Sure* you do!" He laughed, then shot on down the trail.

I stood there a moment, alone in the dark. He was as vile a man as ever I'd met—the stuff from which nightmares are spun.

Old Rompe followed me back through the yard and into the open kitchen. Ressaca, still growling, stayed at the gate.

I put the burlap sack on the table, then the envelope and the flashlight. Grabbing some matches from the drawer, I lit the oil lamp, trimmed it back and took a seat. "What we got here, dog?"

If Rompe knew the answer, he wasn't telling. Shaking the rain off his back, he curled down under the table and went to sleep.

Opening the sack, I found a thermos bottle sheathed in foam—about the size and shape of an artillery shell. Though it appeared new, the foam had cracked along the bottom and was seeping beads of cold, clear water.

More intriguing still were the elaborate wax seals that protected its contents. Someone had gone to a great deal of trouble, pouring rounds of hot red wax across the seam—one to either side—and pressing their signet ring upon it:

Jl

I examined the thermos up close, turning it slowly, giving it a little shake. Though I was bursting with curiosity, I dared not open it.

The envelope was more revealing. Though the flap had been sealed with the selfsame wax and impressed with the same initials, the paper was thin and translucent.

I held it up to the lamp and peered in close. The things inside it were silhouetted by the lamp and revealing to the touch. To one end was a short, cylindrical object that felt spongy when I pressed it. I could tell, even before I smelled the burnt tobacco, that it was a cigarette butt. *But why? What possible value could it have?* Bunched in the other end were curls of short, dark hair. Whether from an animal or person I couldn't be sure. *Had someone scooped them off a barber shop floor? Maybe a shop that catered to big-time clients? To people like Ivanildo Bonfim ...*

"What are you doing, Pai?"

I jumped in my seat and turned. There stood Rafael, rubbing the sleep from his eyes.

"You startled me, boy."

His eyes shifted to the envelope, then to the thermos, and finally back to me. "Who was it, Pai? What did he bring us?"

"No one," I said. "Just the dogs and me. Some thunder rolling through ..."

"I heard someone talking."

"No boy. It's nothing. You go back to sleep now."

He gave me the strangest look, full of yearning and innocence. "Are you all right, *Papai*?"

"Sure," I said. "Go on now. Be quiet not to wake your mother."

"She's not sleeping either."

"No?"

"She's just lying there with her eyes open. You know how she does?"

I knew.

"Maybe you could talk to her, Papai. Tell her everything's okay?"

"Sure," I told him.

But never did.

I walked through a chorus of crickets and night birds that had roused themselves after the rain. The trail to Alzira's was slick and dark, but I knew it well by now—every root and rock and turn.

Never had I come this way—never could I go—without a tribute in my hands. A brace of chickens ... a sack of farinha ... something to appease her.

Tonight it was the thermos I carried, and the envelope, and a pocketful of change that was bound to infuriate her.

Off in the distance I could hear a line boat chugging away from the dock. That would be Leiteiro's boat, headed up the river. *Had he come all the way from Belém just to give me the thermos bottle and an envelope? Or did he have other stops along the way, other deliveries—the way a "milkman" makes his rounds?*

Dalvina was waiting for me at the gate. I could tell by her expression, squeezed from a lime, that she had been standing there for a while. Her eyes fell quickly on the burlap sack, as though the thing were somehow speaking to her. When finally her trance broke off, she opened the gate and walked me to the patio.

There was no sign of Alzira, nor any trace of her bastard dog. I could only hope that he'd fallen off the bluff maybe or drowned in the river.

I pulled up a chair and laid the sack on the table.

Dalvina gestured with both hands. *Give it to me!* I was impressed again by her muscles and the prodigious size of her head, and how clearly she expressed herself without words.

I pointed to myself. "That's all right. I'll give it to her."

She wagged her finger at me—*No!*—then slapped herself on the chest to make the point clear. *I'm to take them!*

"It's my business," I argued. "I'll give them to her."

She squinted at me in a most unpleasant way. Here was a woman who had received her orders and was hide-bound to carry them out.

"All right," I relented. "*Take* them."

She grabbed the sack and the envelope, gave me a little parting look of triumph, and marched off into the house.

I waited and waited, and no one came. The river seemed very close tonight, crunching away at the shoreline below. Lulled by its churning, murmuring voice, I fell asleep in the chair.

"Senhor Zé."

A voice was poking into my slumber.

"*Wake up.*"

I hoisted myself up in the chair and spent half a minute trying to remember where I was.

"You are with *me*," Alzira said. "You will *always* be with me." She sat in her usual place, with the ledger opened on the table between us. With no makeup to hide the years or witchery at work, she showed herself a woman of sixty, decidedly unappealing.

"I brought you a drink," she said.

A little tumbler sat on the table before me, just half full, hardly worth the effort. *I didn't know they made shot glasses for midgets,* I thought. But dared not say it aloud.

Little by little she had been cutting back on the drinks, as though cachaça were in short supply. With every visit the rounds were fewer and the portions smaller, reduced now to this—a thimble of a glass. Likewise her chocolates had dwindled away, from ten to five to two, till at last the plate itself had vanished. Truth was, her "hospitality" knew nothing of grace. Rather, she applied it like grease to a stubborn gearbox, to keep it from whining.

"Drink up," she said. "What's *wrong* with you?"

With one quick swig I finished it and laughed at the portion. "*Nossa! Tudo isso só para mim!*"

Her fat green eye bulged out of its cavern, probing me hard. "So you met Leiteiro?"

"Yes."

"An unfortunate necessity he," she said. "*Mas, assim é a vida.*"

"*Assim é.*"

She craned forward and tapped the ledger with her index finger. "So where's my money?"

Her look was so infused with superiority, so openly disdainful, I felt like a cockroach pinned beneath her shoe. Whatever happened to those sweet words she'd spoken? Has ever a man been so quickly demoted by a woman, from "*meu amor*" to "*amigo*" to "*cara?*" And what of that soft brown eye of hers, with its playful wink, that had urged me into dark and intimate fantasies?

"You can forget about ever sleeping with me," she said.

My God, the woman was a razor!

"It's never going to happen," she finished. Then threw me away with a look, the way a child flings off a toy.

"I never thought of it," I lied.

"Of course you did," she laughed.

Thus can a woman humiliate a man to the point where he has but two choices. To hang his head in silence or grab her by the throat.

"So, where's my money?" she repeated.

"I didn't bring any," I said. This, too, was a lie. I did have some money in my pocket, from the bets that I'd won on the kite. But to offer it now—a pittance really—seemed worse than nothing. "I'll bring some next week," I promised. "I have a deal in the works. A *cash* deal."

"You'll pay additional interest then." She picked up her pen, entered some fresh numbers in the ledger, and calculated the results. That done, she wrote the number on the flat of her palm and held it out for me to see, a little closer to my face than was really necessary.

I was stunned by how much I owed her, and deeply discouraged. After all the payments I'd made, I owed her half again more than when I'd first signed the contract. Two weeks earlier, in a moment of clarity and courage, I had actually challenged her on the numbers. "How is it I pay and pay and pay, and still the numbers grow?"

Patiently she'd brought out the contract and explained Clause 5 and Clause 8 to me in excruciating detail. It was then that I saw the light. Which looked a lot like darkness.

Clause 5 was long and loaded with mumbo. But the essence was this: *My payments were to be made in cash, gold or silver. Any bartered payment—that is, payments made in goods or services—would be credited at only* half *their market value, which value should be determined exclusively by the service provider.* The "service provider" (though the contract never mentioned her by name) was Alzira herself.

Clause 8 stated (in even more confusing language) that *any unpaid balance would be assessed an interest charge of twenty-two percent, compounding weekly.*

If ever I should become a professional man, I would like to specialize in *compound interest.*

Now she pulled back her hand, glanced again at the happy number, and smudged it off with her thumb.

"I've been paying you in good faith," I said. "Most every week I give you something."

"So you have, *cara*. But you haven't been paying on time. And you haven't been paying in cash. And you haven't been paying in full. Do you think Leiteiro works for free? And what about *me*? Do you think *I* work for free?"

I was exhausted and defeated. I grabbed my cap and pushed back from the table, wanting just to leave.

"*Wait*," she said. "I'm not through with you."

I slumped back into the chair.

"Tell me about the foreigner," she said.

"What?"

"The red-haired man with the loose mouth."

It took me a minute to make the turn with her. "The Irishman, you mean?"

"Yes," she said. "The one who *slanders* me with every breath."

I could see now, in her scorching look, that she had believed the lies about Mick and was sharpening her teeth on them.

"It's nothing but *fofoca*," I said. "He's never said anything against you, Dona Alzira. *Nada*."

"I hear otherwise," she retorted. "And I hear it often."

"I tell you, Dona Alzira, it's nothing but chatter. Lies from the tongues of liars."

She folded her arms across her chest, brittle and cold.

"It's from Nina you've heard it, isn't it?"

"Where I get my information is none of your business."

"She's a silly little mouth," I said. "She'll say anything to get your attention."

"*Careful*," Alzira warned. "Nina belongs to me. Or soon will ..."

I had no idea what she meant by that, but I didn't like the sound of it.

"He calls me a *witch*, I believe. The *worst* of all witches. And curses me in public."

"Believe me," I said, "he doesn't speak the language well enough to curse you. Nor does he have any reason to."

"You're close to him, aren't you?" she concluded. "I can see it in the way you defend him."

I shrugged and waved him off. "He's nothing to me, Dona Alzira. Just a fool who washed up on the shore one morning."

"A missionary, I hear."

"One and the same," said I.

"Says he'd rather *die* than have my help," she fumed. She looked off into the night and washed her hands of him. "So let him die."

"He *never* said that," I countered. "Nina made it up."

"You call my little girl a liar?"

"It is what it is, Dona Alzira. *Fofoca!*"

Her lewd green eye began to spasm, then to water, then to peer at me in a most dreadful way. "I'll have that freckled bastard by his ears," she hissed. "I'll give him warts where least a man should want them."

"Why?" I made one last plea, "He's never said a word against you. I tell you true. *Nenhuma palavra.*"

"Then to test his faith," she said sweetly. "By *fire* the metal's tempered, isn't it? Isn't that what his faith teaches?"

"I don't know," I admitted. "I don't listen much."

She dismissed me with her hand. "It's time for you to leave now, sweetie. I suggest you *distance* yourself from him, so the sparks don't catch your hair."

Without a word I got up, put my cap on, and slumped off across the patio.

Alzira rose from her chair and followed me to the gate. Her parting words seemed to take on wings and follow me down the path: "Pay me what you owe me, Senhor Zé. Do what you're told. All will go well ..."

CHAPTER 17

SAMBÃO SAT ON THE EDGE OF HIS DINGY LITTLE BED IN HIS HOT little cabin, inspecting the assortment of goods I'd brought him. Four bottles of copaíba oil. Five bottles of andiroba. Two tubs of turtle fat. Índio's finest.

"This is pure?" he wondered, holding one of the bottles up to the light.

"*Puríssima*," I said. "Straight from the trees to the Indians, and from the Indians straight to me."

With a sniff and a snort he sat the bottle back down on the deck, in line with the others. "*Ótimo!*" he said. "*Vamos lá!*" He reached under his bed and pulled out a hard leather suitcase that was so badly slashed and battered it barely held together. One of its brass corners had been crushed by some indescribable force. Another held to the leather by a single rivet.

"Machete attack?" I asked dryly.

He laughed at me, long and hearty, his belly jiggling along in rhythm. "She's been around the world and back, this one," he said. He patted the suitcase as if it were an old friend. "See here in back where she took a bullet for me. Blew a hole right through my underwear! Ha, ha, ho ..."

I squirmed around on my stool, trying to avoid the nail head that was thrusting upward into my butt. Rivers of sweat poured off my face, my armpits, drenching the sides of my shirt, streaming down the back of my legs. His cabin sat directly over the engine room, which made it the hottest, noisiest, smelliest place on the boat. So cramped we were in the little metal box that our knees were almost touching.

By the looks of it, the *Boa Fortuna* was ten years past its prime and screaming for an overhaul. The boat was about thirty-five meters from prow to stern, dinged and battered hard, colored and discolored and uncolored with four or five generations of disintegrating paint. Every second Wednesday it would put into Jacaré for an hour or two, take on whatever passengers and freight it could find, then chug on down the river to Belém.

Sambão was a master of engines—eighteen years on the river, he'd told me—and also (more discreetly) a master of contraband. I didn't know the full range of his trafficking and was smart enough not to ask.

From out of his pocket he brought a long string of keys, jangled them around for a moment, singled out a little brass one from the bunch, and popped open the suitcase.

There before my happy eyes lay carton after carton of American cigarettes, nestled neatly into an assortment of other profitable goods! Here was my dream fulfilled and my heart delighted! Our little trading company was up and running now, selling real products for real money!

"Ten cartons of Marlboros," said Sambão. "Eight for you ..." One by one he pulled these out of his suitcase and put them in my tote bag, counting as he went. "And two for me." These he set gently on the bed beside him.

"One carton of Lucky Strikes," he said, and placed that too in my bag.

Inside *that* one, I knew, would be my share of the money. Jamela, my clever and industrious cousin-in-law, had resealed the end of the carton so no one would ever notice. What a lucky strike the woman had been for me, full of energy and ideas! Without much help from Ozias, she'd collected dozens of old jelly jars, boiled them clean, filled them with turtle fat (blended with other ingredients of her own concoction), and branded each jar with a hand-made label.

"Ten bags of popcorn," Sambão was counting. "Nine for you and one for me." Again, he put his share on the bed beside him.

Not only had Jamela got our first batch of product ready, but she'd devoted herself to selling it. Along the Avenida dos Heróis and in the plazas across from the big hotels she'd sell the stuff, appealing to worried ladies (and sometimes men) who'd become so wrinkled by their worries that they worried now about their wrinkles.

"Fifty packets of aspirin," Sambão reported. "With four to the pack, that makes two hundred." He smiled broadly and winked at me. "With five held back for me."

Jamela had done well as a vendor, selling every last jar and taking orders for more. The secret behind her success (now translated into *my* success) was obvious. She believed in the virtues of "Amazon Turtle Fat" and promoted it with honest zeal. The fact that she used the product herself and owned a youthful, cherubic face became a winning part of her testimony and pitch. Crowds of badly wrinkled people would gather around her and see in her softly glowing cheeks the possibility—even the *likelihood*—that they could unwrinkle themselves for the price of a good dinner. Thus did Jamela prove again what every good salesman knows: whether you're peddling guinea eggs or hand grenades you *have* to believe in the product.

"And two ... three ... four large boxes of matches," Sambão finished. He dumped these into my bag and rubbed his happy hands together. "That's everything, Zé. Except *this* ..." He pulled a little glass jar from the corner of the suitcase and handed it over. "Hot from the pot," he laughed. "Jamela says to tell you everything's good on their end, and to give you a hug." Sambão crinkled his nose at me and shook his head. "Way too hot in here for hugging."

I took the little jar and turned it in my hand, admiring her work. The label was much improved over her first designs, but still hand-lettered and colored in with love:

Jamela's
100% Pure
Amazon Turtle Fat
Your Miracle Cure for Wrinkles!

"You ever use that goop?" Sambão asked me.

"No."

"You might try it on your *dimples*," he laughed, running his finger down his cheek. He grinned on for a long moment, waiting for me to laugh. "Sorry," he said finally. "Didn't mean any harm."

The whistle sounded, loud and shrill, signaling an end to our business.

Sambão stood up, put his hands on his hips, and hiked up his pants. "*Tá bom então*," he reckoned. "Two weeks from today? Is that the deal?"

"What about the magazines?"

"Oh, the *magazines*!" he blurted. He yanked at the lobe of his ear and shook his head. "I had some for you, Zé. Good ones too! But the first mate got hold of them and I haven't seen them since."

I cinched up my bag and slung it over my shoulder. "Maybe next time then. Whatever you can get."

"Hold on a minute," he said. "Maybe I can grab you something here." He scavenged around under his bed for a minute, pulled out the dusty remnants of a newspaper, and handed it over.

Though its pages had gone yellow and the headlines were two weeks old, it was still news to me.

I hurried home and laid the bag out across the table. With Ana down at the river and Rafael off playing, I was free to open my prize.

Out came the Lucky Strikes and the sample jar from Jamela. These alone were mine. All the rest would go to Índio.

I took up the carton and caressed it for a moment, imaging the little pocket of treasure that was hidden inside. Here were my first profits from an enterprise that would make me rich in a year or two.

Reckless in my excitement, I ripped off the end of the carton and removed the first few packs of cigarettes. There suddenly was the void that Jamela had left, with a fold of money and a little note attached!

Oi Zé,
We did the best we could. Many, many expenses ...
Abraços,
Jamela

Three times I counted and recounted the money, hoping, I guess, that if I handled it enough it would somehow multiply.

But math knows nothing of hope. No matter how I counted it, it still came out to 460 cruzeiros.

"It's a *lot*," I persuaded myself. "More cash than we've seen in a long, long time."

This was true. But it was also true that it was only half the amount I'd expected from her and only a third of what I dreamed.

I would have to pay two hundred to Alzira—and that just to stay even. Then put aside some money for drink. There was coffee and cooking oil and batteries to buy. And some bung and tar to fix my canoe. Everything else, I realized sadly, would have to wait. No books for Rafael. And no clothes for Ana, who embarrassed me in her bare feet and rags.

Just then I heard her coming up the trail from the river, singing softly to herself.

I swept the money off the table and jammed it in my pocket. This she must never see, for it would only raise questions about the deal. And then the deals *behind* the deal. Questions that I would never want to answer.

CHAPTER 18

For the love of words I read most anything that came my way. Food labels and beer posters. The cautionary print on match boxes and dead batteries. The instruction manuals that came with Chico's generator and television set.

Scavenging off the line boats, I'd come home with puzzle books (with the crosswords already done) and old glamour magazines that had traveled up and down the river so long they barely held together. From those I learned a lot about eyeliners, feminine hygiene products and the importance of wearing contouring bras, though none of those products had any currency in our lives. I learned all kinds of "essential" nonsense about celebrities, astrology, and the importance of special diets, though we river folk aren't so much concerned with losing weight as we are with holding on to the weight we have.

Into this mess of random learning came Padre Xabrega's dictionary, one of the most generous and impactful gifts I ever received.

Every morning, every week, Rafael and I would open the dictionary and have three new words for breakfast. Together we'd relish them, like morsels of delicious food, which enabled us to think in ways we had never thought before, to bejewel our conversations with adjectives that were bright and new!

We began on page one with the A's ... *abdôme* ... *abduzir*... *abeberado* ... and agreed to plow ahead, page by page, until we reached the Z's. Even in the grip of a hangover I'd try not to miss our class ... *agrícola* ... *agricultor* ... *agricultura* ... because it gave me a sense of hope in an otherwise desolate life.

My boy's mind was twice as fast as his feet. After a couple weeks working with the dictionary he looked up at me one morning and said, "Papai, it's going to take us forty-three years to finish this."

"What?"

"Forty-three years," he repeated.

"How do you mean?"

Rafael closed the book and pointed at the title. "Well, on the cover here ... right *here* ... it says there are forty-seven thousand words inside. *Certo?*"

"*Certo.*"

"And there are three-hundred and sixty-five days in a year, *né* ? That's what Aunt Leona told me."

"*Pode ser ...*"

"And we're learning three new words a day, *né* ?"

I thought about it a minute. "So you puzzled that out, did you? That it's going to take forty-three years?"

He nodded.

"How could you know that?"

"It's obvious, isn't it?"

"No, it's *not.*"

"Well *now* it is!" he beamed.

"You never had a speck of math," I told him. It sounded almost like an accusation.

"Well I'd *like* to," he said. "Could you teach me?"

"I'm afraid we're a little weak in the math department," I admitted. The thought rolled along in sadness. "Also in geography and foreign language." With the word "foreign" I suddenly thought of the Irish-man. "Rafael! I just had a *great* idea."

"What is it, Papai?"

"Tomorrow I will tell you," I said. "Or maybe Sunday. I have to see if it's possible."

He whined a little at that, but relaxed again and opened the book. "Are we going to finish the lesson, Pai?"

"Yes. But I'm thinking we could speed things up, you know? Maybe study ten words a day instead of three. To get through the book a little sooner."

He thought it over for a few seconds. "In thirteen years," he said.

CHAPTER 19

THAT SATURDAY, DOWN AT THE SOCCER FIELD, I GOT MY CHANCE. The Irishman was sitting on the sideline, about mid-field, where he could watch the game up close. Though it was just a scratch match between some of the adolescents, he was wildly involved, shifting and shouting and waving his hands.

I meandered up beside him and just stood there, like an egg that'd toppled out of its nest. In light of the rudeness I'd shown the man, I wasn't sure how he'd react. "Senhor Michael," I finally managed. "*Boa tarde para você.*"

He looked up from the game and grinned. "If I'm going to call you Zé, then you should call me *Mick*. Don't you think?"

"Yes," I agreed. "So how are you, Mick?"

"Good," he said. "Got a seat here for you." He patted the ground beside him. "A little damp though."

I sat down alongside him and crossed my legs in front of me. The grass was still wet from the morning rain, and judging by the sky, would soon be wetted again.

"That's your boy there, isn't it?" he said.

Rafael, playing barefoot and shirtless, had just scored a header off the goal post.

I nodded proudly. "That's him."

He shook his head in wonder. "You *lied* to me then."

"*Como?*"

"You told me there was nothing here but ignorance and corruption."

"Did I say that?"

"He makes the birds look slow."

This was true. Though Rafael had just turned twelve, he was already taller and swifter than his friends. Already the muscles were filling in across his chest and shoulders, the baby fat disappearing from his chin. On the field of ultimate glory—*futebol*—he was so quick and unpredictable that no one could stay with him.

"That was his *third goal*," said Mick. "And I've only been here twenty minutes."

For some reason the compliment made me feel small and sad. "They will say of our family that the father fizzled, but the boy was a real firecracker."

Mick gave me a pat on the shoulder. "I don't think they'll say that, Zé. In fact you're looking *fine* this morning."

If "fine" wasn't quite the truth, at least it was relatively so. I had made a big effort to stay sober and clean up a little, so the man might take me seriously.

"It's the boy I came to talk about," I said.

But Mick was fixed upon the game.

One of the older boys, Mimico, had dashed past his defender and came flying up the field toward us. He was big and powerful and battling for glory.

Rafael came up to meet him, refused his fake, and drove his foot into the speeding ball. His momentum carried him forward into Mimico's chest. The collision was so violent that it cracked the air and sent both players crumbling to the ground. The ball shot over our heads like a bullet, arced out over the road and plunged into the shadows beneath the cinnamon tree.

For a horrible instant, it felt as if everything everywhere had stopped—all play, all speech, even our breath! The ball had smacked the side of the iron cage and landed on the grave below. After all this time the mound was still plainly visible, so haunted with death that even the grass had shunned it.

The cage swung gently around, creaking on its chain, speaking to us of things that no one wanted to remember. Inside it, the Colonel's hand, reminded of its long and terrible separation, came crawling forward!

Was that what I really saw? Or was it only the slap of the ball that had rattled things around and set his bones in motion?

Rafael was quick to his feet, rubbing his knee. Mimico was a little slower getting up, but he too was unhurt.

Now we were all on our feet, wondering what would come next. In twos and threes the players drifted off the field and spilled out onto the road. No one spoke, and no one moved to fetch the ball. There in the shadows it sat, with the grisly hand above it and the murdered corpse below. Most of the players were too young to remember the day the soldiers hung it or who was buried there. But *this* they knew: their parents and grandparents never talked of the place or the evil that possessed it, as though silence might somehow purge it from their memory.

The Irishman, gawking around, was obviously confused. "So let's get the ball. What are we waiting for?"

I shook my head. "I think we'll just leave it."

"*What?*" He took a bold step into the road and headed for the tree.

I latched hold of him. "I wouldn't do that."

He looked down at me with those bright blue eyes and a puckish smile. "*O medo não manda aqui,*" he said. *Fear doesn't rule us here.* With that he gently removed my arm, ambled across the road, and walked in under the great dead limbs of the cinnamon tree.

Every eye was fast upon him, every ear attentive.

Without ever touching the cage or stepping on the grave, he toed the ball up off the ground, bounced it smartly off his knee and grabbed it with his hands.

The players cheered—as did I—as he came back across the road.

Mick tossed the ball to Rafael. "*Joga !*" he yelled. "Show us some more of that magic."

And play they did.

But Mick and I stood in the road talking.

"So what was it?" he asked me, in a somber voice. "What happened there under the tree?"

"We don't speak of it."

"A murder? Is that what it was?"

"An *execution*."

"And the cage?" he wondered. "The *bones?*"

"Put there as a warning," I said. "A reminder. There's to be no dreaming here."

He scoffed at me. "A rusty old cage ... some dirty bones ..."

"*Cuidado!* " I warned him. "You touch it, you could lose your hand. You move it, you could forfeit your life."

Mick blew out a little puff of air, declaring it nonsense.

"If you knew what lay at the roots of it you'd quickly learn some fear."

"Maybe," he allowed. "But not enough to let it eat soccer balls."

The wind quickened around us. Rain was sweeping in from the east.

"So what about your boy?" he said. "We never did get to talk."

I glanced at the sky again. "It will have to wait. This is going to be a real *toró*."

"Then come down to the boat with me," he said, gesturing toward the river. "I'll make us some tea. We'll talk things over."

This seemed a good idea, though it wasn't *tea* my tongue was craving.

How strange it felt walking up the gangway onto his boat again—up that fractured old plank, with the rain breaking over us. It swept me back to that dismal afternoon when first I'd gone aboard—with Ana and Nina—hoping for some kind of miracle.

No urubus, I noticed, sweeping my hand along the railing. No ghosts looming over the boat. And no Nina the Gab, for which I was very grateful.

While Mick unlocked the hatchway and rumbled down the steps, I glanced over at the pilothouse, at the shattered glass, and remembered how close I'd come to dying there.

Mick had done his best to patch the broken pane. But the old canvas he'd strung across it had ripped loose now and was flapping in the wind.

Despite the rain, I stopped to tie it off.

Presently, Mick stuck his head up through the hatch. "What are you *doing*?!" he shouted.

"Where did you learn to tie a knot, gringo?!" I shouted back.

"Never did," he laughed. He held up a hand to block the rain. "Let it go, Zé! I'll fix it in the morning."

But I was determined now, and with a couple turns more had the canvas stretched tight across the gap.

Stepping down into the cabin I was met with a nice surprise. No flies. No stench. Just a sniff of diesel fuel in the air. I took off my sandals and left them at the foot of the steps.

Mick had cracked open the port side shutters to let some daylight in and was moving now to light the oil lamp that hung in the center of the cabin. Though the space hadn't grown any, it was clean and tidy now, with some touches of life here and there that made it feel more like a home.

His hammock was rolled up neatly and tied off against the forward bulkhead. Just below it sat a large brown steamer trunk that must have served him as both suitcase and closet.

He had converted the top of the engine cage into a decent table, covered with some well-planed boards and flanked on either side with wooden stools. By the looks of it, the tabletop served his every need, with one corner his dining room, jumbled with pots and tableware, another corner his study, piled with books and pens, and yet a third become his vanity, where he kept his shaving mug and toothbrush. I wondered, with such a mess, if ever he got his beans mixed in with his paperclips.

Mick had trimmed the lamp now, filling the cabin with amber light. He walked past the engine and into the room beyond, which was partitioned into a tiny little galley, a tiny little closet, and a tiny little toilet. All this in a space about three meters square, to accommodate a man who was big as a tree. So tight was the headroom that Mick had to slouch around the cabin, ducking his head this way and that, to keep from banging the wooden beams that supported the deck above.

"Have a seat," he said, pointing to one of the stools. "*Fica à vontade.*" He filled his little alcohol burner with fuel and struck a match to it, then set a pan of water atop it.

I sat down on the stool, took off my rain-soaked cap, and considered the odd and many things that were hanging along the facing hull. Strings of dried garlic and peppers dangled from the beam above, with a bunch of overripe bananas drooping sadly in their midst. Farther down was a fine brass compass, swinging on its leather collar, and the small brown knapsack that he liked to carry. Finally, and most interesting, was the string of photographs that he'd hung using clothespins and a stretch of cord that draped forward to the bulkhead. The pictures were hung side by side along the string, like clothes put out to dry.

I leaned forward to get a better look at them: a dark blue lake with strands of mist along the shore; a pretty girl with a beautiful smile; a bunch of friends gathered on the steps of an old stone church. Photos of faraway places and pink-skinned people—of Ireland, I guessed, and Irish people.

Mick had taken the stool opposite me now and was rummaging through his tableware. Presently he found a pair of metal cups, two metal spoons, and some fresh teabags.

"Who is the girl with the dimples?" I asked.

He didn't understand the word *covinhas*—that is, *dimples*—until I poked my cheeks to show him. "There," I said, pointing at the photo. "The pretty redhead?"

He turned and followed my finger. "Ah," he said. "That's my little sister Anne. She owns the sweetest voice in Ireland, I'll tell you. And probably Scotland too."

"And the lake?"

"Lough Gill," he said. "Close by the place where I was born. Clear and clean and deep. Colder than you can imagine, Zé."

I pushed myself into the photo a ways and tried to imagine what it would be like living in a land of pink-skinned giants, fishing in cold blue water, building fires to keep yourself warm. "You have snow there, do you?"

"Sometimes."

"I would someday like to see it snow. To see it falling. To catch it in my hand."

"A thing of real beauty," he agreed. "When the flakes come dancing..." His eyes drifted away, back to Ireland I guess, to places that only he could know.

We sat there in silence for a while as the rain drummed against the hull.

When the water came to a boil, he rose from his stool to get it. "You are actually my first real guest," he said, pouring the cups. "Not counting the beggars and the buzzards."

Though his smile held fast, his eyes revealed a very different mood. Of loneliness. Of a homesick heart. Of a mission that had lost its way.

"Sorry I don't have any sugar," he said.

"*Não precisa*," I told him. "*Tá muito bom assim.*"

He put the pan back on the burner and returned to his stool, then took a careful little sip from his cup. "Only two things the English ever got right," he said. "Tea and ceremony."

I had no idea what he meant by that. "*Como?*"

He waved it off with his hand. "Nothing," he said. "An Irish joke, for a stormy night."

Indeed, the lightning was cracking around us now, the wind tugging the boat hard against its lines. Together we listened as the rain slashed and hammered across the deck above us.

"How did you come to own this boat?" I asked. "Did you bring it from Ireland?"

"No," he laughed. "To sail from Ireland in this little tub would take a bigger fool than I." He rolled the thought over for a moment and playfully added, "Though not by much."

"How then?"

"By plane to Rio," he said, "then on to Manaus, where Josué and the boat were waiting. It belongs to the mission actually."

How vast and wonderful his travels seemed! "I would like to fly in an airplane someday. To look down on the world the way the eagles see it."

He winked at me. "Someday you will, Zé. And more ... More than you can ask or imagine."

"I'd like Rafael to go with me," I said. "To share it all."

"Course you would."

"There's no age limit, is there? On airplanes?"

"No, Zé. No limits at all."

In the blink of an eye the images began to rise, from the colorful ads I'd seen in the magazines and the travel adventures I'd read in the papers. Of silver planes with whirling props, bound for who knows where. Up the metal stairs we'd climb, with other happy travelers, ushered into a cabin trimmed with velvet, pampered by a crew of beautiful, efficient ladies. I'd care not where the plane was going, really, anywhere in the world. Nor care too much if it never came back.

"What would Rafael think of *that*?!" I laughed. "Eating dinner in the clouds!"

"I think it would thrill his heart," said Mick. "I think you need to admit the possibility, Zé. To go ahead and dream."

This I tried for a long, hard moment—to really *admit* the possibility. But felt myself sinking sadly back to earth. For every thought that imagined it "possible," a counter thought reared up to declare it "foolishness." *Não pode.*

"Truly, Mick, I did not come to talk about airplanes. I came to talk about English and math and geography."

He looked over the rim of his cup, through little wisps of steam. "How do you mean?"

I leaned in across the table. "Do you think you could teach Rafael, Senhor Mick? Teach him all the things that I don't know?"

He returned my look with wonder and incredulity. "If I understand you correctly, Zé, I am deeply honored."

"What could you teach him?" I pressed. "What do you know?"

He shrugged at the thought and laughed. "You should have asked me back in the sixties, amigo, when I knew almost *everything*."

"Seriously, could you teach him arithmetic?"

Mick mused it over, as though to puzzle out an equation. "I could teach him some math," he said. "If you can find me a workbook."

"I'll get you a workbook," I promised. "Could you teach him English?"

He nodded again. "Sure. But it's Gaelic that my heart loves best."

"I've never heard of it," I said. "Who speaks Gaelic?"

"Well the *Irish* of course," he groused. "And the *Scots*."

"It must be a very small tongue."

This irritated him further and caused him to mutter—in Gaelic I assumed.

"I'm sorry, Mick. I didn't mean to hurt your feelings."

"Of course you didn't," he said, finishing off his tea.

"But still, I think we should stay with English."

He puckered his lips, clowning for me. "If that's what you want—high tea and pomp—then that's what I'll teach."

"What else do you know?"

His eyes rolled off into a thoughtful corner. "I like to play chess," he said. "I could teach him a bit of that, if you like?"

"That would be good," I agreed. "It's a gentleman's game, isn't it? For nobles and deep thinkers."

"Well, that puts me out of it," he laughed. "I learned it in a pub."

"What else could you teach him?"

"I'm very good with pies," Mick said. "A *champion* actually."

"*Pies*? Can that be true?"

His smile wilted into confusion. "No, not pies," he caught himself. "I mean ... ah, what's the word?" Frustrated, he grabbed a book off the end of the table—his dictionary, I guessed—and thumbed back through it till he found what he was looking for.

"*Swords*!" he exclaimed. "That's what I meant."

Ah, *now* we understood—the slight but important difference between "*empadas*" and "*espadas*!"

"Watch out!" he cried, "or I'll stab you with my *pie*!"

The thought had me thumping my fist on the table, laughing so hard that I spilled my tea. "*Ah, me desculpe.*"

"*Não problema*," he said, handing me a towel.

While I dabbed up the mess, he grew strangely quiet, as though a memory had washed over him that wasn't entirely pleasant. "Have you ever seen a real sword?" he asked.

"No."

He played with his earlobe, tickling out the memory. "Once upon a time, I was the best in all Ireland," he said. "Maybe in all Europe."

The best at what? I wondered.

Mick pointed his finger at me. "Let me show you."

He stood up and made his way forward, ducking through the strings of garlic and bananas, and knelt in front of his steamer trunk. Opening the lid, he rummaged down into its depths for something hidden there. A moment later he was back, carrying a rawhide sheath that was about a meter long, with a soft leather belt attached.

Faster than my eyes could follow, he whipped a sword from the sheath and held it before me. A streak of light exploded from its hilt and raced up the blade, leaping off the tip.

I recoiled from it so quickly, so instinctively, I nearly fell off my stool. The thing was beautiful and wild, like fire, like the flames that must have forged it.

Mick thrust the sword forward, as a knight might brace himself for battle. "I won a bronze medal for Ireland using a sword like this," he said. "Truth is, I was better than the man who took silver—but not quite as sober."

Now he lowered the blade and swung it side to side, as though to recall the touch of an old and intimate friend. "In competition, of course, they blunt the tips and round off the edges ..." Mick gave me a dry little smile. "So you don't cut your opponent in half."

With that, he slowly raised the tip and tapped it against the lamp above. "So what do you think?"

"I think it's the most beautiful thing I've ever seen."

"Its beauty hides its purpose. When my ancestors went to war, they carried this into battle." Mick walked around the end of the table, till he was close beside me. "Here, let me see your hand ..."

I extended my hand to him, palm down.

He laid the blade across my wrist and ever so gently moved it.

I looked on, incredulous, as it shaved away the hairs!

Mick pulled it quickly back, swung it end around, and offered me the handle. "Go ahead, Zé. Give it a try."

Slowly, as one would approach a wild animal, I took the handle and brought the sword up before me. It was much lighter than I would have guessed, and easy to hold. The grip was made of bone, I think, inset with bands of soft black leather. The guard, which formed a kind of metal basket around my hand, was overlaid with gold and silver traceries that were beautifully crafted. Set into the end of the handle was a fine green gem, about the size of a marble. If it was a true emerald, it was worth a fortune.

"It's incredible!" I said, handing it back to him. "But not much good, I think, in schooling my son."

Mick looked disappointed. "I suppose not." With one last flourish, he returned the blade to its sheath and laid it gently on the table.

"Are we agreed then?" I said. "Arithmetic, English, and chess?"

He sat down on his stool and looked me over for a long moment, then pulled a second book off the table. "This is what I should *really* like to teach him, Zé."

I could tell by the way he handled the book, with reverence and familiarity, that it was his Bible.

"I would like him to know Jesus," he said. "In whom all the treasures are hidden."

I nodded pleasantly and determined not to offend him. This was the man's passion, I knew, and a passion offended is an offense forever. Luckily, I had thought it over beforehand and was ready with my answer. "I think we'll leave it up to Padre Xabrega to teach him religion."

Mick grimaced at the thought. "If that's the case, then maybe I could teach him *un*religion."

"I don't understand."

"I tell you true," he said. "Religion is the deadest thing in the world."

What was I to make of *that*, coming from the mouth of a missionary? "I'm afraid I don't understand you. Are you sure you have the right words?"

"Apparently not."

"Can we still have a deal between us?"

"Sure."

"I don't expect you to work for free," I assured him.

He brightened a little at that. "What do you pay a teacher?"

This too I had considered beforehand. "Fresh fish and farinha. Enough to fatten you a little. You must be starving down here, eating finger fish and bananas."

Mick was rubbing his chin now. "Could you get me some *vegetables*?" His eyes widened at the thought. "Some carrots maybe, or tomatoes?"

"Scallions," I offered. "Maybe some collard greens."

"Done," he said.

I reached across the table to shake his hand. It was maybe the strangest deal ever struck, between a little brown man from Jacaré and a redheaded giant from Lough Gill, swapping fish for arithmetic.

Though the rain was still coming hard, I decided to leave.

"You can hang a hammock if you want," he offered. "Stay through till morning?"

"No, it's time to go. Ana will be looking for me." I grabbed my cap and walked forward, stopping at the hatch to put my sandals on. "What are the names for?" I asked, gesturing toward the bulkhead.

In the shadows there I'd noticed them, name after name, written on the pale gray boards.

Mick walked up behind me, clicked on his flashlight, and trained it across the bulkhead. "It's my prayer wall," he said. "The Church of Broken Toys."

Now I could read the names clearly. These were the people— mostly women and children—who had been on the beach that first afternoon, who had heard him preach and gone forward. For reasons that only a lunatic could understand, he had transferred their names from his little notebook onto the bulkhead.

I dared not speak the truth (Why disturb a man in his delusions if they work to bring him peace?) that none of the people on his list, except maybe Kiko and Little Aparecida, were committed to his church.

Mick moved his flashlight methodically down the list, illuminating one name after the other. "Nine men, twenty-two women, and fifty-three kids," he said. "Beloved of the Lord."

I can't describe the tenderness that overwhelmed me then, born of true affection. Out of sympathy I was moved to help him—as one might befriend a homeless dog. "You need to be careful, my friend."

"Of what?"

"Not everyone likes you as much as I do."

"What do you mean by that?"

I found myself leery now, of saying too much and regretting it later. "Some people are in the habit of lying," I said. "Even in their sleep they lie. And others, with anxious ears, are ready to listen."

"Gossip, you mean?"

"Some folks have wild tongues, Mick. Others walk around with rocks in their pocket, looking for a target."

His smile drew thin. "Not so different from Ireland then."

"Be careful, amigo. That's all."

Mick opened the hatchway for me and beamed his flashlight into the night. His eyes were shrewd and perceptive, as if he'd somehow read the secrets of my heart. "You be careful too," he warned.

CHAPTER 20

A<small>LZIRA KNEW JUST WHO TO SEND AND WHEN TO SEND HER</small>. S<small>HE HAD</small> learned every seam and curl in the darkness, the way we fishermen know the depths and currents of the river. It wasn't from wisdom or experience that the witch educed her power, but from instincts sheer and wild—the way a snake knows when to strike—and through the demonic leading of her *orixá*.

On the last day of March, under a full moon, Tatianni went down to the Irishman's boat to seduce him.

In obedience to the one who sent her, she waited for the perfect hour, when the moonlight should play full upon the beach, when her beauty should be illumined with silvery light and purpled shadow.

All preened and pretty she came, with that fabulous black hair of hers, swirling down around her waist like a flight of tyrants. She'd put bells on her toes—*tirim tirim*—to make sure he'd notice her, though only a blind man or a corpse could have failed at that.

Poor Mick, too long alone and missing the tender things of home, was like a chick cut off from its hen.

Dressed in moonlight and bells, and not much else, Tatianni stood at the river's edge, just below the bow of his boat, and called softly into the darkened cabin. With sugared words and songs she summoned him out of his sleep and lured him up on the deck, till he was leaning over the railing just above her. "I'm Tatianni," she purred, with a little thrust of her shoulder. "I've watched you from a distance, Mister Irish. And thought maybe, if you want, we could try it a little *closer.*"

Mick rubbed his eyes in disbelief. He must have thought it a fabulous dream, and flattering too, to have this gorgeous woman before him. And yet, despite the loneliness he suffered and the wild urgings of his flesh, he managed somehow to stop himself. "It's *late*," was all he said.

This surprised her and bothered her some. She had known only three types of men—the roosters, the goats, and the boars. And all of them, without much effort, turned to putty in her hands.

"It's late," he repeated, as though the words might somehow bolster his resolve.

Tatianni postured herself anew, so the moonlight could strike a different curve. "Of *course* it's late," she purred. "I chose it so, *meu amor.* So we can have the moonlight for *ourselves.*" She raised her arms in a very slow and deliberate way, then bunched her hair back into a luxurious ponytail. "See how beautiful it is?" Then freed it suddenly, so it could splash down around her waist.

Mick was forcing his feet backwards now, step by heavy step, toward the hatch. But his eyes were slow to follow.

"Invite me up," she coaxed him. "Just for a *little.*"

Mick was shaking now, sweating rivers down the back of his neck. "I can't," he pleaded. "*Por favor, me deixa em paz!*"

The woman scolded him with her eyes—*Such a naughty boy!*—and pouted her lips in a way that suggested everything. *Soon enough and plenty you'll be thanking me!*

"Maybe tomorrow," he allowed. "We could talk *tomorrow.*"

"If you'll not invite me up, *meu coração*, I'll dance for you here." Ever so slowly she began, dancing across the beach, using the terrible moonlight to accentuate her moves. Faster and faster she carried his eyes, swirling and twirling, till her feet threw sparks across the sand. Her bells were fully excited now, calling attention to her ankles, so her ankles might pay tribute to her calves. Her blue-black hair swirled up and up, whirling around her like a fan.

There was not one man in twenty, I'll wager, or even a hundred, who could have said "no" to what she showed him then, for she was beautiful beyond resistance. "Tatianni the Shape"—that's what we called her—or sometimes "Gatinha," the "Little Cat." She possessed every charm a woman could want, except for good character and a sense of humor.

If Mick had truly wanted to make a stand that night, and brace himself for the nights that followed, he should never have watched her so. For having seen the things she showed him, they could not be easily erased. What's a fire to do once it has tasted the ready thatch?

Against all odds Mick dragged himself back through the hatch— his heart throbbing like a drum—and locked himself in the cabin.

Brash and insistent, Tatianni skipped up the gangway after him, sat close beside the hatch, and spent the next two hours whispering through the cracks.

Down below, Mick lay in a heated sweat, listening to her songs and juicy innuendos, wondering what in God's name he was going to do.

Finally, just before dawn, she slipped away and left him in peace.

In obedience to her mistress and the rhythms of the moon, Tatianni returned the following night, about an hour past midnight. She'd wrapped herself in scarlet and put silver rings on her fingers. Her hair was braided now into three luxurious strands, interlaced with bright white flowers that jostled down around her hips.

Tatianni had given much thought to the foreigner—for he'd become a provocation now and a challenge—and decided that she would call him "Micky" (which she pronounced "Meeky") and treat him with a little more finesse. If he wasn't a goat or a boar, she reckoned, he must then be a rooster, who liked to have its feathers preened and be applauded for its crow.

Mick had given a lot of thought to her as well—not all of it healthy

—and ended up on his knees in prayer. At one point, with his emotions churning, he couldn't be sure which troubled him most: the thought that she might return that night or the thought that she wouldn't. Over and over again he reminded himself of what she was—a prostitute, plain and simple—and of the malignant spirit that controlled her. With that set before him, he knew just what to do. There was only one way to pull the fuse on this kind of explosive, and it must be done fast!

Close by the bow she clapped her hands and called to him, "*Boa noite, amigão!*"

Mick leapt up the cabin stairs and walked boldly forward, gripping the rail. She looked ravishing in the moonlight. More beautiful even than he'd remembered. Surely she'd planned it all, he reminded himself, the way an assailant chooses his spot and readies his knife.

The woman turned herself just so and smiled. "*Oí, Meeky* ! How *handsome* you are in the moonlight. And how *big*! I was hoping—all day long I was hoping—that you'd come out to meet me." She took another step toward the gangway. "It's chilly tonight, don't you think? And *lonely?*"

He balked for a horrible moment, not knowing how to address her. She wasn't a "Senhora" or a "Dona"—that much he knew. "Senhorita" would have been flattering, but also laughable.

"Tatianni ..." he said.

She considered it a victory that he had called her by name—"*Sim?*" —and also an invitation to move closer.

Mick held up his hand. "Listen to me, Tatianni. I don't have any money. Neither do I have anything of value to barter. No rings. No gold. *Nada.*"

He let go a little sigh of relief. The truth was out. The fuse had been pulled.

Had Tatianni not been such an accomplished and disciplined actress, her smile would have collapsed and away she'd have flown. But here she was bent to the will of her mistress, who wasn't after his money.

She took another step forward, showing herself wounded, offended even, by his words. "But I didn't come for money, *Meeky*. Only for *you*. Such a big man, and *wonderful*."

This cut him off at the knees—his defense thrown into shambles—and left him speechless.

Tatianni could see now that her rooster was tied at its feet and laid upon the block. Up the gangway she went, tossing her braids back over her shoulder, showing him everything.

With his hand over his eyes, Mick stumbled backwards through the hatch and locked himself in. "Go away, girl! Leave me in peace."

But she could hear the weakness in his voice. "I know what you want, Meeky. *O que tu quer ...*"

Thus did the contest resume, with more watchers in the night than either of them could have guessed.

Tatianni sat outside the hatch, lauding his "beautiful blue eyes," his "curly red hair," his soon-to-be-proven virility.

Mick lay in his hammock with his hands over his ears, praying aloud, and louder still, then chanting limericks and dithyrambs—anything he could think of—to drown out her voice and the relentless tinkling of her bells.

"*A pedra perto do pé de Pedro é preta,*" he chanted. It was a little tongue twister the kids had taught him, summoned now to occupy his mind. Over and again he repeated it, then summoned up another silly to take its place: "*Lá em cima daquela serra tem uma arara loura. Fala arara loura ...*"

"*Fala arara ... fala arara ...*"

It was the scent of her perfume—of jasmine and lust—that finally pushed him over the edge. Rolling out of his hammock, Mick stripped down to his shorts and slipped quietly out the rear hatch. For a long and anxious moment he stood there on the stern of the boat, hidden from view, peering into the water. The wind rippled softly across its face, clipping the moonlight into jittery little shards. Pushing away his fears, he muttered a prayer and quietly lowered himself into the river.

Despite his desperation, Mick must have known how foolish this was. To go swimming at night, by our reckoning, is a form of suicide, and one that's fairly common along the river. It's not for *nothing* that our village was named Jacaré. There are gators in the river and back in the marshes that can finish a man—even of Mick's size—in three or four bites and leave nothing for his kin to bury. So too, as I'd often warned him, there are poisonous snakes and piranhas and giant fish that come up from the depths. Especially at *night* they come ...

By the luck of the Irish, I guess, Mick survived his foolishness. Swimming and wading, he made his way down the river a few hundred meters and dragged himself up on the shore. He was exhausted by the trial and disappointed at the way he'd handled it. There on the sand he slept, unharmed, till the sun was three hands high.

As Mick lay sleeping on the beach that morning, Rafael was clapping at his boat. The boy, shot full of excitement and great expectations, had risen with the sun and run down to the boat early. Though punctuality is not much our habit here, Rafael was determined to respect the Irishman's wishes, which meant that class should start at eight.

For half an hour the boy stood by the bow and clapped. But no one appeared. *Could Senhor Mick be sleeping still?* he wondered. *Or off in the village for something?*

This was the day that Rafael and I had so long awaited—the first day of class—when the Irishman would explain the mysteries of arithmetic and English, and perhaps pull out his chessboard if time allowed. It was hard to say whether the student or the student's father was the more excited by it all. Secretly (and maybe not so secretly) I'd wished that I could study too. How often do we get the chance—living on the edge of the world—to sit in the company of a foreigner, to hear about foreign lands and foreign peoples, of foreign ingenuity and foreign strangeness? *Gente*, it would be almost as good as getting on an airplane and traveling into the foreignness yourself.

Rafael had dressed himself in his finest shirt that morning—smart and clean—and rubbed a squirt of *babaçu* through his curly black hair. He carried a brand-new workbook and pencil, luxuries that Sambão had brought up the river for me.

Rafael finally grew tired of clapping and waiting. The sun was up over the palms now and hot across the sand. As one last try, he went up the gangway a little and shouted, "*Bom dia!* " But the cabin was locked down tight and quiet as a leaf. *Senhor Mick had forgotten him!*

When Rafael came home that morning and told me there had been no class, I was as much disappointed as he was. And also puzzled. *It was odd that the Irishman should let us down that way. And where in our little village could a man so large and conspicuous have vanished to?*

"We'll go find him," I told the boy. "*Já já.*"

But "*já já*" is a very loose and unpredictable measure of time, especially on the lips of a drunk. In our house, it generally meant, "Ask me again when I'm sober."

Tatianni was at it again that night, dressed in bright orange shorts and a halter top that was barely there. She had perfumed herself with a strange and intoxicating agent made from the flowers of the muruci, which Alzira herself had supplied.

But the moon was waning now, and so was Tatianni's enthusiasm for the project. The man had become tedious to her, and irritating. She could not, in her shallow thinking, imagine the source of his hesitation. Some men balked for lack of money, which was easy to understand. *But how could money be the problem when she'd never asked him for it?* Other men, she knew, were hindered by their fears, thinking their wives or lovers might find them out and shame them in public, or worse, look for the perfect moment to castrate them in their sleep. But the foreigner was single, and obviously alone. *Puta que pariu! What held him back?* The question slipped a little wedge of insecurity into her perfect beauty and poisoned her thoughts toward him.

It was about two in the morning, that third night, when she went down to his boat again. "*Boa noite, Meeky! Venha ver o luar!*" Come see the moonlight!

The hatch creaked open for a moment, then quickly closed.

Though Tatianni was not to see him at all that night, she faithfully took her post and carried on, chatting at him through the hatch.

As time wore on her overtures became increasingly short and bitter, lapsing into catcalls and jeers that suggested he was either impotent or queer. Now her truest character was foaming to the surface, not a lovebird at all, she showed herself, but an ill-tempered lynx.

"Maybe you are not so big down below as up above, Mister Irish? *É isso o problema?*"

Mick had burrowed down into his hammock and wrapped himself in a blanket. He'd stuffed his ears with toilet paper and covered his head with a pillow. Scratchy as it was and suffocatingly hot, it seemed better than risking the river again. But not by much ...

So till dawn the duel played itself out, when finally she retreated, and Mick slipped into a tortured sleep.

I felt well enough the next morning to walk Rafael down to the boat and see what was going on.

The *Jornada de Fé* looked lonely and abandoned in the early light, and longing for some care.

Rafael and I stood by the bow, clapping. The forward hatch and shutters were closed up tight, with no sign of the Irishman. Though I couldn't explain it, I knew the smell of trouble, as if the air itself were braced for battle. I thought back to the long patrols I'd made in the army, pursuing Gasolina and his gang through the unforgiving jungle. Though we always had more men and firepower at our disposal, the advantages of time and place were always his. He could choose, at his own pleasure, to elude us forever ... or in a heartbeat come out of the brush and murder half our squad. It was *that* kind of tension that hung upon the boat, waiting for the evil one to show his face.

I think we might have turned and left had Rafael not caught the sound, ever so faint, of music coming from the cabin.

"Listen, Papai! He's playing his harmonica!"

It was true. When I inclined my ear, I could hear it softly humming. "I want you to stay here," I told Rafael. "Just there in the shade. I won't be long."

Walking up the gangway and onto the deck, I could see something written across the face of the hatch. It took me a moment to figure out what it said and a moment more—running my hand across the letters—to realize that it was written with lipstick.

Faggot!

I tapped softly against the metal plate. "Senhor Mick? Are you in there?"

The harmonica stopped. The silence that followed was long and ruminating.

"Are you all right, Senhor Mick? It's Zé here."

At last the bolt slid back and the hatch swung slowly open. I'm not sure which of us was more shocked; he, by the sudden burst of light that poured in upon him, or me, coming face to face with a cadaver.

I reached out and put my hand on his arm. "*Meu Deus,* what's happened to you?!"

With bloodshot eyes he considered me, like a hermit peering out of his cave. His lips were cracked and drawn, the cheeks gone pale. Stranger still, a twist of toilet paper hung from his ear, bunched back into the hole and spotted with blood.

The Irishman swallowed hard. "I've not been sleeping good."

"Not been *sleeping?* What do you mean?"

He backed slowly down the steps and waved me in. "Come sit."

The place stank hard of sweat and rotten bananas, and something else that I couldn't quite put my nose on. I walked along the starboard side of the cabin, opening the shutters.

Mick shuffled over to his hammock and plopped himself down. With a little push of his foot he set it into motion, swinging himself gently back and forth.

I grabbed a stool and sat down in front of him. "Are you sick?"

He thought about it a moment and shook his head. "No. But Alfredo's not so good." His hand came off his lap and opened slowly before me. There, in the curl of his palm, lay the little turtle.

I could tell by its color and the nasty odor that it was dead.

"I forgot about him," Mick whispered. "Forgot to give him water." He stared down at the blue and yellow shell. His eyes were those of a little boy, too innocent yet to really believe in death. "I shouldn't have brought him here ..."

"Animals pass on," I said. "Same as humans."

The Irishman's head drooped forward. "I shouldn't have juggled with him. He never liked it ..."

"Here, let me take him," I suggested.

Gently, Mick handed the turtle over, his eyes stricken with grief. "We got to bury him, you know?"

"Sure we do. Sure. I'm good at that."

I took Alfredo outside and set him on the deck, then shouted down to Rafael, "Go home, Filho! I'll be there soon."

The boy stretched out his hands. "What about my class?"

"Not today."

"What about Senhor Mick? Is he okay?"

"You go home now, boy. I'll see you there."

Rafael turned slowly, his shoulders slumping, and walked back up the path.

With a long, deep breath, I descended into the cabin again and took up my stool. "What's happened to you, Mick? Tell me."

Back and forth in the hammock he rocked. Back and forth. "Do you know a woman named Tatianni?" he said.

This caught me by surprise and fired my curiosity. "Everyone knows Tatianni. What about her?"

Over the next few minutes he told me everything that had happened the past three nights ... this amorous dream that had roused him from his sleep ... no dream at all, it turned out, but a woman of striking beauty ... dancing in the moonlight ... exciting things inside him that had long been checked. Then back again the following night, he said ... with her juicy invitations and intoxicating scent ... forbidding him sleep ... forcing him finally into the dark, cool river. And again last night ... the dream become a nightmare now ... filled with raunchy taunts and sass ... forcing him to hide inside his hammock and stuff his ears with paper.

When he finished his story, I was so overcome with sympathy and anger I didn't know what to say. Then leaned forward and grabbed him by the arm, "Listen to me, Mick ..."

His eyes were glazed with exhaustion and darting every which way.

I leaned in closer. "*Look* at me, Mick."

He blinked hard and did his best to focus.

"You must never go into the river again at night ... *ever*! Do you understand?"

His brows bent hard upon the warning.

"You're lucky," I told him. "Luckier than you know."

"Yes. Very lucky I am."

I shook my head in wonder. "*Meu Deus*, why would she do this?"

Mick shrugged at me.

"You have to tell her that you got no money," I said. "That she's got nothing here to gain."

"I *told* her so," he pleaded. "She says she's not interested in money."

"Not interested in money?!" I hooted.

He nodded. "That it's *me* she wants."

I tried to unravel that twisted little thought and found it wouldn't give. "Are you sure you used the right words, Mick? That she understood you?"

"I'm sure."

This broke hard against the prevailing currents. *Tatianni not interested in money?* Could a fish suddenly lose interest in water? *Caramba*, she breathed the stuff and built her nest upon it.

Out of my confusion I tossed him some easy advice, "*Meu bendito*, if it's free, why not go ahead and screw her?! *Aproveite!*"

Mick blinked at me two or three times, then answered softly, "I couldn't do that, Zé."

"Why not? It's *free* isn't it?"

He put his foot down on the deck and dragged his hammock to a stop. "It would be like a dog returning to its vomit."

I leaned forward, straining to understand.

His voice was pleading now. "Don't you see, Zé? I've already slept with her a hundred times before."

He was, without a doubt, the most perplexing man I'd ever known. Between his fumbling Portuguese and inscrutable character there was nothing but confusion. "Look," I tried again, "the woman comes clapping in the night. The woman says it's free. So why not make love?"

"'Cause it's got nothing to do with love," said Mick. "Or even lust."

"What then?"

"*Chains*," he said.

"What?"

"If you have the eyes to see them ..."

"You're not making sense, Mick. You're tired."

He sat perfectly still, staring at me. "You're not as stupid as you pretend," he said. "You *know* the devil of whom I speak."

I looked quickly away, so he couldn't read my eyes and see how painfully close to the truth he'd struck. A *drink* was what I needed, to ease my way around it.

"In costumes and perfumes he approaches me," Mick said. "With tender lies. The same way he approaches you."

The last thing in the world I wanted was to focus the conversation on me. "What are you going to do?" I asked.

He thrust his chin forward. "Stand!" he said defiantly. "That's all. By the grease of God ..."

It took me a second to untangle that last bit of confusion. "*Grace*," I said. "I think you mean *grace*."

To some things we're elected, without knowing why. To other things directed, without knowing who. Why is it, I wonder, that a man can believe so faithfully in the unseen powers of gravity and magnetism, yet fail and fail again to recognize the hand of God?

I could say with some honesty that it was the moon that woke me up that night and curiosity that walked me down to the beach. But there was someone else involved who had not yet been revealed.

Tatianni was standing at the river's edge, not far from the boat, using the moonlit water as her mirror. This way and that she postured herself, with self-adoring eyes. Then began to comb her splendid black hair, slowly, slowly, so that every stroke might be prolonged and lovingly approved.

Rumor had it that she owned a thousand mirrors and six hundred kinds of perfume. That was nothing but the talk of jealous women and exaggerating men. I can tell you for a fact that she had nowhere near that number of mirrors. Maybe ten, I think—hung here and there around her house. (Don't ask me how I know.)

In all of this she was a child of vanity. But also—perhaps unwittingly—its mother. While the older women aggressively hated her and slandered her at every chance, some of the younger women and girls— some not even come to puberty yet—secretly admired her. They found her glamorous and exciting in her way and could see for themselves how successfully she attracted men. Whenever these young apprentices got the chance, they would paint their eyes (though crudely) with the selfsame colors and glitters that Tatianni used and adjust their skirts just so. Some of them—the daughters of my friends and family— would one day take a boat to Manaus or Belém and disappear into the world of prostitutes.

So absorbed was Tatianni in herself that night, I was able to walk right up behind her without being noticed. "*Boa noite.*"

The woman spun around with a start and clamped her hand across her breasts. "You?!" she blurted. Her look quickly dissolved into scorn. "Zé Licata."

I nodded at her. "You are a long way from your mirrors, Tatianni. What are you doing down here?"

Now she turned defensive, and insolent. "I do as I *please.*"

"Strange that a flower should leave its bush and go looking for bees," I said. "Has the line grown short at your bed?"

She smiled at me, with those beautiful, empty eyes. "They all come up to see me eventually. If not in person, then in their dreams."

"Except for *him*," I said, gesturing at the boat.

Her eyes fell away and narrowed upon the thought, as if a scorpion had appeared on the sand. Despite her skills as an actress, she could not quite conceal the damage that he'd done. Could it be—*yes*, I spied it there!—a hairline crack in her vanity.

The woman drew back, rallied herself to her beauty, and began with fresh determination to comb her hair. "It must be really *frustrating* for you," she said.

"How's that?"

"To not be able to afford me anymore. To have turned into a mean little drunk."

"Yes, that's true," I admitted.

She looked at me as if I were a piece of bread. "I remember when you came home from the army, with your pockets full of cash. You enjoyed me well enough, didn't you?"

I winced at the memory. "Yes, those were the days ..."

Tatianni shooed me away with her hand. "Why don't you go home now," she said. "And *reminisce* ... "

"Because you bother my friend," I said.

"Is that so?"

"*Olha,* Tati, why waste your time on him? I tell you true, he's got no money. The man's living on skinks and water lilies."

"I know that."

"*Why,* then?"

She lifted her face to the moon, so its light could play across her cheeks. "Because it's fun," she giggled. "It makes him crazy. He groans like an oxcart loaded with rocks."

With that little spurt of wickedness the truth revealed itself. "You're working for Alzira, aren't you? Here to torment him."

Tatianni tossed her hair from side to side, delighting in the feel. "I do as I please, *matuto.*"

"Sure you do. But I need to tell you something, Tati—for your own good. It's not *safe* down here."

She stopped suddenly and pulled the comb from her hair. "What do you mean?"

"I have this dog, see? Well, actually I have *two* dogs. Now old Rompe, he's pretty well behaved, I guess. But the other one, Ressaca, he—"

"What's this got to do with me?" she cut in.

I stepped a little closer. "He's all teeth, you know, and not much brains. He gets loose at night sometimes, because the fence is broken. And runs wild, you know, down here along the river. Right about *here.*"

A cloud pushed over the moon and cast its shadow upon her, distorting her face into something that was very unlovely. "I wouldn't threaten me if I were you, *meu safado*. For there you cross my mistress, who likes you little enough already."

"I am just telling you, Tati. This is *not* a good place to be."

The woman turned her back on me then, as rude as she could make it. "I do as I *please*," she said. "Now go home and *dream* about me ..."

Exactly as she pleased, Tatianni returned the following night.

And so did I, waiting in the shadows with Ressaca.

I would like to say that I wrestled long and hard with the decision before I turned him loose. But the truth should speak, whether it speaks kindly of me or not.

When I saw her there, approaching Mick's boat, I slipped the rope off his collar. "Go get her, boy! *Vai*!"

It was a very stupid and immensely gratifying thing to do. With every confidence in the world, she'd assumed that I was bluffing. Now I smugly played my ace.

Ressaca ripped across the sand, howling like a wolf. The same moon that propelled her beauty into the eyes of men now spurred my dog into murderous pursuit. (Proving I guess that dogs and harlots have something in common.)

Tati took one look at him and fled for her life.

Who could have guessed, had it not been proven there, that the woman could run so fast?! (Who knows, maybe in another time and place, favored by another culture, she'd have become a true Olympian.) One thing is sure, the bells on her toes never jangled like *that* before, racing through the village like a deer.

Fearing that Ressaca might actually catch her and do real damage, I chased along behind them and tried to whistle him back. I was much relieved, and proud of him, when he came trotting back through the trees a moment later. I had told her the truth, you know, when I'd called him a brainless and disobedient creature. (A description, I guess, that also fit his master.)

Excited by the chase, Ressaca rushed in around my feet, leaping on his hinds, thrashing his wild tail.

I knelt down beside him and rubbed his worthy head. "Good boy! You are a bone-chewing devil blaster if ever there was!"

He looked up at me with those big sad eyes, his ears drooping low. With a little yowl he expressed his disappointment: *I had her, you know?! I could have brought you a piece of her leg ...*

"I know you could," I told him. "I *know*. But you don't want to be chewing that kind of meat, boy. That meat's gone *bad*."

By fate or chance there were half a dozen witnesses that night—some sober and some not—who caught a glimpse of Tatianni as she sprinted through the village.

Ajuba Barbosa, who was staggering from someplace (he forgot just where) to go some other place (he couldn't remember why) just about whenever it was, said there were two women and three large dogs involved, which might in fact have been wolves, or maybe hyenas.

Ney Let The Fire Go Out, who has to involve himself in everything, was busy painting the wind when the girl flew by. "Three more days," he told her. "Just three more days ..."

The most reputable witness was Paulo Adário, who was just coming out of his latrine when this "mostly naked, hysterical girl" flashed past him with a "ferocious dog" on her heels. "I thought she was dead and chewed," Paulo told the boys up at the shack. "Then the dog just stops, turns himself around, and trots off into the night. Never seen such a thing before ... and wouldn't mind seeing it again."

So far as I know, Tatianni never went down to Mick's boat again or otherwise bothered the man. Though I have no way to prove it, I suspect something cracked inside her soul that night that she was never quite able to fix. Vanity, in the end, is a very fragile goddess, who bruises at the least rebuke and never ages well.

Freed from his midnight struggles, Mick was able to get some rest in the days that followed and begin his classes with Rafael. In that, as in everything else, he gave credit to God.

"She has not come back!" he told me excitedly. "I have *prayed her away!* "

I didn't have the heart to tell him that Ressaca had spoken to the woman on his behalf and persuaded her to move on.

"God is great!" Mick proclaimed. "And *greatly* to be praised!"

Who was I, least of all men, to argue the point?

CHAPTER 21

THERE'S A SAYING HERE AMONG THE FISHERMEN THAT YOU CAN'T piss into the wind and expect to keep your pants dry.

So knew I that my foolishness would not go unanswered. Once Alzira learned what had happened—if not from Tatianni herself then from some bustling gossip—I would have to pay.

Still, it surprised me how fast the summons came—the following afternoon already—and how wretched it made me feel.

It was Dalvina, her lumbering servant girl, who delivered the note. She arrived in the very heat of the day, when most everyone (like me) was laid back in their hammocks or loafing in the shade.

I went out and opened the gate to her, but we kept our distance and offered no smiles.

Her massive black face was glistening with sweat, which pooled here and there into rivulets and trickled down her heavy neck. Her look was plainly smug, and filled with relish, as one who goes early to the gallows and waits with glee. What did she need with a sneering tongue when her eyes so clearly spoke? *Agora tu vai apanhar, seu safado nojento!*

I took the little scrap of paper from her and unfolded it. Never, I think, was so much malice expressed in so few words:

Tonight at 11
Be Sober!

Twenty minutes early and cold sober I arrived at Alzira's that night. I had in my pockets every last centavo I could gather, hoping, I guess, that money would somehow smooth things over.

It came to 628 cruzeiros in all. Everything that Jamela had sent me over the past few weeks plus everything that Ana had hidden away for emergencies.

Puxa, if this wasn't an emergency, what was? *Soon, and very soon, I swore, I'll put the money back into Ana's jar.*

I stood clapping at the gate, wondering how I'd come to this. The place was deathly still. Even the wind had died away. A pair of timid candles, placed high in the rafters, flickered across the patio and into the tall, shadowy grass.

Suddenly the door to the house opened and out she came, sifting across the patio like a phantom. Her gown, of white gossamer, drifted along behind her like a veil of cobwebs.

Never had I seen an Alzira quite this old or quite so feeble, nor dressed in such priestly garments. Slowly she approached me, her head bowed low, lost in deepest thought. Never once, crossing the yard and opening the gate, did she look up at me. "Go sit!" was all she said.

I found my usual chair, there on the patio, and took a seat, so depressed and intimidated that my hands began to sweat.

Three times she circled the table, mumbling to herself, then stopped directly behind me, leaned in close upon my ear, and whispered, "God but you make me old."

A furious silence followed, then she craned in over my shoulder and shouted, "Why would you *do* such a thing?!" Her horrid, bulbous eye drew closer. "Have you lost your mind?!"

I shut my eyes to that malignant orb, lest it freeze my heart.

"Why?" she pressed.

Like steam from an overheated boiler the words spewed out of me, "'Cause she was torturing my friend! That's why!"

She fell back a little, startled at my bluntness.

"Because she's a nasty little whore!" I finished.

For a long moment, Alzira stopped breathing. Then, ever so gently, with her emotions under perfect control, she whispered, "Listen to me, Zé Licata."

Her mouth was very close to my ear now. I could feel her breath upon it, like a chilling mist.

"Are you listening?"

"Yes."

"If you ever cross me again, you'll wonder how hell got hold of your balls. You understand me?"

I wanted to grab her by the throat.

Her voice grew louder. "Do you *understand* me?"

I could have slapped her face, had I not been so afraid.

"You do well to fear me," she said. "And more, to fear the one we serve. It's not just *me* you've crossed, *Caboclo*. But Xangô himself, to whom your vows were made."

She waited for the words to wash over me, then ripped me again. "You fool! You're lucky to be alive. All day long and half the night I've been praying for you. Making fresh sacrifices. Even so, you will feel his whip across your ass."

I thought suddenly of Ana, alone at home. Then Rafael, asleep in his hammock. What a fool I was, out dancing with the Devil, assuming that he would leave my family in peace. Overcome with guilt and fear, my hands began to shake.

Alzira rounded the table and sat down across from me. Her head slumped forward, resting on her arms, and there she stayed for a very long time. "God but you make me old," she muttered.

When finally she looked up, it was a kinder, younger Alzira that faced me. "Are we in this together or not, Senhor Zé? Tell me plain."

No! my thoughts rebelled. *I'll wash my filthy hands of you! And never return!*

"Your wife and boy are safe tonight," she assured me. "Because of *me* they are safe. Because I have intervened on your behalf."

"Forgive me my lack of gratitude."

"You'll thank me in the end. Once we succeed in our business."

For the first time all night I thought of Ivanildo Bonfim and the untold suffering he'd caused us.

"*Yes*," she sang out. "Fix your mind on the enemy and keep it there. Soon comes the moment you've been waiting for, Senhor Zé. To put him down."

"Yes," I repeated numbly.

Out of the shadows welled his image, fractured and inflamed ... of fat, bejeweled hands and golden teeth ... of that arrogant, thrusting belly ... so sure of himself and his great estate that he gloated over his fraud. Out of that same sordid hole crawled another image—of Jarbas, his goon—dragging us out of the office, heaving poor Chico down the stairs. With horrible clarity I recalled the moment, and then the sound, of Chico's bones cracking against the marble. Then saw his blood there pooling on the steps.

"Leiteiro tells me the man is a glutton of unusual proportions," Alzira supplied. "That there's not enough wine in all the world to fill his belly, nor money enough to line his pockets, nor little girls to satisfy his lust."

Now the images were freshened and alive before me, and with them the vigor of my hate.

"Come now and let me get you a drink," she said cheerily. "And show you what I've made."

She rose from her chair and headed for the house. "Put your money on the table," she called back. "I'll count it later and apply it to your debt."

I was thirstier now than I could ever remember, and profoundly confused. In lame obedience I emptied the money out of my pockets and laid it on the table, stacking the coins into four neat piles and laying the bills beside them.

Alzira returned with a very large drink in one hand and a handsome white box in the other. It was half a meter long and a full hand wide, inscribed across the top with flowery letters,

Feliz Aniversário!

She sat the glass down in front of me and placed the box beside it. "Drink up, Senhor Zé. *Desfruta!*"

In that I needed no encouragement, swilling the whole of it in two or three bolts.

She brought a lamp over, put a match to it, and trimmed back the wick; then came around the table, standing just beside me, and placed her hand on the box. "We shall approach him with a tribute," she said, "as the Greeks approached the Trojans."

There she had lost me.

"You wouldn't know of the Greeks, would you?"

"No."

"With a gift we will honor him," she explained. "To stroke his pride, to overcome his caution."

Now my curiosity was roused, and with it a dark excitement. I could see that the box alone had cost us plenty. How special then should the thing inside it be!

"You will take this to Belém," she told me. "With the greatest care, at the perfect hour, in the perfect place, you will set a *mesa branca* for him."

"Belém?"

"Yes. You'll be leaving on the sixth of April."

I'm not sure which irritated me more, her presumption or her tone.

"I can't just walk out of the house and go to Belém," I said.

"Of course you can."

"What should I tell Ana?"

"Lie to her, of course. Same as you always do."

"How?"

"Tell her you're going to see Jamela, your industrious cousin, and her lazy husband, Ozias. Tell her it has to do with your business there. With turtle fat and copaíba."

"How could you know all that?"

Alzira tossed it away with her hand. "Everything is known in the end," she said. "It's knowing things *beforehand* that really counts."

The woman was full of taunts and teasers. Like iridescent fish they flashed and played beneath her surface, rising now to wow your eyes and make you wonder, then slipping into the depths again.

"You're to take the *Estela Maria* on the night of the sixth," she said. "You will hang your hammock apart from the other travelers, alone as you can make it, and be ever watchful of the things you carry." Her hand was stroking the top of the box now, as though her favorite cat had reclined there on the table.

"That should put you in Belém on the morning of the ninth. Leiteiro will meet you at the docks and help you with your preparations."

"Maybe Leiteiro could just *do* it for me," I suggested. "We could pay him something extra and—."

"No," she cut me off. "This is your *despacho*. There can be no substitutes."

"Jesus!"

"He will have no part in this," she said.

"Listen, I don't know how to do this."

"Leiteiro will provide you everything you need. Treat him as kindly as you can, despite his—" She looked off into the darkness, at a loss for words. "Despite the way he is," she finished.

"And the box," I wondered. "What's in the box?"

She ignored me and went on with her instructions.

"You are to set the *mesa* on the night of the tenth, then have our little gift delivered to Ivanildo Bonfim on the eleventh. Without fail, it *must* be delivered to him on the eleventh."

"Why?"

"Because eleven is a good number, my friend, and because his birthday is on the fourteenth."

Stranger and stranger the plan emerged, too fast for me to grasp. "How can you know all this?" I asked her again.

Alzira pulled over a chair and sat close beside me. "Leiteiro, despite his—ah, *unhappy* appearance—is quite good at what he does. In this case it wasn't much trouble for him to gather the things we needed, to learn what's important to know. Senhor Bonfim is a very public man, and loves it so, always cutting ribbons and preening for the cameras, always promoting himself in the press. What's not been revealed in the newspapers is easily learned from his old girlfriends and gardeners, who aren't very fond of him. Thus we know that he aspires to be governor of Pará and will do whatever it takes to put himself there, that he's on his fourth wife now, and courting her replacement, that he has a serious weakness for cognac and Cuban cigars."

"Is that what's in the box?"

"No," she smiled. "But the idea has merit ..."

"What then?"

With great tenderness and pride she leaned forward and removed the lid.

Inside the box, displayed on a bed of smooth white cotton, lay a collection of beautiful agates, laid out like slices of luminescent fruit. Clearly, they'd all been cut from the same splendid rock, showing similar bands of red and rose, with an innermost eye—about the size of a pea—that was blood red.

As I leaned closer, in awe and admiration, I could see that each of the agates—nine of them in all—had been drilled at the top with a tiny hole and threaded with a fine silver wire. The wires, each cut to a different length, ran to the top of the assembly and passed through a large wooden ring, or harness. Above the harness, the wires were bunched together and drawn into the bottom of a beautiful wooden sphere, about the size of an orange. By the looks of it, the sphere had been carved out of solid wood, hollowed out in its center, and master-fully engraved. A fantastic menagerie of animals and birds played across its surface, created from myth and wild fancy.

For half a minute I couldn't fathom what the thing was, then remembered something that I'd seen—a long, long time ago—hanging in the Colonel's garden. "A wind chime," I said.

Alzira was beaming over her creation. "Yes. A thing of irresistible beauty."

"To carry our *maldição* ..."

She stiffened at the word. "I told you before. I don't *like* that."

I shrugged. "What then? *Feitiço*? Does that sound any better?"

She said nothing.

"I think I have the right to know, don't I? Considering the money I'm paying?"

I could hear the frustration in her sigh, and then her voice. "We will sing him to sleep," she said. "We will sing him a lullaby of our own choosing."

"Jesus!" I cried. "There's something inside it!" Indeed, something small and black and very fast had flashed around the sphere and vanished darkly into one of the holes.

Instinctively I reached out to kill it. "It's a damned *cockroach*, I think."

She seized my wrist. "No!"

I was startled at how quickly she moved and the sudden pressure she inflicted on my wrist.

"You are *never* to touch it," Alzira warned. "*Ever*. And after tonight, never to look on it again."

"Let me *go*," I finally had to say.

Slowly, as a vice releasing, she withdrew her hand.

"How can we know he'll even accept the gift?" I said.

"Because he loves himself to death," she explained. "Because my orixá—and yours—will coax him toward that end."

The plan had become a little too real for me now, and deeply involving. I could feel my poor sad heart, overwhelmed with shadows, thumping inside my chest. In desperation I took the empty glass and raised it to my lips, up and up some more, hoping to lick out a final drop or two.

Alzira placed the lid back on the box, pulled a hank of light blue ribbon from her pocket, and worked cheerfully—like a flower girl humming over her work—till the ribbon was neatly tied and twirled into a bow. "There," she said. "Just right!"

Off she scurried then, into the house again, and appeared a moment later with a small flat package and a gunny sack. "Here, help me with this," she instructed.

I opened the sack and held it as she slipped the box inside.

"There," she said. "Plain and simple. Not to arouse curiosity where none we want. *This* ..." she added importantly, holding out the package, "is the cloth I've made, to set the *mesa*. There is none like it in all the world, consecrated for its purpose." With great reverence and care she slipped it into the sack and tied it off. "Done."

I pushed back from the table and grabbed my cap. To get home and into my hammock was all I wanted, to find a place of shelter and quiet drink.

Alzira raised a kindly finger, as a mother would remind her little one to wipe his chin. "One thing more," she said. "You must renew your vows."

Like a distant bell I heard the warning sound, to hold me off the shoals, but could not resist the chance before me ... *to make that bastard pay for all the suffering he'd caused ... to stop him from doing more!*

"You *do* remember your vows, don't you?" she whispered.

"No. Not exactly."

"Of course you do," she encouraged me. "*Try.*"

As I opened my mouth the words were supplied me. "Xangô, you are the fountain of all my favors ..."

"Good," she said. "Remember the night we danced before him, when he placed his hand upon you?"

"... You alone are my satisfaction and my consolation." I could sense the spirits rising now, like moths from the darkened grass, beating their anxious way toward me.

"Go on," she said.

For the life of me I couldn't remember the rest of it and was too bewildered to try. Like naughty children the spirits swarmed around me, pressing in to hear.

"I declare and plead ..." Alzira prompted me.

Out of the shadows it suddenly echoed, my own dead voice falling upon my own dead ears. "I declare and plead that the injuries inflicted upon me by Ivanildo Abreu Bonfim shall be avenged in full and six and twenty! That he shall become the refuse of my intestines, an object of wrath! That he shall be plundered by your many hands and several, O Xangô, through *Desânimo* and *Depressão*, empowered by our prayers, our faithful service, and the blood of those you crave."

The mob fell away. Silence like a grave enwrapped me.

"And the rest," she pressed me. "Don't forget the rest."

"I, Zemário Luan Vasconcelos dos Santos Licata, declare anew that I am your apparatus, given wholly this night and complete."

Like a little girl she clapped her hands. "Now we are of one accord," she said, beaming. Then clapped again, with purpose and authority, to dismiss the cloud of witnesses that danced around us.

Exhausted, I rose from the table and took up my sack.

"I feel renewed and encouraged in this," she said. "You will too, Senhor Zé, once you take hold of it. You must put to death that odd reluctance that holds you back. Take hold of your power and wield it. Watch your enemies dissolve."

Depressed and confused, I stumbled toward the gate. A sewer of malicious thoughts and horrible images went coursing through my mind.

"Go ahead and speak them aloud!" she ordered me. "Prophesy!"

"I mean to cut this man in half and leave his entrails for the dogs."

"Yes!" she agreed. "I can see him there, in his lavish home, reclined in his soft and pillowed bed. Behind his gates and guards he imagines himself secure. But soon enough our melodies will find him, to steal away his sleep. Then shall his wheels begin to turn and churn and finally break upon themselves."

"It will be slow?"

"Yes," she promised. "Because you wanted it so."

I passed through the gate and let it close behind me.

"One thing more," she added. "You will need money, Senhor Zé. *Lots* of money. To set the *mesa* right."

I looked wearily back at her, with my empty pockets and my empty soul. "More money?"

"Yes," she informed me. "Two thousand cruzeiros. Maybe more."

"But I don't have any," I murmured. "Everything I have is on the table there. Every centavo.*"

With a flip of her hand she brushed my concerns away. "I shouldn't worry, Senhor Zé. Loans can be taken. Credit given. A clever man finds clever means ..."

On down the trail I walked, into the empty night.

"What is left to *you* ..." she called, "is to listen close and do exactly as you're told."

At first light, with the roosters crowing, I hurried up the path to home.

Faster and faster I had pushed the trail, sensing that something horrible lay ahead.

Now I could see the gate, broken off its hinges, flattened in the dirt.

"Jesus!"

He will be no help in this.

Into the yard I ran, wild with fear. "Ana?!"

How loudly the silence screamed!

Meu Deus! Where were the dogs?! "Ana!"

"Here," she answered softly.

Now I could see her, in the corner of the kitchen, hiding in the shadows.

I rushed in beside her and laid hold of her arm. "What's happened, Ana? *What?!*"

Slowly, very slowly, she looked up at me. Her eyes were wet with horror, her voice so weak and wretched that I could scarcely hear her. "Something came into the yard."

"Speak up, woman! What?!"

"Into the yard it came," she muttered. "I cannot say ..."

Even so, you will feel his whip.

"Where's Rafael?!" I shouted. "Where?!"

She gestured toward the house. Now she was weeping into her hands.

Back through the bedroom I dashed and into the little room beyond.

O blessed mercy! The boy lay safe in his hammock, peering out at me.

"Papai!" he shouted.

"Are you all right?"

He nodded.

With a trembling hand I instructed him, "You stay right there, boy! You *understand?*"

"Sure, Pai. Right here."

I hurried back into our room, pitched the gunny sack into the corner and threw open the wardrobe.

Because of me your wife and boy are safe tonight. Because I have intervened on your behalf.

I snatched the Colt off the shelf, threw the safety, and hurried out.

Sunlight was sifting into the kitchen now. I could see that Ana was still in her slip, her hair a jumbled mess. "What was it, *amor*? What came in the yard?"

She shook her head. "I don't know, Zé. A jaguar maybe."

That I couldn't believe. There had not been a jaguar on the island in twenty years.

"Did you get a look at it?"

Again she rattled her head. "We barred the door. The windows tight. I dared not look, Zé. I dared not look. Just prayed to God, with all his saints, that it not come in ..."

"Where are the dogs?"

"Just prayed," she rambled on. "That's all ..."

"Where are the *dogs*, Ana?"

"Ressaca's dead," she blurted.

"What?"

"When I came out, Zé ... when finally I looked ..." She pointed off into the yard. "I found him there."

"I don't see anything."

"I took him away," she cried. "I didn't want Rafael to see him. What was left ..."

"Jesus."

"I carried him out back and put him under," she sobbed.

You will feel his whip across your ass!

Her voice was shaking with horror. "It could have done worse, Zé. Could have killed us both."

"Where's Rompe?"

"Hiding," she said. "Under the house I think."

Since when had Rompe been afraid of anything?

Into the yard I walked and looked around. Now I spotted the place, where the ground was roughed and broken, where splotches of blood lay moist upon the dirt. Here and there, embedded in the mess, were bits of fur remaining. Just bits of fur ...

I could see from the tracks that it hadn't lasted long. Mixed with Ressaca's familiar prints were some giant others, half again the size of my hand. There was no cat in all the world that would leave a track like that. But there was a dog ... if a *dog* you'd call it ... sired of a wolf and whelped from a Doberman bitch.

Pesadelo.

Ana had stopped crying now and followed me into the yard. "Why should it kill the dog?" she said. "Why didn't it go for the chickens?"

"It wasn't after food," I whispered.

"What then?"

"Listen to me, woman. I want you to get your broom and come sweep these tracks away. Every last sign of it, you understand? So far as Rafael is to know, Ressaca passed away in the night. That's all. Just passed away."

"Yes, Zé."

I walked down the side of the house, past the latrine, to the place where she had buried him.

There in the fresh-turned earth I saw the price of evil and knew I owned the blame.

"I am sorry for this," I told him. "Truly I am."

Even from a pup he had been loyal to me. Not very smart, you know, but ever loyal and always brave.

"Truly, you were a better dog than I a man."

CHAPTER 22

I KNEW, EVEN AS I PACKED MY BAG, THAT I WAS ON THE VERGE OF drowning. I knew it in my heart and sensed it in my soul, yet could not escape the sticky deal I'd made.

Once it's done you will be free of it, I reasoned. *A few more days is all. Then only to wait for the chips to fall ...*

In some odd and twisted way I thought myself a champion, willing to sacrifice myself for something noble. If not for me, who would stop this thieving bastard from his work, who distilled our dreams into cognac and blew away our children's future in the puff and glow of his fine cigars?

Others, with more honest eyes, could see that I had fallen into the rapids and was being swept away. One after the other they came to warn me, to offer love's good counsel, like ropes thrown out from the shore.

Slowest of foot, but first to speak, was old Aunt Leona, who had loved me longer than anyone. With no invitation or warning she appeared, like a hornet buzzing into the room.

"So here stands the fool in the midst of his folly," she observed.

I shrugged off the sting and tried to generate some pleasantness between us. "How are you this morning, Auntie? Feeling well?"

"How I am is not the question, Zé! You're the one with his pants on fire."

"I'm fine, Auntie. *Really*."

"Sure you is," she mocked me. "When rats ask cats to dance." Now she had spied my travel bag, spread open on the table. "It's true then, is it? You are going to Belém?"

"Yes, Auntie. Day after tomorrow."

"And that's why you've hocked your ass, is it? To make this trip?"

Since I didn't have the heart to lie to her, I kept my mouth shut.

With enormous effort she inched herself forward and let fly her thoughts. "You been out asking money, haven't you, Zé? From one end of the island to the other you been asking. But from me you didn't ask. Not from *me*. Because you *know* what I would say."

She tried to lift her walking stick, to smack me, but was too feeble to do it. Her bitty arm began to twitch and tremble with the effort, to no effect.

Finally, as the spasm passed, her arm grew still. Left and right she gawked around, looking for a place to sit.

I got her a stool from the corner and helped her down, right there in the doorway.

With her deep brown eyes she examined me and licked her lips for another round. "A poor man can find wealth in a field well worked," she said. "'Less evil sweeps it away."

To that I had no answer, except to look the other way.

"It's trouble you're after, *né verdade*?"

I stared into the folds of my bag and shuffled the clothes around.

"So will you answer me or not?"

"I'm going to see my cousins, Auntie. That's all. And do a little business."

"Don't you lie to me, Zé Licata. You don't have the face for it."

Tá bom, thought I. *Then I will answer you with silence.*

"Stay home and work your land," she urged me. "The manioc should come in good this year if you care for it."

There was wisdom in her words, I knew. Though not much tenderness.

She wobbled on the stool, swallowed hard, and fired off another piece of her mind. "Why not go fishing now that the fishing is good? And take the boy along. The moon is right and the weather fair. The men are bringing in pacu by the baskets full."

"I *have* to make the trip," I told her. "There is no way out."

"And so you must," she said, her voice trailing off. "So you must. Until foolishness bears its fruit."

Yes, the words resounded, *till foolishness bears its fruit.*

"Come over here then," Auntie whispered, "and let me kiss you."

The only way that that could happen—so bitty she was and seated low—was for me to kneel on the floor beside her. This I did with honest reverence, for reverence she was due.

Auntie laid her ancient hands upon me, stroked my cheek, and with great tenderness kissed me on the temple. "So much anger," she lamented. "Like your father and grandfather you have it, and all their fathers before. Can you not lay it down, Zé?"

"How do you do that?" I asked her. "How?"

She was silent then. With all her years to draw upon, with all the history and experience contained in her encyclopedic brain, she could not produce an answer.

Late that night, as a storm came off the river, I heard Ana get out of her hammock and come timidly over.

For hours I'd been turning and twisting in my hammock, afraid of what my dreams might bring. Compared to the demons that raged inside my head the storm was a baby's lullaby.

I could tell from her fragrance and the brush of her hair that Ana had drawn close. Then felt her hand on my shoulder, tracing its way down my arm, till it found its place in mine.

Lightning flashed around the shutters. A blast of thunder, like cannon fire, shook the walls.

Ana waited for it to roll away, then leaned in closer. "Could you not be persuaded to stay, *meu bem*? To stay here with Rafael and me?"

Here was love's sweet voice, from the lips of one who cared.

With another flash I saw her eyes, like a mother worrying over her child.

I took a deep breath and whistled it slowly out, so frail a note that only I could hear it.

"I'm afraid, Zé," she whispered. "Afraid without knowing why. It hounds my very sleep it does."

"You'll be fine," I said. "You will be protected here."

She had no idea what that might mean, and I no way to tell her.

"It's not for me I fear," she added quickly. "It's for *you*, Zé. I dreamed that you were chained and thrown in the river, there to drown before me, with nothing we could do."

So closely were her fears inlaid upon my own they seemed to feed upon themselves and multiply. "I'll make the trip as short as I can," I promised her. "Seven or eight days. Nine at most."

How strangely the silence possessed us, despite the thunder and rain.

Ana lifted my hand out of the hammock, brought it to her lips, and kissed it.

How odd to be kissed that way, twice in a single day, with such sadness and soft farewell.

"*Eu te amo de coração,*" she said.

"I know you do. Otherwise you wouldn't put up with my crap."

A tear splashed softly on my wrist.

"You are my hero, Zé. You have *always* been my hero."

Here she spoke from memories long burned out and sentiments exhausted. Here her mind would surely know what her heart could not admit, that her "hero" was a drunk, that he'd abused her with his mouth and sometimes with his fist, that he had descended now into things so dark that she dared not ask.

"Go now and get some sleep," I told her. "There is nothing more to say ..."

Rafael and I were into the C's now, sipping our coffee milks and eating fresh *beiju*. Twice he had picked up the dictionary and read our assignment for the day—"*cadastro ... cadáver ... cadeia ...*"—without absorbing a single word.

"So where are you this morning?" I asked him, snapping my finger.

His eyes swung back from some faraway thought, clouded with worries. "You are in trouble, aren't you, Pai?"

I nodded at him. "You were listening in, weren't you, when Aunt Leona was here?"

"She talks very loud," he said.

"Yes she does. It's because she's a little deaf that she talks that way. And because she wants to hammer important things into wooden heads."

Rafael studied me so intensely that I felt like crawling under the table. "Are you going away?"

"Yes."

"No matter what she says?"

"I have to."

"No you *don't*," he objected. His face suddenly brightened. "You could stay home and work on the campaign! It would be fun!"

"Campaign?" I repeated dully. "What campaign is that?"

"You *know*, Pai. To get rid of Duba. To make you community president."

"You've been talking with Chico again, haven't you? About the elections?"

He nodded eagerly. "Yes, Pai."

So innocent was his look, so unguarded his affection, it nearly broke my heart.

"Chico's got you on the ballot," he said.

"So I heard."

"It's a great number, don't you think? Two-two-two?"

"Yes," I agreed. "Easy to remember."

His enthusiasm was soaring now. "And look here!" he exclaimed. "We're going to make some banners for you." He grabbed his book, fanned it open, and spun it around so I could read it:

Since Duba Don't Do Nothing
Don't Do Nothing for Duba
Vote 222

I could tell by his grin and the cock of his head that he was very proud of his work. Indeed, the letters were nicely penned. Scaled up a bit, they would sit just fine on a poster board.

"So what do you think, Papai?"

I read it again and had to laugh. "It's obvious isn't it—so *subtle* the message and cleverly rhymed—that *Chico has done it again!*"

"*Sim, senhor,*" the boy confirmed. "He's the one who thought it up."

"Always the poet he."

Now he had caught the sarcasm in my voice. "Seriously, Pai, what do you think of it?"

"Seriously?"

"Seriously."

"I think that Duba's gonna pee red when he sees it," I said. "And once he's thought it over a while, he's going to send one of his sons—probably Joberto—to smack Chico in the head."

Rafael took a little bite out of his thumbnail. "Maybe we should soften it down a little, you think?"

"That would be up to you and your poet."

"Well how about this one then?" Rafael offered. He flipped the page over and showed me the other side:

Zé Licata
Hometown Hero
Vote 222

He held it there a moment, waiting for me to catch fire. Then saw that my tinder was wet. "You don't like this one either, do you?"

I reached over and put my hand on his wrist. "Look Rafael, you know how I feel about Chico. Same as you do. But you also must know —and I'm sure you do—that he's not quite ... eh ... *anchored.*"

The boy closed his notebook and pushed it aside. "Normal, you mean."

"*É isso mesmo.* That's it exactly."

"Well maybe that's why we like him so much," he retorted.

"*Claro que sim.* But he gets these wild ideas upon him. I don't know from where they come. Out of the great beyond, I guess."

"Like a dream you mean?"

"Yes, like a dream, more or less. A dream that grabs hold of the helm and won't let go."

All the excitement had drained out of him now. "So you don't want to be president?"

"No, son. Never did. It's something that hatched inside Chico's head—a long, long time ago—and won't let go."

I had made the boy sad now. But it was good for him to grip the truth.

"There's a special word that describes Chico's situation," I told him. "Right here in the dictionary." I turned the book around and searched back through the pages. "Here it is. *Delusional.* A persistent false psychotic belief regarding the self, or a person or object outside the self.' Can you follow that?"

"No."

"Neither can I exactly. But that's the word. *Delusional.*"

"So what's wrong with dreaming?" he asked. "You told me it was good for a man to dream."

"Yes I did."

"Well we're dreaming that you're going to win! *That's* what we're dreaming!"

With that I decided to put away my paddle. "All right then," I sighed. "If that's the way you're going. But you need to remember something, Filho—and maybe remind Chico too—that I won't be campaigning with you. And when the time comes, I will *not* be voting for Zé."

His mouth gaped open with disbelief. No matter how long he struggled with the idea, no matter how I should explain it to him, Rafael would never forgive me the thought of voting for Duba Escobar.

"Duba is the laziest man alive," he said.

"Yes he is. Too lazy even to make a good crook."

His eyes began to tear, but he was too much a man to let them run.

"I love you, *meu filho*," I said. "Forgive me for the things I am not."

He bit down on his lip, for the truth was hard and bitter. "Let me go with you then!" he blurted.

"What?"

"To Belém. To help you."

"No, Filho. That's not possible."

"Yes it is," he insisted. "I could be a *help* to you." His voice was full of manly promise, his face with courage.

I turned him down as gently as I could. "It would be great to have you with me, Rafael. Truly it would. But the work is tough and the business serious."

"I'm tough," he asserted. "I can be serious."

"I know you can. I *know*. But this is a dark and peculiar thing. Something I have to do myself."

Wiping the tears off his cheeks, Rafael closed the notebook, got up from the table and walked away from me. Though he could never have guessed the real purpose of my trip, the boy somehow knew, in his innocence and his youth, that it was serious unto death. And that I'd not seen fit to include him.

CHAPTER 23

THE *ESTELA MARIA* WAS TWELVE HOURS LATE WHEN SHE LIMPED UP to the dock in Belém. A light rain drifted across the wharf as the crew secured the lines and pulled the gangway down. It was two-thirty in the morning.

I gathered up my things and moved quickly forward, anxious to get off. The trip had stretched into four long days and brought me nothing but sleeplessness and worry. Now, to top it off, the rain had followed us in.

With a few tired others I descended the gangway and walked up to the old terminal. Most of the passengers had remained in their hammocks, choosing to sleep on through the night and get off in the morning.

There in the shadows, under the drippy metal roof, Leiteiro was waiting for me. He was hunched over, his head craned forward, wearing the same green slicker as before.

"You're *late*," he said, pulling the hood up.

"We threw a prop coming out of Monte Alegre," I explained. "No spare of course. We've been limping along on one engine."

"Well, it's put a spider in the soup," he grumbled. "Maybe ruined everything."

With that the man turned and hobbled off the platform, moving so fast that I could barely keep up.

The parking lot was nearly empty and poorly lit. Leiteiro led me to an old gray sedan that was parked—for obvious reasons—directly under a streetlight.

"Not a good place to leave it," he said. "Not a good place to *be*." His nose jutted out from under his hood, sniffing the air for predators.

I rounded the car to the passenger's side, noting the odd assortment of panels and off-color fenders that had been used to patch the vehicle. Though there wasn't much chrome left—just the bumper in front and the left-side mirror—it was polished up nice.

Leiteiro was in the driver's seat now, reaching over to open the door for me. "Put your things in back there. Then lock the door."

Three or four times he cranked the motor, with no success.

"*Vai pegar*," he assured me, pumping the gas.

Sure enough, after much wheezing and belching, the engine started. With a blast of cool blue smoke emitting from the rear, we shot off into the night.

"*Tá vendo?*" he said, shifting up the gears. "It's just cranky on the start."

"Jesus, what's that smell?" I said. "Is that coming off the engine?"

"Kerosene," he said. "I use it for my asthma."

I rolled the window down.

"It's better than menthol, you know, when you rub it on your chest."

"Must make you popular with the ladies," I remarked.

He was irritated now and showed it in his glance. "You don't smell so good either, amigo. Like old *fish* actually."

"There was no shower on the boat," I told him.

"That would explain it," he said. Then added pointedly, "Some of it anyway."

I ignored the remark and tried to get my bearings. "Where are we going?"

"Off to the south a little," he said vaguely. "You got the cloth with you?"

"Yes."

"And the gift?"

"Yes."

"No one messed with them on the boat, did they? No questions asked?"

"No. They're in the sack. Everything's safe."

Out of long habit, I guess, or suffering from a nervous tic, Leiteiro kept thumping his thumbs on the steering wheel. This went on and on, as though he were counting off the blocks. "You don't have to like me," he said.

That's good, I thought, *because it's probably not possible.*

"But you do *need* me," he added. "So be smart, and don't piss me off."

"*Tudo bem.*"

"So no more talk about how I smell, okay? Or how I look ..."

"*Tudo bem.*"

His hood had slipped back onto his shoulders now, revealing a massive scar across the side of his head. The wound must have been very old, judging by the way his hair had grown in around it. That he had survived such a horrible blow, from a cleaver maybe, or an ax, seemed almost a miracle.

"You got money?" he asked.

"Yes."

"These people don't work on credit."

"I got money."

Leiteiro drove us into a dingy commercial district, filled with dozens of dark little shops and bars that bordered on a run-down plaza. It looked like a fine place to get murdered.

He rounded the plaza a couple times, parked and turned off the lights. Then, with no explanation at all, settled back into his seat and closed his eyes.

"What are we doing?" I asked.

"Waiting," said Leiteiro. "Get some sleep if you can. There won't be another chance."

"Waiting for what?"

"For the shops to open," he said. "Everything we need is within a block or two."

Never in my life, before that fateful day or since, have I spent so much money in so little time. Or enjoyed it less.

The dinner plate alone cost me sixty cruzeiros, and the goblet to go with it, of fine crystal, another eighty. These were sums for a prince to pay, not a pauper. With every purchase came a little twinge of guilt and a sense of loss.

One after the other, Leiteiro led me into the peculiar little shops I needed. When I suggested at one point that we buy simple steel cutlery instead of plated silver, he pulled me aside and scolded me, "You must not cheapen the *mesa* in any way. It must be a true sacrifice from a true servant. You *understand*?"

When I said nothing, he pressed in closer. "You *are* a true servant, aren't you?"

I swallowed hard and spoke the truth. "Yes."

Shop by shop the list was filled: An eight-inch cigar imported from Cuba. Five black candles. A bottle of fine cachaça. A half kilo of liver, butchered fresh that morning. A hunter's knife with a seven-inch blade. A flashlight with fresh batteries.

All these went back to the car in turn, locked in the trunk and covered with a blanket. Finally, late that afternoon, we finished the list and drove away.

"Do you know where you are?" he asked.

"Not really."

"Good. For a while now you will have to know even less." With that, he pulled a green bandana out of the glove box and laid it across my lap. "Fasten this over your eyes," he instructed. "It's best for everyone."

And so I traveled blind—blinder than I knew—to some hidden rendezvous ahead. For a while the traffic was thick and noisy around us. The man drove hard, cutting his way through. Once we braked so hard that it threw me forward in the seat and punched the air out of me. Leiteiro stood on the horn and cursed the other driver, then pushed our car still faster, as though a new burst of speed would prove him right.

After a while the noises of the city fell away and the road turned rough, exposing the sad condition of his shock absorbers.

Ten minutes on, Leiteiro stopped the car, but left the engine running. "We're close," he said. "You can take it off now. For a minute."

I pushed the bandana up and peered out into the night. The headlights were trained forward into the darkness, revealing a narrow dirt road that must have been cut for horses and oxcarts. To the left, pressed close against the car, was a wall of thick jungle that ran on as far as I could see. To the right lay an open pasture, overgrown with weeds, with an old post-and-wire fence strung along its border.

"I'll need your money here," he said. "Four hundred cruzeiros."

Though I knew what the money was for, and that it had all been planned ahead, the thought of it repulsed me. "Is there some way we can do without this part?" I said. "Some way to get around it?"

Leiteiro looked at me as though I were an idiot. "Do without it?" he sneered. "It's the blood that draws them, Licata. It's the blood that gives it *force*."

I wished suddenly that I had never come down this road, that I had gone into the favelas along the river and hired an assassin to do the job. "I need a drink."

"No drinking," he told me. "After we're done, then you can drink."

"Jesus. Just to steady my nerves," I pleaded.

He could see now that my hands were shaking, and the need was urgent. "Maybe," he relented. "We'll see. Now the money, please."

I pulled out my wallet and sadly counted out the cash, borrowed from Domingos and Lula and Leo the Boatman. "*Cristo*, I am a poor man becoming poorer."

"You have still to buy me gasoline," he reminded me. "But we will see about that later. Now cover up your eyes."

So into blindness I returned, at the mercy of my agent.

We drove a short ways on, pushed through a sharp curve, and came to a stop. Leiteiro turned off the motor and got out.

I sat there in silence, clasping my hands, desperate for a drink. The darkness that cloaked my eyes was nothing compared to the darkness that invaded my heart.

A few minutes later, I heard the trunk open and felt the weight of something placed inside it—then voices, Leiteiro's and another, constrained to whisper, compelled to finish their dark exchange as fast as possible.

Another minute passed, then the door beside me abruptly opened.

A little breeze whiffed through the car, and with it a confusion of odors: of cigarette smoke ... then fresh manure and the stink of goats ... and finally, hopefully, the delicious scent of cachaça.

"I have a drink for you," Leiteiro said. "Just this one." He leaned in through the door and pushed a glass into my grateful hand. "Leave the blinder on," he said.

I drank it all in one great swallow and felt enormously better.

He took the glass away and slammed the door. The smell of goats and whiskey lingered.

A minute more and we were on our way again, turning the car around, speeding back into the city.

An hour passed before Leiteiro finally stopped again.

"You can take it off now," he said.

I removed the bandana and rubbed my tired eyes.

We were parked on the edge of a little roundabout that played off into three nicely paved streets. The one to the right, which descended into a gentle curve, was lined with large, gated houses that rose like castles behind their fortified walls. Never, except in the magazines, had I seen such a stunning display of wealth.

"He lives right there," Leiteiro said. "Just beyond the curve."

"I had not expected this," I admitted.

"We must be quiet," he whispered. "We must be quick." He jerked his thumb back over his shoulder. "The house back there's got a watchdog."

My breath was starting to run away with me now, my pulse to quicken. "Where will we set it?"

"Just there," said Leiteiro. "In the roundabout. You will place things in the order I say, *exactly* as I tell you."

"*Está bom.*"

He looked at his watch. "It's midnight. Time to move."

As I reached for the door handle I realized my hand was shaking.

"Let's try not to use the flashlights," he said. "There's a little moon to help us. Maybe it'll be enough."

"*Sim.*"

Leiteiro must have seen the reluctance in my face and sensed how scared I was. "It will be fine," he assured me.

"*Sim.*"

"Why not enjoy it? You've waited a long time, haven't you? To get even with this bastard?"

"Yes. Long enough."

He glanced at his watch again. "All right, *vamos.* Be quiet with the door."

Like a pair of shadows we moved, taking the sacks from the trunk and carrying them into the center of the roundabout. There, inside a ring of bushes, Leiteiro pointed me to a patch of open, sandy ground that was mostly hidden from the street.

"First, the cloth," he whispered.

I pulled it from its package, unfolded it, and spread it quickly across the sand. I could see now that it was made from two triangular pieces—one red and the other black—stitched together to form a perfect square. Inexplicably, the center of it had been stained with something that was dark and irregular.

"*Caramba!*" I muttered. "Look at *this.* Something's spilled on it?"

"No, it's as it should be," said Leiteiro. "Go on now!"

In quick order I set the plate in the center of the cloth, with the knife and fork to either side, and placed the goblet near. Then took the bottle of cachaça from him, opened it and poured the goblet full. The smell was so delicious, so enticing, I couldn't let go.

"Put it down," he ordered me.

I barely heard him, so strongly did the scent attract me. *A swig was all I wanted! To wet my tongue and calm my hands!*

"Don't!" he threatened me. "Put it down!"

From behind us a car approached, coming slowly down the grade.

"Jesus!" Leiteiro cursed. "Get down."

We ducked low and froze as the headlights swept over the circle. My heart was in my hand and my hand was on the trembling bottle.

The car crawled around the circle and descended the hill.

Now the dog was barking and wouldn't shut up. Soon enough, the noise would raise a watchman, who'd surely find us out.

Leiteiro handed me the cigar. "Set them down!" he hissed.

Out of fear I placed the bottle and set the cigar beside it.

Last out of my sack came the slab of liver, plopped hastily on the plate, then the five little candles, squat and black. These we set at careful intervals around the cloth, to form a circle.

"Faster," he urged, handing me the matches. "Go!"

One by one I set the wicks aflame, then stuffed the matches in my pocket.

Now he had untied the second sack and pulled out the goat, holding it up by its hinds. In the flash and flicker of the candles I could see that it was perfectly black, with its muzzle taped shut to keep it from bawling.

Before I could say a word or think a thought, Leiteiro handed it to me, and then the knife. "Hold it over the plate," he said. "Say your vows. Slit its throat."

Now I had it in my grip. A small thing really. A yearling still wanting its mother's milk.

"Go ahead," he pressed. "Be quick!"

The animal was quivering with fear, its eyes wide open, fixed hard upon the knife. Though I had butchered tapirs and boars and chickens by the hundreds, I could not bring myself to do it.

"Kill it!" Leiteiro ordered.

"I can't."

"Say your vows!"

Though only minutes had passed, it seemed like hours.

"Go on!" he hissed.

With a dry and halting tongue I finally spoke: "Xangô, you are the fountain of all my favors. All my fountains are in you. Receive this gift upon your altar. *Faça o que estou pedindo ...*"

From out of the cloth a shadow rose, like a curl of smoke, ever larger, ever darker, emitting a stink too horrible to breathe. *What stays your hand? Do as you are told!*

Leiteiro reached over and slapped me on the arm. "Go *on*, goddammit!"

Out of fear I gripped the knife. Out of vengeance I slit the animal's throat. The kid bucked and jerked and kicked me in the chest, bleating through the open wound. From out of its throat the blood spurted down and splattered off the plate, till its heart could pump no more. Then hung there limply in my hands.

From out of the shadow I heard my orixá, purring with delight. *Well done my good and faithful servant. We hear your plea and rise to help. We shall lessen him and lessen him, till finally he lessens himself.*

"Drop the knife," Leiteiro urged me. "Leave it!"

But my hand held fast upon the grip, as drop by drop the animal bled its last. I gazed upon the altar with morbid fascination, infused with power. A breath of chill dark air curled around me and licked the flames up off their wicks.

"Throw it down!" Leiteiro barked. "Let's go!"

Without a care I dropped the bloodied knife and flung the carcass in the bush.

Leiteiro rushed back to the car and jumped in.

How thoroughly cold and hardened I felt as I trailed along behind him. How impervious and proud!

We had driven only a mile or two when suddenly my stomach soured. "I'm going to be sick," I warned him.

"There's no place to pull off," Leiteiro said. "It's dangerous here."

"I'm telling you, I'm going to be sick."

"And I'm telling *you*, there is no place to pull over."

I struggled to open the window, but the glass stuck part way down. I held my stomach as long as I could, then threw up with such explosive energy that it splattered all over the dashboard.

Leiteiro braked hard and yanked us off the road into a bank of weeds. "Get out!" he shrieked. "Look what you done to my car! Mother of God!"

Somehow I managed to open the door and stumble away. I fell hard to my knees and emptied my belly into the ditch.

Out of the darkness I could hear Leona whisper, *"The fool in the midst of his folly."*

Then heard Leiteiro's voice, shouting at me, "You are going to clean up my car, *seu safado*! You *hear* me?! You are going to get a bucket and sponge and clean all this up."

The next morning we approached the house again, this time from the other end of the street. We parked and waited, close by a bus stop, till a young man came pedaling up on his bicycle and stopped alongside us. He was dressed in a crisp blue shirt with gray epaulettes and a stiff-billed cap that gave him a professional look. I noticed, as he parked his bike, that it had an oversized basket in front, the kind that mail carriers and delivery boys used.

The exchange was quick and efficient.

Leiteiro rolled down the window, nodded at the boy, and handed him the box. "House 331," was all he said.

The boy took the box and placed it gently in his basket, then returned to the window with his hand outstretched.

Leiteiro put some money in it—*my* money—and gave him a final instruction. "Say as little as you can. Disappear quickly. You remember what I told you?"

The boy nodded, stashed the money in his pocket, and climbed back on his bike.

From our hiding place, shielded by a hedgerow of ferns, we watched him pedal down the street and dismount in front of Bonfim's house.

"He's perfect," Leiteiro said. "Just right for the part, *né?*"

Indeed, the boy, who must have been sixteen or seventeen, projected a certain wholesomeness and nonchalance that was very convincing.

"He specializes at bits like this," Leiteiro said. "Though not exactly cheap."

Now the boy was at the gate, gift in hand, ringing the bell.

"Do you know what's in the box?" I asked.

"No," Leiteiro replied. "And please don't tell me. In fact, the less we talk, the better things will be."

Though I had cleaned up the mess in his car and apologized to him, the man was still irked.

Now the gate had opened, and who should appear in the doorway but the great man himself, dressed in a fine white robe. Even at a distance I could see his belly thrusting forward, his hand reaching out, anxious for his gift.

The boy was delivering his lines now, with an ingratiating mix of politeness and apathy. *No, there was nothing to sign,* he'd explain. *The gift was from a secret admirer, for the gentleman's birthday.*

The great man smiled, with hardly a question, and took the thing in.

"Too bad we can't attend the party," I said, as we drove off. "Help him celebrate his birthday."

Leiteiro was peering thoughtfully ahead, drumming his thumbs against the wheel. "I expect it will be his last," he said.

A few hours later, Leiteiro left me at the docks with nine cruzeiros, three oranges and a bottle of cachaça. He said not a word as I got out of the car, a reminder of how fond we were of each other.

I roamed the docks for a long hour, looking for a way home. None of the regular line boats would take me, despite my pleading, despite my promises, before God and all the Saints, that I would pay them on the other end.

"Sorry, no credit."

Dejected and alone, with no plan at all, I came across a shabby little freighter—the *Três Irmãos*—that was sailing for Manaus that night. I found the first mate, a rough-cut man with short, reddish hair, smoking a cigarette at the foot of the gangway.

"No passengers," he said. "The boat's not licensed for it."

I dug the last cruzeiros out of my pocket and offered them to him. "Look, brother, I got no other means. *Please.* I'm begging ..."

"Sorry. It could get us in big trouble."

"I could do some work for you. Pay my way along."

He eyed the cash, winced at the risk he was taking, and snatched it out of my hand. "You can hang your hammock aft, over the onions," he said. "No meals included. *Entende?* And twice a day you clean out the heads."

"Beautiful."

Before he could change his mind, I hurried up the gangway and down the breezeway. The afterdeck was loaded with boxes of canned goods and cooking oil, cases of bottled beer and soft drinks, and sacks of onions piled high across the stern. It was there, above the onions, close by the railing, that I found a little nook to string my hammock.

Though I was broke and alone, with no prospects at all, I took pleasure in what I'd done and relished the raw, invigorating power it gave me. The curse would ravage my enemy's life and eviscerate his spirit, the way a cancer eats away the flesh. No matter that Ivanildo Bonfim was a big shot minister with lots of money. Mine would be the victory now, and mine the vengeance, for all the kids he'd cheated, for all the schools he'd never built, for all the villages left in darkness.

I crawled up into my hammock, peeled back an orange, and delighted in my revenge.

Not the end...
RIVERS WILD
Book Two:
The Third Promise
... Available soon from Brimstone Fiction!

CHARACTER NAME KEY

Key to Pronouncing Characters' Names
(Listed alphabetically. Pronunciations are approximate.)

Ajuba Barbosa /ah-JHOO-bah bahr-BAW-zah/
Alzira /ahl-ZEE-rah/
Ana Paula Bezerra /AH-nah PAOW-lah beh-ZEH-hah/
Aparecida /ah-pah-reh-SEE-dah/
Cassilda /kah-SEEL-dah/
Chico /SHEE-koo/
Chocolate /shoh-koh-LAT-chee/
Duba Escobar /DOO-bah es-koh-BAHR/
Ivanildo Abreu Bonfim /ee-vah-NEEL-doo ah-BREOO bohn-FEEHN/
Mateus Izquerda /mah-TEY-oos ees-KEYR-dah/
Jamela /jhah-MEH-lah/
Jarbas /JHAR-bahs/
João Silveiro /jhoo-ÃOW seel-VEY-roo/*
José Nery /jhoh-ZEH NEH-ree/
Kiko /KEE-koo/
Leiteiro /ley-TEY-roo/
Leo /LEH-oo/

253

Leona /leh-OH-nah/
Nonato /noh-NAH-too/
Ozias /oh-ZEE-yas/
Paixante /paee-SHAHN-chee/
Pega-Ficha /PEH-gah FEE-shah/
Rafael /hah-fah-EL/
Ribeiro /hee-BEY-roo/
Tatianni /taht-chee-YAH-nee/
Vinícius /vee-NEE-see-yoos/
Xabrega /shah-BREH-gah/
Zé Licata /ZEH lee-KAH-tah/
Zemário /zeh MAH ree yoo/

* In Portuguese, the "tilde" diacritic over a vowel (e.g., ã or õ) indicates nasal pronunciation.

PORTUGUESE GLOSSARY

(Defined in context, alphabetically. Pronunciations are approximate.)

A

abduzir /ah-bee-doo-ZEER/ to abduct

abeberado /ah-beh-beh-RAH-doo/ watered, drunk

abraços /ah-BRAH-sos/ hugs

açaí /ahs-sah-EE/ a type of palm tree prized for its fruit and hearts of palm

acerola /ah-se-ROH-lah/ an evergreen shrub or small tree that produces red, cherry-like fruit

agrícola /ah-GREE-co-lah/ agricultural

agricultor /ah-gree-kool-TOR/ farmer

agricultura /*ah-gree-kool-TOO-rah*/ agriculture

amante /*ah-MAHN-chee*/ lover

andiroba /*ahn-jee-ROH-bah*/ a tropical, rain forest tree valued for the medicinal properties in its bark, leaf, oil and fruit

aproveite /*ah-pro-VAY-chee*/ enjoy; take advantage of

arara /*ah-RAH-rah*/ macaw

B

babaçu /*bah-bah-SOO*/ the babassu palm, prized for its oil, with properties similar to coconut oil

Banco Federal /*BAHN-koo feh-deh-RAHL*/ Federal Bank

Bandeirante(s) /*ban-dey-RAHN-chee(s)*/ a heavy-duty pickup truck with a jeep-like cab, built in Brazil by Toyota from 1968–2001; *also*: 17th-century Portuguese settlers in Brazil who were rugged frontiersmen and fortune hunters

barraca /*bah-HA-kah*/ a rough little shack or hut

Bateria Mallet /*bah-teh-REE-ya mah-LEH*/ a Brazilian artillery command in the War of the Triple Alliance

beiju /*bey-JHOO*/ a type of bread, pancake or crepe made from tapioca, especially popular in rural areas of Brazil

Belém /*beh-LEHN*/ the bustling capital of the state of Pará, Brazil, where the Amazon River empties into the Atlantic Ocean

besteira(s) /*bes-TEY-rah(s)*/ nonsense, rubbish, stupidity

Boa Fortuna /*BO-ah for-TOO-nah* / Good Fortune

bossa nova /*BAWS-sah NAWV-ah*/ a lyrical fusion of samba and jazz that was first popularized in the 1950s

brasileiros /*brah-zee-LEY-roos*/ Brazilians (*singular*: *brasileiro*)

C

caboclo /*kah-BO-klo*/ mestizo or half-breed (in this context, derogatory)

cachaça /*kah-SHA-sah*/ a distilled spirit, generally 80 proof, made from fermented sugarcane juice (also called "*pinga*")

cacique /*kah-SEE-kee*/ tribal chief

cadastro /*kah-DAH-stroo*/ register

cadáver /*kah-DAH-veyr*/ corpse

cadeia /*kah-DEY-yah*/ chain, prison

caju /*kah-JHOO*/ a tropical evergreen that produces the cashew nut and edible red or yellow fruit

calma /*KAHL-mah*/ calm; stay calm

candomblé priestess /*kahn-dom-BLEH*/ an Afro-American religion that recognizes and worships numerous gods; every practitioner is believed to have their own tutelary orixá (lesser god or spirit) that controls his or her destiny; a person's character or personality is strongly linked to their personal orixá

cara(s) /*KAH-rah(s)*/ guy(s), man (men)

caramba /*kah-RAHM-ba*/ dang

centavo(s) /sen-TAH-voo(s) / cent(s)

chapinhar /chah-peehn-YAHR / to splash

como? /KOH-moo?/ how's that? what?

copaíba /koh-pah-EE-bah/ various species of trees found in the Brazilian Amazon that yield a colorless to light-yellow oil prized for its medicinal qualities

covinhas /koh-VEE-nyas/ dimples

credo /KREH-doo/ geez

cruzeiro(s) /kroo-ZAY-roo(s)/ the currency of Brazil from 1942 to 1986, eventually replaced by the *real*

cueca /KWEH-kah/ men's underwear

cuíca /KWEE-kah/ a Brazilian friction drum with a broad pitch range

cuidado /kwee-DAH-doo/ be careful, beware

curandeira(o) /koo-rahn-DAY-rah(-roo)/ witchdoctor, spirit healer

D

depressão /deh-pres-SAOW/* depression

desânimo /dehz-AH-nee-moo / discouragement

descuidado /dehz-kwee-DAH-doo/ careless, reckless

descuidar /dehz-kwee-DAHR/ to neglect

descuidista /dehz-kwee-JEES-tah/ neglectful or careless person desfruta /*dehz-FROO-tah*/ enjoy

despacho /*dehz-PAH-shoo*/ dispatch, order, message

destinado /*des-chee-NAH-doo*/ destined

droga /*DRAW-gah*/ dammit; *also*: drug

E

eita! /*EY-tah!*/ hey!

empadas /*em-PAH-dahs*/ pies

encantada /*en-kahn-TAH-dah*/ delighted

espadas /*es-PAH-das*/ swords

estimado /*es-chee-MAH-doo*/ esteemed, dear

entende? /*en-TEN-jee?*/ understand?

F

farinha /*fah-REEN-yah*/ ground manioc

favela(s) /*fah-VEH-lah(s)*/ slum(s)

feitiço /*fey-CHEE-soo*/ hex, spell

filho /*FEEL-yoo*/ son, boy

fofoca /*foh-FOH-kah*/ gossip

futebol /*foo-chee-BOHL*/ soccer

G

gatinha /gah-TCHEEN-yah/ little cat

gaúcho /ga-OO-shoo/ a native of the Brazilian state of Rio Grande do Sul

gente /JHEN-chee/ people, folks

gripe /GREE-pee/ flu, cold

guaraná /guah-rah-NAH/ a climbing plant native to the Amazon basin; its berries and seeds, which contain high concentrations of caffeine, are rendered into a pulp or liquid that provides quick energy and endurance

I

ingá /een-GAH/ a long, bean-like fruit that grows from the tropical plant of the same name; the pulp, which covers the seeds, is sweet and edible raw

Irlanda /eer-LAHN-dah/ Ireland

J

Jacaré /jhah-kah-REH/ the name of an Amazon village, meaning "caiman" or "alligator"

jambo /JHAHM-boo/ a small- to medium-sized tree that bears white, pink or greenish flowers, producing an edible fruit similar to a guava

joga! /JHAW-gah!/ play!

Jornada de Fé /jhor-NAH-dah jee FEH/ Journey of Faith

Jornal do Brasil /*jhor-NAOO doo brah-ZEEOO*/ a prominent Brazilian newspaper

L

leiteiro /*ley-TEY-roo*/ milkman

M

macumba /*mah-KOOM-bah*/ a Brazilian religious cult that practices spirit worship, using sorcery, ritual dance, and fetishes

macumbeira(o) /*mah-koom-BEY-ra(-roo)*/ a person who practices macumba

mãe /*mãee*/* mother

mãe de santo /*mãee jee SAHN-too*/* mother of [the] saint[s], a candomblé

malandros /*mah-LAHN-droos*/ rascals, bums

maldição /*mao-jee-SÁOW*/* curse

malquerente /*mao-keh-REHN-chee*/ bad guy

malquistar /*mao-kee-STAHR*/ to malign

malquisto /*mao-KEE-stoo*/ disliked; unpopular

maluco(s) /*mah-LOO-koo(s)*/ lunatic(s), crazy

mamãe /*mah-MÃEE*/* mama

Manaus /*mah-NAHWS*/ the capital city of the state of Amazonas,

Brazil, situated deeply inland, where the confluence of the Negro and Solimões rivers form the Amazon.

manda-chuvas /MAHN-da-SHOO-vahs/ bigwig, mogul; *literally, "rain commander"*

mano /MAH-noo/ brother, bro

marginais /mahr-jhee-NAEES/ riffraff, punks

matuto /mah-TOO-too/ country bumpkin, simpleton

mergulhar /meyhr-gool-YAHR/ to dive

mesa branca /MEH-za BRAN-ka/ *literally* "white table"; in certain religions, an informal altar or gathering, often including food, drink and tobacco, used to attract, appease or employ a spirit

mingau /meen-GAO/ mush, porridge

moleque(s) /moh-LEH-kee(s)/ brat(s), imp(s)

moto /MAW-too/ motorcycle

muruci /moo-roo-SEE/ a tropical plant valued for its sweet yellow fruit and fragrant flowers

N

nada /NAH-dah/ nothing

nadar /nah-DAHR/ to swim

não /nãow/* no

né(?) /neh(?)/ right(?) Isn't that so(?)

novela /no-VEH-lah/ soap opera

nunca /NOON-kah/ never

O

Óbidos /AW-bee-doos/ river port, positioned 67 miles west of Santarém, at the narrowest and swiftest part of the Amazon

obrigado(a) /oh-bree-GAH-doo(-dah)/ thank you

oi /oy/ hi

olá /oh-LAH/ hello

olha /AWL-yah/ look

onça /OHNS-sah/ jaguar

ordem /OHR-dehn/ order

orixá /oh-ree-SHAH/ in some Afro-American religions and cults, a lesser god or spirit that influences an individual's personality and character, and controls his or her destiny (see "candomblé" and "macumba")

ótimo /AW-chee-moo/ great, fine

ovelha /oh-VEH-lyah/ sheep

P

pacu /pah-KOO/ a South American fish that grows up to 3.5 feet in length and over 85 pounds

pai /paee/ father

palma /*PAHL-mah*/ in this context, a handful of bananas; *also,* the palm of the hand, or a tropical evergreen tree

papagaio /*pah-pah-GAEE-yoo*/ kite; *also*: parrot

papai /*pah-PAEE*/ papa

papo /*PAH-poo*/ chitchat or gossip

pesadelo /*peh-zah-DEH-loo*/ nightmare

polícia militar /*poh-LEE-see-yah mee-lee-TAHR*/ military police

porcos /*POHR-koos*/ pigs

porra(!) /*POH-hah(!)*/ *{vulgar}* crap(!); *also*: dammit(!)

pousada(s) /*poh-ZAH-dah(s)*/ hostel(s)

primo /*PREE-moo*/ cousin

puríssima /*poo-REE-see-mah*/ very pure, purest

puxa(!) /*POO-sha(!)*/ wow(!), gee(!)

R

rápido(!) /*HAH-pee-doo*/ quick(!), fast(!)

S

Santarém /*sahn-tah-REHN*/ river port located midway between Manaus and Belém, at the confluence of the Tapajós and Amazon rivers

Sateré-Mawé /*sah-teh-REH-mah-WEH*/ an indigenous people of Brazil that dwell mainly in the state of Amazonas

Senhor /sehn-YOR / Mr. (*abbrev: Sr.*) *also*: Sir *or* Lord

senhor(es) /sehn-YOR(-ees) / sir(s), gentlemen

senhora(s) /sehn-YOR-ah(s) / (*abbrev: Sra.*) Mrs., madam, ladies

senhorita /sehn-yoh-REE-tah/ young miss; maiden

sim /SEEHN/ yes

T

tamanduá /tah-mahn-doo-WAH / anteater

taperebá /tah-peh-reh-BAH/ a tropical tree that grows up to about 65 feet, producing sweet-scented flowers and small, yellow, edible fruit

tirim tirim /chee-REEHN chee-REEHN/ (*sound*): the tinkle or jangle of bells

toró /toh-RAWH/ cloudburst

Três Irmãos /TREYZ eer-MÃOWS/* Three Brothers

U

unha-de-gato /OOHN-ya jee GAH-too/ "cat's claw"; a tropical plant with distinctive thorns that resemble a cat's claw; its leaves have long been used to make medicinal extracts and creams

urubu(s) /oo-roo-BOO(S)/ vulture(s); buzzard(s); *also*, the Rio Urubu (Buzzard River)

V

vai /vaee/ go

vamos(!) /*VAH-moos*/ let's go(!); also *vamos lá!* (let's go for it!)

velha /*VEH-lyah*/ old woman; old

X

Xangô /*shan-GO*/ a superior god or *orixá* worshipped by those who practice candomblé, an Afro-American religion that is prevalent in Brazil; Xangô is sometimes referred to as the "King of Candomblé" and pictured or sculpted with a crown on his head (*see also*: "orixá" and "candomblé")

* In Portuguese, the "tilde" diacritic over a vowel (e.g., ã or õ) indicates nasal pronunciation.

PORTUGUESE PHRASES

(Defined in context, alphabetically.)

- Ah, me desculpe – Oops, sorry
- A pedra perto do pé de Pedro é preta – *A nonsensical Brazilian tongue-twister; literally:* the rock near Peter's foot is black
- Abre as janelas – Open the windows
- Agora tu vai apanhar, seu safado nojento! – Now you're gonna get it, you disgusting scumbag!
- Assim é – That's right
- Até mais – See you later
- Boa noite – Good night
- Boa noite, amigão! – Good evening, big friend!
- Boa tarde – Good afternoon
- Boa tarde para você – A good afternoon to you
- Bom dia – Good morning
- Bora levar ele para o hospital! – Let's take him to the hospital!
- Cala a boca! – Shut your mouth!
- Certo? – Right?

- Claro que sim – Yes, of course
- Corre e corre e nunca se cansa – It runs and runs and never gets tired
- De onde? – From where?
- De que fala? – What's it say? What's it about?
- Deste tamanho! – This big!
- Deus me livre – Heaven help me; God forbid
- E aí, Primo, você está? – Hey, Cousin, are you there?
- É isso mesmo – That's it exactly
- É isso o problema? – Is that the problem?
- É mesmo – Yeah, you're right
- É não e pronto – The answer's "no"; it's decided
- É só conversa, sabe? – It's just talk, you know?
- Eh, seu cachorro! – Hey, you mongrel! Dog!
- Ele quer subir mais! – It wants to go higher!
- Entre, meu amor – Come in, my love
- Escuta, cara – Listen, man
- Está bem? – Are you okay?
- Está bom – All right
- Estou te esperando – I'm waiting for you
- Eu sei – I know
- Faça o que estou pedindo – Do what I am asking
- Feliz Aniversário! – Happy Birthday!
- Fica à vontade – Make yourself at home
- Formalmente batizada – Formally baptized
- Gente boa, sabe? – Fine folks, you know?
- Gente rica e poderosa – Rich and powerful people
- Já já – Right away
- Lá em cima daquela serra tem uma arara loura. Fala, arara loura, fala ... – *A Brazilian tongue-twister*; *literally*: On the mountaintop there sits a blond macaw. Speak, blond macaw, speak ...
- Mais ou menos – So-so
- Malucos! – Morons!
- Mas, assim é a vida – But, that's life
- Meu amor – My love

- Meu bem – honey (as in darling)
- Meu coração – My heartthrob
- Meu Deus – My God
- Meu filho – My boy; my son
- Meu prazer – My pleasure *(spoken incorrectly by a foreigner)*
- Meu safado – You scumbag
- Meu(s) bendito(s) – My blessed one(s)
- Minha nossa Senhora – Oh, my Blessed Mother (as in the Virgin Mary)
- Muito bom – Very good
- Muito obrigado(a) – Thank you very much
- Não pode – You can't
- Não precisa – It doesn't need it
- Não problema – No problem *(spoken incorrectly by a foreigner)*
- Né verdade? – Isn't that true?
- Nenhuma palavra – Not a word
- Nos perdoe, senhor – Excuse us, sir
- Nossa Senhora(!) – Blessed Mother(!) (as in the Virgin Mary)
- Nossa! Tudo isso só para mim! – Wow! All this, just for me!
- O medo não manda aqui – Fear doesn't rule us here
- O que tu quer – What you want
- O rato roeu a roupa do rei de Roma! – *A Brazilian tongue-twister; literally*: The rat chewed the king of Rome's robe
- O Veleiro do Céu – Sky Sailor
- Papagaio gigantesco – Giant kite
- Para libertar o povo! – To free the people!
- Passa daí! – Get away from there!
- Pode ser – Could be; Maybe so
- Por favor – Please
- Por favor, me deixa em paz! – Please, leave me in peace!
- Puta que pariu! *{vulgar}* – Hell!
- Puxa vida(!) – Oh my goodness(!) Holy cow(!)
- Que besteira! – What baloney!
- Que legal! – How cool!
- Rapaz, que coisa boa! – Man, that's a great thing!
- Seu safado! – You scumbag!

- Só brincando – Just kidding around
- Solta! – Release it! Free it!
- Sou teu maior amigo – I'm your best friend
- Tá bem? – Okay?
- Tá bom então – Okay, then
- Tá maluco! – You're nuts!
- Tá muito bom assim – It's just fine like this
- Tem, sim – Yes I do (have them)
- Tu mesmo! – Yeah, you!
- Tudo bem – All right; Okay; That's fine
- Um pouco – A little
- Um ... dois ... três e já! – One ... two ... three, go!
- Vá pro inferno – Go to hell
- Vai pegar – It'll start
- Venha ver o luar – Come and see the moonlight
- Vira já! – Turn now!
- Viva a revolução! – Long live the revolution!

ABOUT THE AUTHOR

From Puerto Rico to Paraguay, from Rio de Janeiro into the wilds of the Amazon, Don Best has lived the adventures of an expatriate writer and Christian missionary.

Fluent in Portuguese and Spanish, Don came to love the people he writes about by living among them. *The Gravedigger's Dream*, Book One in the *Rivers Wild* series, was inspired by ten years of laughter, tears and lessons hard-won in the heart of the Brazilian Amazon.

With his wife and colleague, Elizabeth, Don now explores the teeming jungles of South Carolina.

Learn more at www.donbestauthor.com.

Don Best is available for interviews, lectures and readings. For more information, email him at author@donbestauthor.com.

Made in the USA
Middletown, DE
29 July 2021

45007137R00170